MURDER BY ARTIFACT

MURDER BY ARTIFACT

THE MURDER QUILT

BARBARA GRAHAM

FIVE STAR

A part of Gale, Cengage Learning

GALE
CENGAGE Learning™

Detroit • New York • San Francisco • New Haven, Conn • Waterville, Maine • London

GALE
CENGAGE Learning

Set in 11 pt. Plantin.
Printed on permanent paper.

LIBRARY OF CONGRESS CATALOGING-IN-PUBLICATION DATA

Graham, Barbara, 1948–
   Murder by artifact : the murder quilt / Barbara Graham. —
1st ed.
   p. cm.
   ISBN-13: 978-1-59414-828-6 (alk. paper)
   ISBN-10: 1-59414-828-7 (alk. paper)
   1. Sheriffs—Fiction. 2. Tennessee—Fiction. I. Title.
PS3607.R336M85 2009
813'.6—dc22   2009027522

First Edition. First Printing: November 2009.
Published in 2009 in conjunction with Tekno Books and Ed Gorman.

Printed in the United States of America
1 2 3 4 5 6 7 13 12 11 10 09

This book is dedicated to all the caregivers. Theirs is a difficult and often thankless job.
And as always, with love to Dennis, Justin and Alexander.

ACKNOWLEDGMENTS

The altogether wonderful Museum of Appalachia in Norris, Tennessee, has a "murder quilt." I was so enthralled by the name, I had to write a book with such an artifact. They also have a great collection of flax hackles. Inspiration comes from all places.

To Alice Duncan for seeing the promise in my manuscript and guiding me through the edits. Without her, the book would be a mess. Thank you, Alice.

Thanks to Michelle Quick, a great friend and pattern tester.

Special thanks to K. T. Irwin of Northwest K-9 Search and Recovery of Cody, Wyoming. In addition to providing me with expert information, she and her search dogs work long and hard, helping those in need.

NIGHT ON THE MOUNTAIN

A MYSTERY QUILT BY THEO ABERNATHY

The finished size is suitable as a wall hanging, lap or crib size top of approximately 42" by 54".

All fabric requirements are generous and based on standard width fabric of approximately 40" of usable fabric. The instructions assume familiarity with basic quilt construction and an accurate 1/4" seam.

Fabric requirements:

Lights—3 light prints, 1/4 yard each (fat quarters work fine). If all are from same color family (like yellow) they should be different values.

Medium or Dark—2 different prints in one color family (like blues). Mediums need to contrast with the chosen lights.

Medium or Dark #1—1 1/2 yards

Medium or Dark #2—1 1/4 yards or scraps of various fabrics in same color family as Medium #1.

Cutting instructions: Make sure to label pieces by color number and size.

From Light #1—cut 6 squares 3 3/4" *and* cut 24 squares 2 1/8"

From Light #2—cut 6 squares 3 3/4" *and* cut 12 squares 4 1/4"

From Light #3—cut 30 squares 2 1/8" *and* cut 20 squares 1 3/4"

From Medium/Dark #1—cut 4 strips 4 1/4" by length of fabric *and* 4 strips 2 1/2" by length of fabric

from remainder—cut 17 strips 2 1/8" by 10 1/4" *and* 32 squares 1 3/4"

From Medium/Dark #2—cut 72 squares 3 3/4" *and* cut 12 squares 4 1/4"

CHAPTER ONE

"There's a huge old bloodstain in the center of it."

"On what?" Theo Abernathy pressed the tiny telephone to her ear while she walked around her studio, only half listening to her mother-in-law's phone conversation. Theo wondered if she had time to put the finishing touches on her newest quilt pattern before it was time to pick her sons up from day camp. She still had a few hours. It might be enough.

"On the donation called 'the murder quilt.'" Jane's honeyed voice flowed through the receiver. "Honestly, Theo, aren't you listening to me? That's what the paper pinned to the front calls it. There's a short history written on the exhibition release form. I think you need to come see this quilt, and soon."

Theo didn't want to admit she had not been paying strict attention. If she did, Jane's feelings would be hurt and Theo wanted to avoid doing that. "How soon?"

"Now." Jane's voice held a fascinating mixture of excitement and command.

"Okay." Theo conceded, recognizing a summons from her mother-in-law when she heard one. "Who donated *this* quilt? It's certainly a catchier name than 'grandmother's favorite.'"

Jane didn't quite snort. Her soft laugh sounded like an agreement to Theo.

"Well, it's not exactly a donation," said Jane. "You'll never guess who's offering to loan it to the museum for a while." Without waiting for a response, Jane hung up on her.

Theo doubted Jane and her sister had expected such an enormous outpouring of family artifacts when they announced their plans to create a folk museum in Park County, Tennessee. Many of the relics were more trash than treasure. People left boxes of chipped canning jars, scythes, flax hackles, magazines and whatever else they wanted to get rid of at the new museum site. At last count, the ladies had eighteen horse collars stacked in a storage shed. None of them were in good shape.

In the past month, Theo had received several summonses to come see antique quilts. As a dedicated quilter and owner of Theo's Quilt Shop, it was her pleasure. Usually. A few of the items were excessively worn, dirty and smelled of mildew. The owners of those either hoped for a cash buyout or for major, free repairs. The ploy wouldn't work. Some things shouldn't be saved.

As long as she wasn't getting any work done, Theo decided to drag Nina along as reinforcement. Her best friend loved spur-of-the-moment activities almost as much as she loved chocolate. When Nina answered the phone, Theo spoke without preamble.

"You have nothing better to do now that school's out, so put some shoes on. I'll be by to get you in five minutes."

Nina snickered softly. "Okay, will you at least tell me what this is about?"

"Someone donated a quilt Jane's all excited about and she won't tell me where she got it." Theo disconnected the call.

Pulling her keys out of her purse, she clattered down the stairs from her studio into her fabric store and nearly plowed into a customer. Summer brought lots of tourists into the shop. "Oops, pardon me."

The shopper turned and smiled. She held a small, dark-eyed boy in her arms. "Hello, Theo, do you remember me?"

Theo paused, considering. The woman looked to be in her mid-thirties like herself. Attractive rather than pretty, she had large blue eyes, short dark hair and a wide mouth coated with flame-red lipstick. Theo thought maybe they had been in school together, but which one? Silersville High or the University of Tennessee? "You do look familiar." Theo tilted her head. "I'm afraid your name escapes me."

"You were talking to my uncle just the other day." The boy squirmed and the woman changed her grip, exposing a deformed thumb.

The sight of the unusual thumb jogged her memory. "Vicky Parker." High school. Vicky had lived up the road from Nina for only a few months and they had all gone to high school together. Theo remembered Vicky had an unsavory reputation and a nasty attitude for which she had earned the nickname "Icky Vicky." Theo smiled. People grew up a lot after high school. "How are you? Have you moved back here?"

"No. We're just visiting." She squeezed the little boy and he giggled.

"You've certainly got a handsome little boy." Theo grinned at the child.

"Thanks." Vicky ran a protective hand over his shoulder blades, holding him still. "I wanted to come by and say hi. You're about the only person I liked when I lived here."

"Really?" Surprised, Theo considered their history. She doubted they had exchanged more than twenty words in the short time they were in school together. Vicky had actually been in the class behind hers.

"Yeah. I felt sorry for you 'cause you lived with those creepy old people." She leaned closer, invading Theo's space. She reeked of cigarette smoke. "I heard they wouldn't even let you watch television or talk on the phone and treated you like a slave."

Theo felt like she was trapped between an ashtray and the wall. In a lightning quick move, Vicky's little boy pressed sticky

11

fingers on the lenses of her glasses.

Theo slipped her glasses off and cleaned them on the bottom of her shirt. "They were my grandparents and I wasn't a slave."

"If you say so." Vicky lifted her eyebrows.

Although she loved her grandparents, Theo had to admit Vicky wasn't too far off the mark about some of their rules. Stepping out of the little boy's reach, she replaced her glasses and glanced at her watch. She began to sidle toward the back door. "Sorry, Vicky, I'm late for an appointment and have to leave now." Before she could stop her mouth, she found herself saying something she knew was stupid. "Come by again when you're in town and we'll have a nice talk. Over lunch maybe."

"I'd love to." Vicky grinned and followed Theo through the doorway, watching her. She spoke softly to the boy and waved his little arm with her hand. "Say bye-bye, Theo." Vicky's smile, as wide as it was, didn't reach her eyes.

Theo thought her expression looked oddly like triumph. But why?

With a groan, she climbed into her car and turned the key. For a change, the minivan started immediately. Theo put it in gear, thinking she and Vicky didn't have enough memories in common to get them through ordering coffee.

She mulled over the unexpected interaction as she drove to Nina's house. Something about it disturbed her. Goose bumps rose on her arms. Theo wondered what put such a satisfied expression on Vicky's face. It was as though she had wanted Theo to invite her to do something together but not for the expected reasons.

CHAPTER TWO

Addressed to "Sheriff Marc Antony Abernathy, Personal," a plain white envelope rested on the top of Tony's morning mail. He glanced at the envelopes under it. As usual, most of the rest of the mail was addressed impersonally to Sheriff, Park County. Half curious and half irritated when someone used his whole name, Tony slit the top of the envelope.

A newspaper photograph fell out and fluttered to his desk. Tony left it there while he read the accompanying note. Written on an ordinary index card, it simply read, "There's more." Although scribbled in green crayon, there was nothing childish about the message.

His eyes moved to the fallen rectangle of newspaper. The photograph showed his own face and the bones of a human hand he held. The article had been torn from the *Silersville Gazette*, their twice-weekly local paper. There was no date on the clipping. Tony didn't need one. It was now June, and he remembered the incident had happened in March.

The sudden chill running through him had nothing to do with the refrigerated air blasting from the overworked air conditioner. An unexpected weather front had trapped a pocket of unusually hot and humid air over East Tennessee.

The headline read, "Sheriff's wife finds body." Mesmerized, he continued to read. "Skeletal remains were discovered today by Theo Abernathy. Mrs. Abernathy said she was looking for wildflowers in McMahon Park when she saw bones protruding from the ground. The bones have been sent to the state laboratory for testing and identification. No other details were available at this time."

Tony reached for the envelope. This time, he held it by only the very edge. The postmark was Cincinnati, Ohio, and mailed only two days earlier.

"Ruth Ann! Wade!" Tony bellowed, not wanting to take the time to use the intercom.

Ruth Ann, his secretary, arrived first. Her desk sat opposite his interior door. Her dark eyes were wide. A tissue adhered to her wet fingernail polish.

Deputy Wade Claybough crashed into her back and spun into the hallway. Straightening, he gathered his dignity, and when he walked in, only the flush on his high cheekbones betrayed his embarrassment.

If Tony had been in a better mood, the scene might have entertained him. He loved the Marx brothers. Instead, he glared at them both and reached into his desk drawer and retrieved three evidence bags. He left the pair standing at attention while he slipped the note, the newspaper clipping and the envelope into separate evidence bags.

"Tell me about this envelope." Tony held the bag out to Ruth Ann.

Ignoring the flapping tissue dangling from her half-lavender fingernail, Ruth Ann took the bag. She lifted her shoulders and let them fall. "It arrived in the mail this morning, along with all the rest." She handed it back. "I never open your personal mail."

Taking it back, he passed it to Wade. "I need you to do your fingerprint magic on this envelope and these." Tony added the rest.

The block letters were easy to read. Ruth Ann's eyes widened as she read the note. "More? As in more bodies?" If her skin weren't so dark, a shade she referred to as Godiva dark chocolate, she'd look like a ghost.

The flush left Wade's cheeks. "I doubt I'll find anything but your prints, Ruth Ann's and Fred the mailman's. I'll get right on it."

"Ruth Ann," said Tony. "I want you to stir up the state lab. They've had our bones for about three months now. I know they would have called if they made an identification, but I want to know what they do know."

Watching the pair of them charge off to their tasks, Tony settled back onto his chair and reached for the jumbo jar of antacid tablets he kept on his desk. He pulled a well-worn road atlas from the bottom of a stack of papers on the floor.

At just over three hundred miles from Silersville to Cincinnati, it would be an easy enough drive, mostly interstate highway. Someone could make it round trip in a day. He rubbed his bald head and tried to ease some of the rapidly building tension from his shoulders.

He wanted to march down to the office of the *Silersville Gazette* and ask to see a list of out-of-town subscribers. Only knowing Winifred Thornby, the cantankerous editor, would turn his question into a front-page story stopped him.

Lots of people in the area had relatives in Cincinnati and northern Kentucky. The out-of-state subscriber list was probably longer than the list of locals in their tiny county.

His desk phone rang, startling him. He reached for the receiver and pressed it to his ear. "Sheriff."

The high-pitched whine pouring through the earpiece sounded like some kind of siren wailing. He jerked upright in his chair. A second later, he realized a woman was crying into his ear. He felt more like joining in than asking the problem. He'd heard the same sound too many times not to recognize it.

"What's the problem, Blossom?" Tony eased the receiver away from his ear and held it about two inches from his head. With his free hand, he began sorting the rest of his mail. If Blossom held true to form, the conversation would continue for a while before she got to the point.

"That devil woman messed up my yard." The whine rose another octave.

"What woman?" Tony tossed several pieces of junk mail in the direction of the trash can. One went in.

"You know who I mean. Queen Doreen, the mayor's wife."

Tony had no trouble visualizing the mayor's wife. The petite woman could freeze anyone with a single haughty glance. Tony tried to visualize Blossom's yard and failed. Only the image of Blossom herself came to mind. An extremely large woman, she loved to dress in bright colors even though they clashed vividly with her impossibly orange hair. Tony enjoyed knowing her hair was nearly as thin as his own. He guessed her age at somewhere between twenty-five and thirty.

"What did Doreen do?"

"She stole my little donkey and cart planter." The whine eased a bit. "And she dumped the petunias out on the grass."

Ah, now he could see the yard in his mind. Blossom and the rest of the Flowers clan enjoyed the liberal use of plaster figurines in their landscaping. The particular planter in question sat close to the road and leaned against the pole supporting the mail box. The paint job was reckless at best. As Tony recalled, the donkey itself had three neon green eyes, a trait he believed to be very unusual in the donkey family. Not only was the thing hideous, it also had to weigh almost as much as Queen Doreen. She was not a large woman.

"How do you know she took it?" Tony's gaze wandered over the piles of papers stacked on his desk and thought he really ought to do something about the mess. Instead, he rummaged in his top desk drawer and found the extra staples and proceeded to refill his stapler. "Did you see her do it?"

Silence, broken only by the sounds of something being chewed, was her response. After a bit more smacking, she answered, "Not exactly, but . . ."

The image of a cow chewing a cud sprang into Tony's mind. "But?" He rested his elbow on the nearest stack of papers and leaned his forehead against his fist.

"Who else woulda taken it? I heard her threaten to have Marmot-the-Varmint pick it up with the rest of the trash." Her dissertation was punctuated by juicy-sounding hiccups. "It's none of her business what I put in my yard. Even if she is married to old Calvin. Bein' the mayor's wife don't make her God, you know."

Tony wanted to bang his head on the desk or the receiver. How had he ever let his wife talk him into moving back here once they had escaped? Silersville in general and the job of Park County Sheriff, specifically, were turning him into an old man, and he wasn't even forty yet. "Okay, Blossom. I'll have someone check into it."

"Thank you, Sheriff." Her voice took on a tone of incredible sweetness. "I'll be waiting for you."

Tony knew the drill. If he sent Sheila or another deputy by her house, Blossom would still have some excuse why she had to talk to Tony in person. Not in his wildest dreams had he ever imagined he would have a groupie, at least not in his capacity of sheriff. Occasionally, he let his errant thoughts tempt him with fame as a noted author, celebrated for his bestselling novel of the Old West. As yet he hadn't finished it, much less achieved kudos.

He groaned. If it turned out someone really needed to interview Queen Doreen, the responsible deputy would manage to shove the duty off on him. No one could tolerate the woman, and she had zero respect for anyone she considered second banana.

The sheriffs of larger counties didn't have the problem of deputies pushing work onto the boss. Tony knew for sure because he'd asked some of them. Their jobs were largely administrative. With an accepting shrug, he reached for more antacids. He might as well admit the truth to himself: being a paper pusher held no appeal for him, either.

Being lazy worked for him.

CHAPTER THREE

Outside of town, Theo urged her minivan up the hill to the back of Nina's house. Unlike Theo's ancient home in town, Nina's beautiful house was spacious and constructed to take advantage of the spectacular view. It sat on a ten-acre lot. Built on part of the old family farm her father converted to high-priced lots when he realized selling real estate paid better than farming in poor soil; the modern brown brick house had an unobstructed view of the Smoky Mountains. Today the distinctive haze did make them appear mysteriously smoke-blue.

Nina's copper-red hair glowed like fire. She stood near her driveway, examining something in the flowerbed. The way her fists rested on her hips and the line of her spine said someone was in trouble. Deep trouble. Theo assumed it must be one of Nina's children.

Across the road was McMahon Park, the center of the loosely constructed subdivision. More nature preserve than park, it was beautiful and wild. Only a small section of it had been tamed into a playground area. Theo had been looking for wildflowers when she wandered in there a few months ago. Instead of flowers, she had discovered the bones of a hand. Every time she visited Nina, she wondered about them. Tony hadn't mentioned anything about them in weeks.

"The damned deer ate all the buds." Nina jumped into the minivan. "What's this all about?"

"Jane wouldn't say much. It sounds like someone may give

the new museum a quilt labeled 'the murder quilt.' "

"Well, no wonder she called you." Nina laughed. "Either one of those words would drag you out of your studio. Using both magic words in one phrase—wow, I'm surprised you slowed down to pick me up."

With a laugh, Theo stuck her tongue out. "One of your old neighbors came into the shop this morning."

"Who?"

"Vicky Parker."

"Icky?" Nina's eyes twinkled. "I see her uncle from time to time but I haven't seen her in ages. She only lived up there off and on. Never for longer than a couple of months at a time." Nina pointed to a small white house on the next hill over. "Since the county built the new road, Nelson doesn't drive past here anymore."

Theo frowned. "If she calls me for lunch, you have to come, too."

Much later, Wade came back into Tony's office waving the envelope. "No one, not even you, Sheriff, left a clear print on the paper."

The information didn't surprise Tony. The day didn't feel like one during which anything was going to come easily.

"I could send it off to the FBI. In the class you sent me to, they trained me to do fingerprint analysis on reasonably normal surfaces." He leaned forward over Tony's desk and tapped the bag holding the card. "They might be able to raise a print where I failed, although it won't be fast."

Tony doubted anything would come of sending the envelope to the FBI. "I guess it wouldn't hurt to try. Let's wait until we decide if there is something to this or it's just some prankster."

He leaned back in his chair. "Speaking of pranks, someone has stolen a large yard ornament from in front of the Flowers' house. I'm going over now, and I want you to follow me for backup."

"Backup?" Wade's dark blue eyes sparkled. "Are you expecting trouble? Should I call the TBI? FBI? Maybe Blossom and the rest of the Flowers are terrorists using the lawn ornament as an excuse to lure you out of your office."

"Very funny."

Still stewing over the newspaper clipping and the note, Tony drove past the Flowers home. Set back from the road, the rambling structure was a lot like the family that lived inside. There were lots of Flowers, and each was a petal or two off in Tony's opinion.

The center of the large yard was a well-manicured grass lawn. Around the perimeter of the grass grew a small forest of crape myrtles and rhododendron. Blossom kept her collection of yard ornaments in plain view. Tony was not a connoisseur of plaster figurines, even so, he suspected these had to be factory seconds.

A large, red-coated gnome squatted next to the driveway holding a hand-painted sign. Uneven letters spelled "Flowers." There was something about the gnome's pose that conveyed an impression of discomfort, like the little guy was searching for the outhouse and may have waited too long to begin his search. Overall, Tony thought the Flowers family presented a more tasteful display than some in town. Few homes in Silersville didn't have at least one gnome, fairy, frog or dragonfly parked in the vegetation.

Thinking how he preferred the goofy animal ornaments to the ones painted to look like the back end of a woman bending over, her skirt sliding up, he parked across the road and walked toward the Flowers' yard. His arrival stirred up a pair of spotted hounds. Jumping to their feet, they stood behind a screen door baying like they'd treed a raccoon. Tony tried to ignore them as

21

he wandered around with a camera and snapped a few pictures. It was easy to see where the donkey and cart had been. Mud and grass had been churned up as the thief had wrestled with the unwieldy piece.

Wade pulled up behind Tony's official green-and-white Blazer. Wade was Tony's unofficial chief deputy and full-time assistant. "What's up?"

"Someone took Blossom's donkey and cart." Tony stepped back and took a photograph of the street near the site. "She called me claiming Queen Doreen had done it."

"You could have sent Sheila or me out to take the pictures."

"Yeah, I know." Tony straightened. "Then it would automatically become an official investigation and I'd have to do more damned paperwork."

Wade climbed out of his car. His curiosity, like Tony's, had been piqued. "How'd they get it out of there without breaking it to bits? Or did they?"

"And why?" Tony pointed to the gnome with the dyspeptic expression and several other smaller items, like a cross-eyed frog and a turtle holding a pink umbrella. "Those would be a lot easier to pick up."

"Why does Blossom think it was the mayor's wife?"

"I gather it's a feud with some history." From behind him came the aroma of cinnamon and apples. His stomach rumbled. He saw Wade straighten, and a grin lit his handsome face. Focusing on his deputy's startling good looks, Tony realized it was time to take Wade off of street patrol. During the height of tourist season, carloads of giggling girls would run stop signs just to get a close look at him.

Tony turned. Blossom churned her way across the lawn. A plateful of something emitting heavenly scents was clutched in her fat fingers. Dressed in an outfit resembling a recycled circus tent of orange and red, she was barefoot. Even her toes looked overweight. A sweet smile lit her homely face.

"I'm so glad you came by," Blossom panted. She lifted the paper napkin away from the plate underneath and exposed a pile of fat cookies. "They're apple. I hear it's your favorite fruit, isn't it? I thought you and Wade might need a little something while you investigate." She batted her stubby eyelashes at both men.

Wade was the first to recover his poise. "Why, thank you, Blossom, you know I can resist anything but temptation." He picked a pair of cookies off the plate with one hand.

Tony hated to see his deputy eat alone, so he took a couple as well. Like everything Blossom cooked, these cookies tasted like a little bit of heaven, warm and moist, apples and spice and, as usual, something he couldn't identify. He stifled his impulse to grab the whole plate and lock himself in the car until he finished them all.

"You are one terrific cook," said Wade.

"Amen," added Tony. He looked past her to the dogs, still baying wildly. "Didn't the dogs bark or wake anyone up?"

Blossom's head moved slowly from side to side.

Wade glanced around. "Is that normal? They're going nuts here in the middle of the day and I'm not stealing anything."

She put on her thoughtful expression. "That must have been the night Daddy and Toot, you know, Marigold's oldest boy, took them coon hunting." She eased closer to Tony.

Anxious to be away from Blossom's adoring presence, Tony sidled toward the Blazer. "I'd better get going." Blossom followed him the whole way, continuing to offer more cookies until he closed the door in her face.

CHAPTER FOUR

Tony decided to visit the mayor's home. In the unlikely event Doreen had taken the ornament, maybe it now sat on the Cash-dollar's lawn. It wouldn't hurt to look. As a stalling technique, he thought it possessed multiple virtues, not the least of which would be visiting the couple outside of their work areas.

Calvin Cashdollar made no secret of his wealth. He had a healthy income from his mortuary business. Those funds, added to the wad he'd inherited, made him rich. If he wasn't the community's richest citizen, he was close to it, or had been until Queen Doreen started shopping. Although Doreen owned a gift shop, she left the actual work to her employees and dedicated herself to buying. Some of the things she purchased actually ended up for sale in the shop.

In spite of criticism stemming from being a mayor who didn't reside in the town he represented, Calvin and the Queen lived in a rambling white-brick home outside of town. Set in the center of thirty acres, it was easily the most luxurious house in the county. Tony had heard once that the house boasted eleven bathrooms. He couldn't vouch for the information because he had never gotten past the foyer and the mayor's home office.

The house was not visible from the road and only a discreet number on the gateposts signaled the beginning of the driveway. The decorative white-brick pillars supported a cast-iron gate. They were topped with urn-shaped decorations. Rumor was one contained Calvin's mother and the other one his father. A winding drive led to an open park with the faux English manor house at the far end.

Tony parked the Blazer at the bottom of the steps and approached the door. Evergreen topiaries, trained and trimmed into spiral shapes, flanked the double oak panels. Steeling himself to talk to Doreen, he rang the doorbell.

From somewhere deep in the house came the sound of chimes playing "Rock of Ages." After a minute of listening to most of the melody, it almost surprised Tony when the door opened.

Pansy Flowers Millsaps stared up at him. Pansy was an older version of her baby sister, Blossom. Whereas Blossom flaunted her size, Pansy seemed to be trying to suppress hers. Squished into a pair of black slacks two sizes smaller than she needed and an equally tight long-sleeved white cotton blouse covered with a black apron cinched around her waist, she looked too uncomfortable for words.

"What?" From her sour expression, it appeared Pansy didn't share her sister's affection for him.

"Good afternoon, Pansy." Tony tried his most ingratiating smile. It had no noticeable effect. He shifted his duty belt and her eyes focused on his sidearm. "Is Mrs. Cashdollar at home?"

"No."

Pansy would have shut the door in his face if he hadn't quickly wedged his foot into the opening. "Do you know where I might find her?"

"Why?"

"I don't have to account to you for anything, Pansy." Tony frowned down at her, annoyed by her attitude. "This does concern a member of your family. I'm looking into the disappearance of one of Blossom's lawn ornaments."

Suddenly the door opened wide and Pansy stepped forward, concerned. "Which one?"

"The donkey and cart."

"Oh, dear, I hope you find the statue for her. It's one of Blossom's favorites." Pansy pulled a dust rag from one of her apron pockets and began polishing the brass door handle. "Her Majesty went over to your mom's new museum with some quilts."

"When did she leave?"

"You just missed her." Pansy stowed the rag and without another word, shut the door in his face.

Faced with the solid oak panel again, Tony turned and left.

The museum project made Tony believe his mother and his Aunt Martha had lost their collective minds. The sisters had purchased an ageing and dilapidated motel on the outskirts of town and had plans to create a folk museum and classrooms on the site. They had enticed Tony's brother Gus to be the contractor in charge.

Only a few months earlier, they had stalled on the museum plan and had talked about going to Chattanooga and resurrecting their childhood sister singing act. Thankfully, a benefactor had donated an ancient barn to the museum's cause. To everyone's relief, receiving a barn set the ladies back on the museum path and away from singing on the road. At the very least the project kept the ghost of Tony's late father from moaning in the dark about his widow singing in bars.

The gift of the dilapidated barn quickly turned into a double-edged sword. Theo claimed it was a case of old man Ferguson seeing a way to get someone else to pay to clean a relic off his farm.

Tony agreed with his wife.

His big brother Gus, who was not usually a man prone to profanity, had begun swearing the second he saw the antique pile of termite-infested boards. He'd been improving his vocabulary on a daily basis since then and had reached expert level a week ago.

Until then, a hint of hope remained. Maybe the barn would survive traveling intact. Alas, the truth quickly became clear. The structure only remained upright because of several strategically placed supports held into the ground with a truckload of concrete. Just using the boards in random order would not work. A "See Rock City" painting adorned the roof and one side of the building. It needed to be reconstructed on site, in the proper sequence. According to Gus, they were going to number each of the boards and haul it on flatbed trailers.

The donation of the barn had inspired countless families to clean out the family attics and barns. While it would be unthinkable to throw away Granny's old butter churn, it would be a public service to donate it to the museum. Because of a widespread school of thought, old items destined for display had begun to arrive long before the ladies were ready for them.

Gus and his crew had been busy. After cutting away a jungle of kudzu, they had razed all of the old guest cabins, leaving a trail of tracks and potholes all over the area. A bulldozer was busy pushing over the cinderblock building formerly used as the office.

Two temporary collection warehouses had been created on the site where a garden would eventually be planted. There was a metal shed containing a host of old harness parts, barn lanterns and farming tools. They had stopped counting rusty hoes. No one understood why donating a hoe seemed so popular. It's not like the technology had changed a lot in the past fifty years.

A mobile home hauled in to be the temporary office became the storage area for smaller, more fragile items. As Tony pulled into the lot, he could see his wife's minivan, his mom's car and a beige Volvo. Queen Doreen drove a beige Volvo. He smiled.

She was trapped.

He parked the Blazer behind the Volvo and walked toward the trailer. Gus intercepted him before he reached the door. Tony grinned at his older brother. Gus might have hair but Tony had the height. Tony's six feet four inches was noticeably more than Gus's mere six feet. He loved to stand toe-to-toe with Gus and irritate him. After all, what else are brothers supposed to do?

He was about to give Gus a ration of grief but the man's expression stopped him. "Having a bad day?"

"Can I borrow your gun?" Gus asked. Desperation oozed from him.

"Maybe. Who are you planning to shoot?" Tony glanced around. Three men stood around a deep hole, inserting rebar into it, reinforcing something.

For just an instant, he visualized a grave. The idea of finding bones down in the pit chilled him. Knowing he would go crazy if his imagination ran wild, he forced a jovial expression onto his face. "The names have to be on the paperwork, you know." He did laugh when Gus rolled his eyes because it made him look just like Tony's six-year-old son, Jamie.

Gus didn't answer the gun question directly. "Your mother is just plain nuts."

"Mine is? Last I heard we share the same gene pool."

"No way. She's all yours." Gus tipped his head toward the trailer. "I sent her into the trailer for her own safety. She wanted to climb down into the hole and measure something. For a little while, I thought I'd have to duct tape her into a chair."

"Maybe we can give her to our sister," said Tony, pushing aside a sense of impending doom.

"Callie didn't move to Memphis by accident. Why do you think our sister lives in the other end of the state?" Gus looked amused and didn't wait for Tony to answer. "It's because she's smarter than any of her brothers."

Tony couldn't dispute his statement.

Stepping up onto the tiny, temporary stoop, he turned the knob on the door and pulled it open. The sound made by five women with different opinions hit him like a brick. He took an involuntary step backwards and nearly fell. The knob came off in his hand as a heavy spring snapped the door shut in his face. Holding the useless knob, he turned to look at Gus.

Merriment erased some of the fatigue on Gus's face. "It comes off all the time. The knob's just on there for show anyway."

Tony heard laughter in his brother's voice. Without understanding what happened, he smiled in response. "How?"

Gus pointed to the additional hardware on the door frame. "They use the hasp and ring and close it with a padlock."

Tony steeled himself and opened the door again. A large open room had been created by removing all of the furniture except two big tables. Floor-to-ceiling open shelves lined the walls, providing storage for numerous assorted items.

Five women stood around the tables, studying a pair of quilts. If expression meant anything, they looked like a group of surgeons performing a heart transplant. Those women were serious.

He could see his mother and her sister standing on one side of the table. They held their hands behind their backs, probably to keep from touching the quilt. Over the past ten years of living with Theo, he had learned a lot about quilts. He knew it was very bad form to touch antique quilts, or quilts in a show, with bare hands. Dirt and oils could damage them beyond repair.

He thought Jane looked quite good for her mysterious age of sixty-something. Her baby sister Martha was only fifty, closer to Tony's age than Jane's and looked even frumpier than ever. Her gray hair didn't look like it had been combed this century. Martha held a notebook and pen.

At the far end of the table, Tony could see Theo's wild golden curls. Her face was turned down as she examined the quilt. His wife's best friend, Nina, stood near her and shielded her expression. Her copper-red hair gleamed like a beacon.

Nearest him, Queen Doreen gripped one of the quilts. White cotton gloves covered her hands. As usual, she was dressed like a fashion plate. Tony didn't think he had ever seen her in jeans or a T-shirt. Her hair was rarely the same color or style. The hairstyle of the week was a white-blond, almost boyish cut. It looked good on her fragile features.

Doreen sounded like a museum docent. "This one is known in our family as the engagement quilt. The one on the table is the murder quilt." She waited while Martha made the appropriate notes and Jane attached tags to them using special acid-free cardboard. "My grandmother Bathsheba Cochran gave them over to me. As the only female member of my family, I am responsible for their care. I won't let you display them if there is any chance they'll be ruined."

Theo's voice sounded muffled. "I can see some pulled threads, and a couple of the fabrics have completely deteriorated on the engagement quilt. This section looks like a cat used it for a bed. Do you want to display it as is or have someone try to restore it?"

"How can they restore it? It is priceless." Disdain lifted one corner of her collagen-enhanced lips.

"I know." Theo's face turned toward Doreen. "Sometimes people will opt to cover the exposed batting with a swatch of the same or very similar antique fabric, especially if the quilt is heavily damaged in one area. This quilt has suffered from hard wear over the years."

"I don't want some amateur messing with it."

The glint in Theo's eyes was one Tony was familiar with. Doreen might not realize she was messing with dynamite. His dainty little wife was about to explode. He cleared his throat, bringing all eyes to him. "Could I possibly talk to you outside, Doreen?"

He wished he had a picture of the five women. It was probably the first time in history all five were silent at the same time. The sound of his voice rendered them speechless. They had been studying the quilt intently. None of them appeared to have heard the commotion with the door and the busted knob. They all jerked upright and swiveled to face him.

Doreen didn't waste any of her pleasant public expression on him. Shooting him the royal glare reserved for the help, she stalked past him and down the steps.

CHAPTER FIVE

Theo craned her neck. She couldn't see anything of interest through the tiny window. Tony and Doreen had vanished. "What do you suppose is going on?"

Nina moved to a different window as if looking at the same view from a different angle would help. "Beats me."

"Never mind what's going on out there." Martha pulled the younger women away from the window. "Before Doreen comes back in, tell us what you think we should do with these quilts?"

Theo spread the murder quilt out on the spotless table. Inspecting it in detail, she admired the beautiful workmanship. What looked like millions of tiny stitches held the patchwork together. Another million created an intricate pattern of quilting, holding the layers of front, back and cotton batting together so closely nothing could shift. She flinched at the sight of a large, dark blotch in the center. Clearly it was a very old bloodstain. A wave of nausea ran through her and was gone in a second. Most likely using hot water and lye soap, the launderer had set the stain instead of washing it out.

By sheer chance the quilt hadn't been destroyed. She wondered when Doreen was going to explain how the quilt was named. If the stain was any indication, it would not be a pleasant story. "How good is your insurance?"

"Okay, I guess." Martha squinted. "Why?"

"Get more if you are going to display her quilts and photograph everything carefully. Document everything and make sure she signs off on it. If there is one stain or loose thread not documented, she's bound to sue, claiming you are the one who damaged it." Theo peered over the top of her glasses. "It is a lovely piece, though. I wonder if I could reproduce the pattern as a mystery quilt. I haven't designed one of those for a while, have I?"

Nina groaned. "And you'll make me test it and I'll end up with one more unfinished project."

"Absolutely." Theo set an elbow into Nina's ribs. "At least three if I'm lucky. Think of all the fabric you'll get to buy at my shop."

Martha looked to her sister for a translation. "What is she talking about?"

"Are you sure we're related?" Jane grinned. "A mystery quilt is constructed without a picture. You just follow the clues, cutting and sewing as directed."

"Does it work?"

"Oh, yeah." Nina laughed. "Some of those turn out prettier than ones where you think you know what you're doing."

Theo glanced up from the quilt when the door swung open again. Expecting Doreen or even Tony, she jumped, surprised, as Winifred Thornby, the editor, reporter and photographer for the *Silersville Gazette* charged inside. She reminded Theo of the pictures of her own namesake, Theodore Roosevelt, charging up San Juan Hill.

Following in her wake, Queen Doreen returned, wearing her haughtiest expression, and didn't look at anyone. Tony ducked and entered. In the small space and surrounded by a gaggle of women, Theo thought her husband looked like he'd grown. Wearing his chocolate brown, short-sleeved uniform shirt and khaki pants, as well as his duty belt with its assorted weapons and tools—pistol, handcuffs, radio, pepper spray, and flashlight—he looked huge. The ball cap with the department insignia covered his bald head but not his expression. Tony stood in the corner, grinning like a pirate. Theo knew and loved that smile. She couldn't wait to learn why he was using it.

Tony thought the combination of heat and limited floor space in the trailer created a claustrophobic's nightmare. Not normally bothered by close places, he began feeling uneasy. To get a breath of air, he attempted to back away from the women and quilts and bumped into a wall.

Winifred began issuing instructions to the ladies about how she wanted the quilts held while she took her photographs. If she wrote the story the way Doreen obviously wanted, the news article threatened to become more of a publicity article for the Cashdollar family than for the new museum.

Peering at them through the camera's viewfinder, Winifred obviously realized there wasn't enough space in the trailer to allow her to take a suitable photograph of the murder quilt. "Everyone outside." She pointed to the older women holding the quilt. "Don't get that dirty."

Tony stayed behind and watched as the flock of women climbed out of the trailer. In a rare moment of cooperation, they all worked together to keep the quilt from touching the ground as it was photographed outside.

Tony glared at Doreen through the tiny window. She might look like Peter Pan with her new haircut but she was no child. She just turned her back to him and walked away. Vastly irritated by Doreen's dismissal, Tony wasn't leaving or letting her leave, until he got an answer to his question about the lawn ornament.

The Blazer parked behind her Volvo might be the only thing guaranteed to ensure her cooperation. She'd talk to him just to get rid of him.

With nothing else to do for the moment, his mind returned

to the mysterious note and newspaper clipping. He really didn't like the image it conjured in his mind. More unidentified bodies in his county! If something turned up, he'd have to call in the TBI, because Park County did not have the necessary resources. The Tennessee Bureau of Investigation would not be thrilled, either. The older the bones, the harder it would be to solve the case. If there was a case. He still hoped the note and newspaper clipping were part of a joke.

If so, it wasn't a funny one.

To distract himself, he turned and began to examine some of the donated bits and pieces lining the open shelves. It was easy to recognize items like old tobacco tins and medicine bottles. A set of surgical tools lay open on the bare wood. Knowing how little regard earlier centuries had for sterilization processes, Tony felt queasy. The crude implements, saws and scalpels, resembled the ones in his brother's toolbox. No, he reconsidered his thoughts. Gus kept his tools cleaner, and he'd bet his brother's saw was sharper.

Tony couldn't erase his memories of being shot and the medical aftermath. If the Chicago doctor who had removed the bullets from his stomach had used those old tools, Tony knew he would be dead, butchered like a hog.

He began to turn away when a stack of unfamiliar items captured his attention. Grateful for the distraction, he stared at them for a long time. What were they? They looked like oversized scrub brushes set with metal spikes instead of bristles. He leaned forward to better examine the spikes. Each one came through the wooden base as a square, approximately a quarter of an inch per side. From there it became tapered and rounded until it finished as a point. The spikes on each "thingy" were uniform length. Some four inches, the longest he saw had six-inch spikes. All appeared to be made of iron, not polished smooth, and the number of rows of the closely set spikes varied as well. The spiked board was attached to a second board, some of which had padded ends. For the life of him, he couldn't decide what purpose they served.

The door opened behind him and the women trooped back inside. The chatter was dying down. Winifred had taken her photographs. When she began taking her notes and continuing the interview, Tony got the feeling she was willing to give the museum project the respect it was due. The newspaper needed articles.

Tony waited until Winifred began to put away her camera gear before he tried to talk to her. "Hey, Winifred?" He took a step forward. "What's the *Gazette*'s out of town circulation? You know, approximately how many out-of-towners will read about the new museum?"

Winifred's perpetual frown deepened, and he was struck once more by how his high school classmate looked older than his mother.

"More than stay within the county. Probably about three thousand."

"All within driving distance of Silersville?"

"Most of them, I guess." Winifred flipped her notebook closed without taking her eyes from his. "A few get mailed out of the country. One even goes to China."

"Where would you say the largest portion goes?" Tony wondered who in China would be interested in local gossip, which was the bulk of each edition.

Her eyes narrowed. "Why the sudden interest in my newspaper? Is there something I should know about?"

Winifred, for all her faults, could smell a story. He shook his head. "My mom and aunt are working hard on this project." He edged around the subject. Although he had gone to high school with Winifred, or maybe *because* he had, the two of them didn't get along very well. "I was just curious about how much publicity they might be getting and where the information was going."

She stared at him for a full minute, assessing his statement. Finally, she appeared to accept his story at face value and reached into her pocket for her keys. "Well, if this is going to make tomorrow's edition, I'd better get going."

Even though she hadn't answered his question, Tony squeezed into the corner to let her pass.

The *Silersville Gazette* came out twice a week, in the evening, and he knew Winifred's part-time reporters couldn't come close to doing it without her.

Once she was gone, he glanced around, his eyes searching for the mayor's wife. He thought Doreen might be trying to hide behind his wife. Good luck with that. Tony slipped an antacid tablet out of his shirt pocket and popped it into his mouth as he looked directly at Theo. When she smiled at him, he tipped his head only slightly. The girl he had married was brilliant. She knew what he wanted. As casually as she could, she pushed Nina out of the way and then dragged her around to the far side of the tables, leaving Doreen totally exposed with no place to run.

Realizing she was trapped, the mayor's wife capitulated. She brushed past him and went back outside.

Tony got right to the point. "Do you know anything about the disappearance of a lawn ornament from the Flowers' home?"

"No." Doreen's lips twitched, deepening the sneer. "I imagine it would be hard to know if one was missing. There ought to be an ordinance against displaying crap like that in public."

"I don't suppose you've mentioned your feelings to any of the Flowers clan?" He'd be surprised if she deigned to talk to Pansy about anything other than the orders of the day. He sincerely hoped Pansy was paid well for her trouble. Housekeeping for the Queen had to be a thankless job.

"I do remember telling Claude Marmot he ought to pick up

some of those things when he's making his trash pick up. They are simply hideous."

To him, the most surprising thing about her statement was learning Queen Doreen had deigned to speak to Marmot-the-Varmint. Claude Marmot was the county trash collector and not well known for his tidy personal habits. Truth be told, he smelled worse than the dump. With the exceptional heat of late, that was saying something. Tony supposed he would have to drive out to the dump. Maybe he'd get Wade to ride along on the fun jaunt. Just in case the donkey was out there, he could have it checked for fingerprints. The county had paid to send Wade to Quantico for special training by the FBI. If Doreen had touched it, Tony wanted to know about it. He backed the Blazer out of the way and watched as Doreen climbed into her Volvo and tore out of the site, her tires throwing clumps of mud and loose grass.

Theo felt as though she had escaped from prison by the time she and Nina got back to her studio. The whole business with Doreen and Winifred had wasted the whole morning. She did like the new pattern idea circulating in her brain and couldn't wait to start working on it.

"You can help me work up the mystery quilt pattern." She reached into a drawer and handed Nina a stack of various cotton fabrics cut into small squares. "Sew these first. Don't worry about the colors matching or anything, just sew any two together, right sides of the fabrics facing to make twosies until you run out. Press the seam toward the darker fabric and then sew two sets together to make a square."

Nina furrowed her brow as she examined the wild assortment of colors and fabrics. "These are hideous together. You've got flowers and plaids and polka dots all mixed together."

"Don't worry about matching the colors or even separating

them into lights and darks, just randomly sew. I know you like to overthink colors. Forget it. You'll love doing this. No thinking required."

Nina's expression remained uncertain. "Slave driver."

"Hey, school's out. You don't have anything better to do until you go to the university for your continuing education stuff. You don't even have mom excuses, because I happen to know the kids are staying with their father." Theo poked her in the shoulder. "You work for me now."

"What's the story with Tony and Doreen? What did he want with her?" Nina went to Theo's spare sewing machine and began stacking her squares. "For a moment, I dreamed he was about to drag her off, handcuffed and screaming."

"That picture does have a certain allure, doesn't it?" Theo grinned at her best friend. "I have no idea what was going on. No one keeps a secret better than Tony does." She handed Nina a new spool of thread. "Unlike you."

"Hey, not fair. I can keep a secret. It's just the people I tell who have loose lips."

CHAPTER SIX

Tony knew Claude Marmot fairly well.

Honest to a fault, the man also had a deep and abiding love of garbage. His one-room house sat just off the road between Silersville and the Park County landfill. Because he retrieved a lot of the discards and decorated his lawn with them, it was hard to tell where the line between his home and the landfill was drawn.

Sitting in the passenger seat of the Blazer, Wade gave a low whistle. "It looks like he's adding on."

Tony pulled into the gravel driveway, carefully avoiding hitting any of the assorted "rescued" items. After he parked, he saw what Wade meant. Slightly behind the house was a skeleton of a building. It consisted of a framework of two-by-fours and some roof trusses.

Claude was in the process of lifting a three-legged table from the back of his battered car/truck, a sedan he had converted into a pickup. Formerly a midnight blue 1989 Crown Victoria, the car had been cut and spliced. The back seat area and trunk became an open bed. The back seat now sat under an awning from the old bank building. The awning dangled crookedly from mismatched salvaged poles, providing cover and shade for the luxury lawn chair.

When Claude spotted them, he smiled, exposing one of the worst sets of teeth in the county. He propped his new find against the side of his unpainted cottage, positioning the corner missing a leg away from the building. As Tony and Wade walked up to him, he continued with his project.

"Afternoon, Sheriff. Wade." Claude released the table, stepped back and looked surprised when the table fell over.

"New treasure?" Tony asked. He was careful to stay upwind of the man.

"Yep." Claude scratched his belly where it was exposed between the bottom of his filthy t-shirt and the top of his even filthier jeans. He was the hairiest man Tony had seen. His belly looked like it was covered with black fur. "People are just too wasteful for words." Claude pointed at the new construction. "Old man Nelson paid me a hundred bucks to take it away."

"Really? Why?" Wade asked.

"Beats me." Claude flapped his beefy arms. "He's been taking the shingles and siding off for months. Then, all of a sudden, he wanted this gone. There was an old freezer inside I wouldn't take 'cause he wouldn't remove the door. Lazy bastard." His toothy grin reinforced the slight rodent quality of his face, part of the source of his nickname. "The old coot called the building a squirrel-infested mess. It looked like a gift to me. I can add it on to my place and maybe have enough space for my wife."

"Wife?" said Wade.

"Yep. I've got her all picked out."

Tony's mind shied away from the idea of what a Mrs. Marmot would be like and what he meant by picking her out. Instead, he focused on the rejects Claude had adopted. Tony didn't see any sign of traditional lawn ornaments. He saw pieces of pipe, discarded furniture, old bottles and even a rusted bicycle with one wheel.

He looked back at Claude. "I understand the mayor's wife suggested you ought to remove some yard decorations in town."

"Oh, yeah. The Queen sure has got some bug up her butt

about those things. She had a whole list of things she thought were 'con-tam-in-a-ting' the town." With each syllable spoken, his expression of disdain seemed to deepen.

"And you?"

Claude grinned and snorted, making his belly bob up and down under his too-short shirt. Resting his fists on his hips, he leaned against the side of the house and began using the rough board siding to scratch his back like a bear against a tree.

"I like them just fine and the county's not paying me to steal folks stuff on the Queen's say-so." Claude surveyed his domain. "It's not exactly my decorating style. I think it cheapens the looks of the place. To each his own." Claude stopped scratching and his eyes met Tony's. "As long as you're here, I ought to tell you she weren't too keen on some of your mom's yard stuff neither."

Tony could practically feel his eyebrows hit the brim of his hat.

"I don't suppose you've noticed if Blossom's donkey and cart appeared in someone else's yard?" Wade asked. He bent forward and tried to pet a tiny striped kitten poking its head out from under a tarp near his feet. The timid creature slipped away. "Maybe it was just moved into another place."

"Donkey?" Claude looked confused for a moment then began to chuckle. "Oh, I know the one you mean. The three-eyed jackass." He laughed harder, his belly bouncing wildly. "Someone stole that? Wow! Your thieves are really strong or used a front loader. The thing has to weigh a ton."

His workday over, Tony parked in front his house. He couldn't help comparing it to the Cashdollar mansion. The similarities ended with two facts. They were both two stories tall and made of brick.

His home sat on a pleasant, tree-covered lot across from the city park. It was the first brick house built in Silersville and some of the bricks had begun to crumble. The bottom line about living in such an old house was everything needed repairs or remodeling. He shook his head. That wasn't quite true. Not anymore. It did have a brand-new heating and air-conditioning system. The old furnace had died in January and would cost more to repair than to replace. Unfortunately, the money earmarked for a new car for Theo had been diverted into the house.

Technically, Theo owned the house. She grew up in it and eventually inherited it from her grandparents. None of their family could imagine living in a different house in Silersville. It had what their house in Chicago never had—history and character. Maybe a little too much character.

But, it was home.

He didn't have time to waste, needing to change clothes before practice started. He didn't want to wear his uniform to the ball fields. Both of the boys had baseball practice and he was the assistant coach for Jamie's team, Ruby's Reds. Theo would make sure Chris made it to his team practice. Chris played for the Gazette Sox. Not for the first time, Tony wondered how single parents got anything done and delivered each child to individual activities, too.

Once practice ended and the family was home again, they had a late dinner of tuna melt sandwiches and soup. The boys ate and ran. Enjoying the quiet, Tony filled Theo in on his day. When he mentioned the newspaper clipping and note, he gained her full attention.

"That's just spooky." Theo paused in the middle of cleaning the table. "Do you think it's for real?"

"I hope it's just a sick joke." Tony guessed it wasn't. He didn't want to say more.

His concern grew as he watched Theo. She seemed so lost in

thought that she didn't even notice she left half of the table dirty when she dropped the rag in the sink and sat down. She looked pale as death.

Theo felt so queasy she couldn't decide whether to throw up or faint first. Little black dots swirled in front of her eyes and she could hear an odd buzzing sound. It was loud enough to block out Tony's voice.

The bones in the woods. She'd found them behind Nina's house by accident. No one knew to whom they belonged. If they were from the time while Tony was away in the Navy or at Northwestern, he wouldn't have known about them. Would anyone have told him about the strange things that happened here so many years ago?

Just before she would have toppled onto the floor, she felt his arms surround her. The nausea stopped as quickly as it started.

"I think you need to talk to Harvey." She tilted her head back and met his eyes. Tony looked scared. Theo couldn't believe her eyes.

"Are you okay?" He clutched her tighter.

Theo swallowed hard and nodded. "I just remembered hearing something terrible happened when you were off kissing the girls in every port."

"What?"

"I think you were still in the Navy. Maybe you were already going to Northwestern." Theo thought he wouldn't have looked more confused if she had suddenly started speaking in Russian. "I'm not sure. I lived on campus and was wrapped up in school when my grandmother warned me about the 'meanness in the world' and said Harvey was dealing with it." Theo felt cold and hot at the same time. "Can I have some water?"

Tony didn't like seeing Theo so upset. If he hadn't grabbed her in time, she would have passed out and fallen off her chair. As it was, he had to help her hold the glass of water because her hands were shaking so badly. Her skin tone was more green than pink.

"I feel so silly," said Theo.

"Nonsense." Tony realized his own hands were shaking, splashing water onto his wife. "Did you remember something specific?"

"Not really." She pushed the glass away. "I've felt kind of off all day and suddenly I remembered a call from my grandparents when I was in Knoxville."

"They used a telephone?" Tony eased himself onto the floor next to Theo. Her grandparents—he always thought of them as "the old people"—had not believed in modern conveniences, including the telephone. They must have been disturbed indeed to have used one.

"I know." Theo gave him a watery smile. "It was probably the only time they used one. I think your dad helped them make the call."

"What was it about? Do you remember any details?"

Theo gazed into space. "Mammaw heard that people were missing. Just vanished into thin air, you know, so she assumed the devil was loose." Her smile showed her love for the old woman. "Of course, if the milk spoiled, she blamed the devil."

Theo seemed better and Tony felt himself relaxing, too. "Did you ever hear more about it?"

She shook her head. "When I came home for a visit, they had forgotten all about it or weren't worried anymore." Pressing her forehead against his chest, she sighed. "They died not long after that."

Tony held her close. He could feel her sorrow for the parents she didn't remember and the grandparents who raised her. Hoping to distract her, he whispered in her ear, "Marmot-the-

Varmint is looking for a wife."

"No way." Theo's expression of mingled horror and delight was gratifying. When she kissed him, he thought, very gratifying indeed.

CHAPTER SEVEN

The first thing the next morning, Tony called on retired Sheriff Harvey Winston. Refusing an offer of coffee, he jumped into the topic. "You remember those bones Theo found this spring?"

"Yep."

Harvey had never been a chatterbox. Tony wondered if his answer seemed more terse than usual—or maybe Theo's comments infused a fair amount of suspicion in his mind. Tony tried again. "It's been a while since I talked to you about them. Do you remember any missing person cases, no matter how long ago?"

"Nope."

"Well, I received an anonymous note yesterday claiming there are more bodies to be found and Theo said I should ask you about something when she was in college. It scared her grandmother and grandfather enough to make a phone call."

"You don't say?" Harvey sat a bit straighter. "A phone call? The Silers?"

Tony didn't answer, letting the older man process the information.

"And now an anonymous letter?" The sleepy tone vanished. Harvey's interest glowed in his eyes. "Where was it mailed? Do you believe it?"

"It was postmarked in Cincinnati. I don't know what to think. Theo was pretty upset last night." Tony leaned back in his chair trying to relax. The memory of Theo's near collapse kept the

47

muscles in the back of his neck tight. "It's a pretty weird practical joke to make from Ohio. If it was mailed locally I'd come closer to believing some kid was having a little fun."

"It's been a while, now that you mention it, I don't think a woman who went missing in the Gatlinburg area of the national park was ever found, and of course there were always rumors of wild pigs eating children in Cades Cove." Harvey was suddenly garrulous, uncharacteristically so. "Of course, neither of those is in Park County. There's no reason to believe anyone was killed. Even if they were, there's no proof they came near here."

"Neither of those scenarios would be likely to upset Theo's grandmother. That woman wasn't afraid of anything." Tony hoped a little humor would loosen Harvey's lips.

With a snort, Harvey dropped his guard. "You are right, of course. She was a lot tougher than me. Now that you mention it, we did have a strange case. Can't imagine how I forgot about it since it scared the snot out of me at the time. I doubt it's what you're looking for." He cleared his throat a couple of times. "There was some animal mutilation. It started with a couple of small animals. A possum, for sure, and maybe a coon. I'm not sure what else. Oh, yeah, someone's goat disappeared around then. It was probably a simple theft. The whole thing ended as fast as it started, after a couple of cattle were slaughtered. A year or so later, I put the file away. It never happened again."

"How long ago?"

"Years." Harvey fell silent.

Tony remembered Theo's timetable. "Maybe twenty years ago? That would be about the time I joined the Navy."

"No. Well, I guess it could be. I was thinking maybe a couple of years later." He gazed out the window and nodded. "My youngest was away at Xavier, playing on a basketball scholarship. I remember being glad that she wasn't around with some freak running loose."

"Isn't she the same age as Theo?"

"Yep. They graduated at the same time. So it's maybe been fifteen or sixteen years."

Maybe this was what had upset Theo's grandmother. It was odd. No one in his family had bothered to tell him about the most exciting thing that had probably happened in Park County since they had moved there.

Harvey laughed. "About that same time there were some reports of space ship landings, aliens loose, some real woo-woo stuff. The closest thing to space aliens I ever saw is that robot statue and life-sized saucer old man Ferguson built out of tractor parts and stuck in his front yard."

"Okay, thanks, Harvey. Call me if you think of anything else."

"Keep your powder dry, kid."

Tony laughed and saluted before leaving the old sheriff.

Harvey had been the sheriff in Park County since forever. He had been the sheriff when the Abernathy family had moved to Silersville when Tony was eight. He was still the sheriff until three years ago when Tony and Theo moved back from Chicago, at his suggestion. With his support, Tony was elected as Park County's new sheriff.

As he returned to his office, he decided being sheriff felt like a game of "Tag" and he was "It."

His musings were interrupted by a knock on the door frame. He looked up to see Deputy Mike Ott. Mike wasn't scheduled to work for two more days. In case he dropped by, Tony had taped a note to his locker. "You wanted to see me?"

"Come in, Mike. Don't worry, I know you're still on vacation." Tony leaned back in his chair. "How'd your trip go?" Mike and his girlfriend Ruby had been out of town, searching for Ruby's little girl. Her ne'er-do-well ex-husband had given her to relatives and they in turn had given, or, more likely, sold her to another family. "Any news?"

"Well, we have another lead to follow. You know how it goes. One thing leads to another." He exhaled heavily and sank onto one of the extra chairs. "Ruby is pretty discouraged, and I have to confess, I am, too." He squeezed his hands together. "If her SOB of an ex-husband wasn't already dead, I swear, I'd enjoy killing him myself."

The flash of pure malice startled Tony. Mike looked as nondescript as paste and usually managed his emotions with an iron control. It made him the perfect undercover cop. Tony wasn't sure how much control he would have himself if something threatened Theo or one of the boys. He doubted he would do half as well as Mike.

Tony shook his head to clear it. "On the subject of leads, I want you to look at this." Tony handed him the bag containing the newspaper clipping.

Mike studied the letters in silence. Finally, he looked up, his clear blue eyes meeting Tony's. "Do you think we missed something out there in the woods? We searched the best we could. Dammit's not trained as a cadaver dog, you know."

"I know, and no, I don't think we missed anything." The search had lasted for days. Mike and his bloodhound Dammit had combed every inch of the park and located just about enough bones to make one body. A couple of the smaller bones of the wrist and ankle had not been found. Those were probably carried off by some kind of critter. "If you had turned up three thigh bones or something, I'd say well, maybe there was something wrong."

A fleeting grin lit Mike's face. "Do you want us to go back out there?"

"No," said Tony. "You've covered it all. Plus, we have nothing for a scent."

"True." Mike looked thoughtful. "How about cold cases? Have you learned anything there?"

Tony shrugged. "I'm not sure. I asked Harvey, and he said there was nothing like that, at least not that he could remember. He talked a while about old cases inside the national park and even mentioned a case of animal mutilation."

"Really?" Mike's eyebrow flew skyward. "But?"

"I didn't believe him." Tony stood and began pacing. "I can't shake the feeling that he was still keeping something from me."

"Who is keeping something from you?" Wade trotted in carrying the mail. On the top of the stack was an envelope in an evidence bag. "Looks like another one."

Tony automatically reached for the antacids and then the bag. The envelope, including the Cincinnati postmark, looked exactly like the one from the day before.

"Okay, Wade, check the outside for prints. I can hardly wait to see what's inside."

Mike and Tony sat staring at the first clipping. It occupied the center of his desk.

Deputy Sheila Teffeteller came to the open doorway.

Tony looked up. Sheila's face looked drawn and tired. The normally immaculate deputy looked like she'd been fighting a wildcat in a dustbin. Beyond her, Ruth Ann sat at her desk watching them carefully. It slowed her application of a fresh coat of polish to her long fingernails. Even from here, Tony could see the green glow. It wasn't a nice green. *Bilious* came to mind.

Mike laughed. "Geez, kid, you fall down a chimney?"

Tony waved her to a chair. "What's wrong, Sheila?"

"It sounds so ordinary. I was driving my route, minding my own business." Sheila settled onto the unoccupied chair and released a weary sigh. "Nellie Pearl Prigmore flagged me down."

"How is the old bat?" Mike asked.

"As mean as new." Sheila fanned her face with her hand. Moisture dappled her fair skin, and her sweat-soaked shirt clung to the body armor beneath it. "She started out by making a complaint about someone stealing some of her yard art."

"I don't suppose it was replaced with a donkey and cart?" Tony still guessed a prankster was simply rotating the pieces.

"Nope. Nothing took its place." She consulted her notebook. "The missing item is a blue and yellow elf sitting on a two-foot-tall pink toadstool and holding a bouquet of flowers. Mostly daisies. According to Nellie Pearl, it was there when she went to bed last night because she remembered seeing it from her bedroom window."

"Did she have any idea who might be responsible?" Tony asked.

"Only everyone in the county." Sheila glared at him. "Then she pulled out the 'poor old woman' routine, and the next thing I knew, she had me carrying boxes of books or lead pipes or something heavy like that, up and down the stairs. I know I carried a plastic crate filled with jars of something containing lots of camphor. Brand-new jars."

Mike pinched his nose with his fingers as he asked, "Is that why she smells like that?"

Tony was preparing his own politically incorrect comment when Wade returned, waving the evidence bag containing the latest mysterious envelope. "It's clean, just like the last one."

Every trace of levity vanished.

Tony took the bag. Using a souvenir letter opener, he slit open the top of the envelope and turned it upside down over a clean sheet of paper on his desk. An index card, seemingly identical to the first one, fell onto his desk along with a larger newspaper clipping. This clipping had yellowed until it was almost chocolate brown. The worn seam and edges made it look like it had been folded and carried in a wallet for a while, but not continuously, for twenty years. Ignoring the clipping for the moment, he read the message on the card out loud. " 'I know where she is. Do you?' "

Tony glanced up and saw all eyes focused on the bit of newspaper. "Those seven words are all that's written on the card." He used the point of the opener to push the card into a plastic bag.

Armed with a paperclip and letter opener, Tony unfolded the newspaper clipping and maneuvered it into a separate bag. At the top of the article was a photograph of an attractive young woman. It was a Knoxville newspaper and the headline read, "Local woman missing in national park." It was dated some twenty years previous.

Tony cleared his throat, preparing to read the clipping to the three deputies and to Ruth Ann, who stood in the doorway not even blowing on her fingernails. The silence almost unnerved him. He began. " 'Mrs. Annabelle Garrison was last seen at the Sugarlands Visitor Center in Gatlinburg. On an outing to the national park with her husband and two children, Mrs. Garrison reportedly had gone to the restroom and failed to return. The family and authorities request anyone with information contact either the Sevier County Sheriff's Office or the national park authorities.' "

"Aw, man, twenty years ago. In the national park?" Tony waved the clipping. "I do remember this now. Harvey talked about it earlier, and it didn't ring a bell. I was in high school and it was just before graduation. It was big news at the time. What have we got to do with it?"

"We must be the gravesite." Mike frowned. "Why here? We must be thirty miles from the visitor center."

"Why and when?" Sheila leaned forward to study the newspaper photograph. "Those bones were not out there for twenty years."

"That's true." Tony massaged the back of his neck. "Don't forget, Theo found a male skeleton. If this woman's here, we haven't found her yet."

"Why the sudden onslaught of clippings?" asked Wade. He moved to look at Tony's big wall calendar. On it were notations about shifts, phases of the moon and vacation time. He turned back to the others. "The moon's not full, so it isn't crazy time. It sounds like someone got away with murder. After all these years, why bring it up?"

Mike tapped the piece of newspaper with his pen. "Do you remember if there was any suggestion of foul play? Could the woman have just run off?"

"I'll call the FBI and check into it," said Tony. "As far as I remember from the news, she just vanished. She could have been abducted by aliens for all anybody told the media." He reached for the telephone on his desk and changed his mind. He rustled in the stuff packed into his pencil drawer and found some sticky notes. "I left days after graduation. They could have found her twenty years ago." He doubted it. If she had been found, he would bet it was her corpse.

He scribbled the woman's name and the date on a notepad and handed it to Ruth Ann. "Do your thing."

CHAPTER EIGHT

Tony called the FBI. They gave him little information.

So, he called Max, his former partner in Chicago. Max joined the FBI right after Tony left. He probably wouldn't know nearly as much as the Knoxville office. Still, it was a good excuse to talk to his friend.

In spite of the serious nature of his inquiry, Tony found himself laughing. Max hadn't changed a bit. Although he morphed into a suit, his irreverent sense of humor went with him. As soon as he recognized Tony's voice on the phone, his former partner started in on him.

"So how's the local yokel? People ever find out you're really a mouse wearing an inflatable sheriff's costume?" Max loved to tell people his old partner moved to the hills and became a sheriff. "Do they let you carry your own bullet around?"

Tony didn't rise to the bait. "Did Luscious Laura decide she would rather be married to a real man instead of a suit?" Tony thought Theo was pretty. Max's wife was stunningly beautiful and apparently blind to Max's faults. "I'll give Laura another week before she runs off with the bag boy at the grocery store."

"Hey, I've missed you, partner." Max sounded serious. "Why don't you bring the family up and we'll all go to a baseball game and you can soak up some civilization. Your kids can eat something besides fried squirrels and baked road kill."

"You help solve my problem and I'll buy you all the hot dogs you can eat and pass the bill on to the county." Tony had automatically dialed Max's number when he finished talking to the Knoxville office. He hadn't been able to tell if the agency planned to take an active interest or not. "It's not your area. I already called the Knoxville office. I'm wondering if I'll soon have every initial in the country running around my county."

"Damn, you sound serious. What's up?" Max became all business when Tony explained about the body and the newspaper clippings. "Man, that's just weird. What other initials are you talking to?"

"I've a DEA group, although they're about gone, and the ATF." Tony heard a rattle like the phone fell into a metal trash can. He moved the receiver away from his ear. "What are you doing now?"

"Hey, sorry about that." Max swore under his breath. "I can't type and hang onto this dinky little phone at the same time and I lost my ear thingy for it somewhere. ATF, huh? Are they up there drinking all the moonshine?"

"Not exactly." Tony wouldn't give out more information than that and Max clearly didn't expect an answer.

Max did confirm that the FBI was very interested in the apparent resurrection of a cold case.

"I'd say that you're about to get lots of visitors in suits."

Theo frowned at the photograph in the evening's *Silersville Gazette*. It covered half of the front page. In the picture, Queen Doreen smiled broadly, her very best political smile, and held one corner of the engagement quilt. Theo thought Doreen looked like a very attractive shark in a size-nothing dress. The caption below it read, "Doreen Cashdollar lends her family heirloom quilts to new museum."

The accompanying article detailed all the family tree beginning with Abigail, for whom the engagement quilt was pieced, and her subsequent death, which led to the second quilt acquiring the designation of the murder quilt. Doreen received the quilt from her grandmother Bathsheba Cochran, Abigail's sister. More rhetoric praised the mayor's father-in-law. Robert "Sonny" Cochran was well known in horse show circles for his fine Tennessee Walking horses. There was mention of the horse farm where Doreen grew up. Another paragraph spread word of Doreen's philanthropic deeds. Only at the very end was the new museum mentioned in passing. It was not the publicity they had hoped to get. The lure of quilts on display was greatly diminished by the blatant admiration of Winifred Thornby for Doreen Cochran Cashdollar.

Theo's outrage grew. The article sounded more like a public relations piece for the Cashdollar and Cochran families than an explanation about the museum goals. She tapped the newspaper with a finger. "I don't see where it says anything about Her Majesty being a royal pain in the butt."

"It also neglects to mention that Saint Sonny is rumored to have spawned children in at least three states and only produced one with his wife," said Tony.

"That's understandable. Have you met the Queen Mother?" Theo teased. "Imagine the world with more Doreens."

Tony shuddered. "Maybe it's a good thing that the museum is not pushed too much for now."

"Why's that?" Theo pushed her glasses up her nose and stared into his eyes. "I thought you were in favor of them pursuing this dream."

"Oh, believe me, I am, especially since it's keeping them from singing in bars." Tony's eyes sparkled. "All I mean is the museum's not exactly finished yet, is it? Is there any sense in making a big publicity push until an opening date can be announced?"

"True." She shifted in her chair and peered over her glasses at him. "Now, tell me why you came to the museum yesterday. I loved the expression on Doreen's face. It has to be the first time anyone managed to silence her without resorting to a gag."

CHAPTER NINE

Another newspaper article arrived in the mail. Again, there seemed to be no way to trace it to the sender. This clipping described a hiker missing on the Appalachian Trail. Evidently traveling alone, a young man whose last contact with his family had been in Pennsylvania, never reported in again. Several hikers remembered seeing him farther north. None had much information to share. No one in Tennessee had seen him. A series of media pleas and posters in the towns near the trail turned up no clues. Several years later, the hiker's disappearance had even been the subject of a national television program. It didn't produce any solid leads.

The note attached to the newspaper article simply read, "I could make a call and be on television tonight. I wanted you to have this."

All information about the case went from his office to the FBI and the TBI. Federal, state and local law enforcement had the same information, or lack of it. The bones Theo had found were examined by forensic anthropologists under the watchful eyes of a host of interested observers.

They determined the bones belonged to a thirty-something Caucasian male. Other than that, nothing. The teeth were missing so dental records would not help. Tony found the number of men missing for at least three months to twenty years staggering. Lots of men had disappeared and could have passed through the area.

Rather than dedicate countless days, weeks or months sifting through the growing list of tragic stories, Tony wanted to throw all of the information into the trash and set it on fire. He wouldn't, of course. As the case continued to worsen, he wondered if it would ever be solved.

By the middle of the following week, at least eight yard ornaments had been reported missing from different sites around town. The thief, or what seemed more likely, a group of thieves, seemed to specialize in the largest ornament from each property struck. Some of them had to weigh almost a hundred pounds, and the odd shapes would make stealing even harder to manage. Prying up these babies wasn't like taking a wallet and slipping it inside your shirt.

Tony had quite a discussion with his regular night deputy, J. B. Lewis. Because his parents had not supplied him with first or middle names, only initials, he was often referred to by his fellow deputies as Jonely Bonely.

"Honest to God, J.B., I don't know any more than I did after the first theft. I really assumed it was a copycat of last summer's migrating gnomes."

"So did I." J.B. sighed heavily, sending the scent of spearmint chewing gum across Tony's desk. "It wasn't until the third one vanished and nothing reappeared that I realized we have a new ornament thief."

Tony rubbed his forehead and reached for an antacid. "I can't exactly post a deputy on each monstrous ornament. We don't have that many deputies to start with, and the tourists keep those busy."

"Speaking of tourists," said J.B., "did Wade tell you about his new admirer?"

Pausing with one hand wrapped around the antacid bottle, Tony frowned. "No."

"I get to be the first to tell you, then." Excitement mixed with merriment gleamed in J.B.'s eyes. "I heard he stopped a girl who was driving a convertible with both tops down."

Feeling mildly confused, Tony popped two antacids into his mouth and chewed slowly. "Okay, I've got the picture now."

J.B. grinned. "He couldn't let the girl drive around like that even if there weren't laws against it. She could cause a major accident, couldn't she? So he pulls her over and goes over to get her to cover herself when she wraps her bra around his neck and pulls him down so she can kiss him."

"Okay, that's it!" Tony reached for his telephone. "Wade is either going to wear an ugly mask or sit at his desk and do nothing except paperwork until September."

On Friday, the morning mail included a new envelope, just like the previous ones carrying cards and newspaper clippings. Instead of an article about another unsolved missing-person case, this one held a ticket to that night's baseball game in Cincinnati. A note on the now-familiar index cards used for stationary read, "Want to solve four murders? If so, Tony, use this ticket." Tony glanced up at the tense faces watching him. "Real cloak and dagger stuff, huh? It gets weirder."

He cleared his throat, preparing to wow his audience. "Park your Blazer in Newport, Kentucky, and walk across the Purple People Bridge. Show this ticket to the elevator operator and go up to the Club level. Plan to be there anytime between five-thirty and the first pitch. I promise you are in no danger. I only want to share some information. You do not need to bring other cops, although I'll understand if you don't trust me. I'll be watching for you."

"Tonight? That's not much notice for a three-hundred-mile drive," said Wade.

"I agree." Tony tapped the ticket on the desk. "Whoever sent this knows exactly how long the drive is and how long it usually takes mail to get from there to here."

Ruth Ann stood in the doorway. Her eyes were focused on the letter. "He, or she, also knows you drive a Blazer."

"And I'd say this person knows you and maybe even knows the FBI has been looking over your shoulder." Wade stared at him from across the desk, surprise and concern in his dark blue eyes. "It sounds like a trap to me. Are you going?"

"It's a trap all right," Tony nodded. "We'll just see who gets caught in it, though." He reached for his telephone. "I don't think this person is dangerous, still, a little backup is a comforting thing."

"Do you think it's just a prank?" Ruth Ann asked.

"Maybe." Tony paused with his hand over the receiver. "I do think this person knows a lot more about what happened twenty years ago than showed up in these newspaper clippings. What really baffles me is why he waited so long to bring it to light."

"Will they let you take your gun into the ballpark?" Wade leaned forward. "I wouldn't be surprised to learn you have a few enemies out there."

"Most of them live in our county jail or prison. I can't imagine any of them would be in Cincinnati." He mentally cataloged the most dangerous ones. There were not many, and none of them would know half of the details displayed in the letter. "I'll find out about the gun. It shouldn't be a problem. Telling Theo will be worse." He rolled his eyes. "She's a lot more dangerous than anyone in Ohio."

He noticed although Wade and Ruth Ann both laughed, neither disagreed.

"And, you can bet Theo will make sure I'm wearing my heaviest vest."

Tony stopped by Theo's quilt shop to tell her where he was going. He told himself she would feel better if she got to fuss and fret a bit and remind him to be careful. His wife had a lot of spunk and was smarter than him. Her views often helped him professionally, however, she did not deal well with being kept in the dark.

Gretchen Blackburn, Theo's full-time assistant, stood behind the wide counter, cutting a length of fabric and chatting with several out-of-town customers. Tony always wanted to call her Brunhild because her voice and body type were Wagnerian. So far he'd managed to stifle the words. When she braided her long blond hair, like she had today, all she needed was a Viking helmet and spear. She looked up and smiled at him. "Theo's in her studio."

Tony returned the smile and nodded as he moved toward the staircase to Theo's studio. From that vantage point, he could see a group of four quilters gathered in the big workroom, quilting on the current charity quilt. A couple of them were tiny old women who looked like garden gnomes and a pair of young women. Susan and Amy, the younger ones, belonged to the Thursday Night Bowling League, a joke name for Theo's quilting group.

Susan's voice carried to him. "I heard Doreen might change her mind about letting the new museum display her great-aunt's quilts."

"That's okay by me." One of the gnomes spoke. "That woman has been a pure aggravation ever since Calvin married her, and I doubt she'll get nicer with more publicity."

Tony noticed Theo had added a chain that went from railing to railing at the base of the staircase. On it hung a small wooden plaque, simple and to the point. "Private." The chain and sign were new.

Wondering why she hadn't mentioned being bothered, he unclipped the chain, stepped past it, and clipped it behind him. At the top of the stairs, he turned the knob and strolled into Theo's world, so different from the one he worked in. Hers was full of light and color and the scents of lavender and fabric sizing.

Tall shelves held full bolts and cut yardage of fabrics arranged more or less by color. White flannel covered one whole wall from floor to ceiling, providing her with a design wall. Because quilt blocks clung to it as if by magic, she used it to audition different designs without having to pin everything. Today there was an assortment of vibrant orange and green blocks scattered across the surface. It was eye-catching even if not his favorite colors.

A skylight installed in the high ceiling was augmented with enough electric lighting to illuminate an airstrip. At one end of the room was a large table with a recess for her sewing machine and next to it, a standard table, not quite as large. His brother Gus had built it to her specifications. Taller than a normal table, its surface was covered with a large, self-healing plastic cutting mat. A nearby rack held plastic rulers in all shapes and sizes. Razor-sharp rotary cutters hung from hooks on the wall next to it.

Theo sat at her laptop computer, playing with her design software. She looked up and smiled when he came in.

"We have a break in our case."

Turning to face him, she ran her fingers through her hair, lifting the curls. "Let me guess." Her grin widened. "The thief tried to steal the statue of Amoes Siler, our glorious founding father, from the park and it toppled over on him."

"Different case." Tony toyed with a little fishing pole leaning against her desk. Spying him, Zoë, the office kitten, dashed from her hiding spot and attacked the fabric fish at the end of the line. He teased the kitten, making the fish jump into the air and Theo laugh as she watched. "I came by to tell you that I have to go to Cincinnati. Now. I'll stop by the house and pick up a few things on my way out of town."

"Why? What's happened?" Theo looked up from the kitten, the smile still lingered on her face.

Enlarged by the magnification of her glasses, her big green-gold hazel eyes appeared huge. Tony chose his words with care. "Our mysterious message-sender has provided me with a ticket to the baseball game tonight. I am to meet him or her before the game starts."

"That's awfully cloak-and-dagger, isn't it?" Theo turned to watch the kitten, hiding her expression.

"Yeah, that's exactly what I thought, too." Tony led the kitten up onto the window seat before putting the cat toy away. "I've been on the phone with the FBI and Cincinnati police for the last hour. If I leave now, I'll have plenty of time to meet with them, check into my hotel, and put on my armor before the game."

"You better call me. A lot."

He nodded. Theo's pretty face had gone pale, and her freckles appeared more pronounced than usual.

"What about Jamie's game here?" Theo smiled. "Am I the coach tonight? I think Marjorie's still out of town."

Tony was proud of her smile. He knew it wasn't always easy for her dealing with the hazards of his job. At least she stayed much calmer now.

He considered her question about Jamie's game. In the flurry of preparations for the trip to Cincinnati, he had spaced out on his six-year-old's baseball game that evening. He was glad she reminded him. She could coach it. She'd done it before when both Marjorie, the head coach, and he were unavailable. Still, he knew she preferred to sit on the bleachers. "I'll stop and ask Gus if he'll take my place. If he has to get back home to Townsend, I guess you'll get to do it. Either way, I'll put the bats and practice balls in your van." He bent and gave her a kiss and ruffled her hair. "Keep your cell phone on. I'll want updates on the game."

CHAPTER TEN

On his way out of town, he stopped by the museum site to talk to his brother. The place looked like organized chaos. Tony grinned at the picture his brother made standing in the middle of the construction battlefield, his fists resting on his hips. All Gus needed was a breastplate, helmet, sword and short skirt to complete the picture. No Roman general ever had a more commanding attitude.

Their mom, a former Latin teacher, had classical ideas. Being named Jane probably encouraged her to steer clear of the ordinary names in the name-the-baby book. Even so, when she named her firstborn son, Caesar Augustus, she probably hadn't planned on people calling him Gus.

Tony glanced around the site. To him, it looked like a fair amount of progress had been made since his last visit, when he came out to talk to Doreen the previous week.

The hole vanished when the foundation was poured. Now Quentin and Mac, two of the day laborers, were framing a wall above it.

Quentin suffered from a long history of drug and alcohol problems. Recently returned from rehab, his health had noticeably improved. Still pencil-thin and a bit twitchy, he managed to hold a two-by-six in place while his coworker, Mac, used a nail gun to attach it to the cross board. A third workman, Kenny, carried a couple of five-gallon buckets down a wooden ladder propped in the space between the dirt and concrete. Kenny reminded Tony of an ant. Small, industrious and pound for pound stronger than anyone else he knew. Kenny was a foot shorter and nearly a hundred pounds lighter than Tony. He managed to haul pipe, boards and tools that probably out- weighed him. Constant labor in the sun had eventually tanned his skin a reddish brown that matched his dark auburn hair and added to his antlike appearance.

Mac looked at Gus and pointed to the thing he and Quentin made. "How's this boss?" The well-muscled man wore his tool belt with the ease only years of practice could provide. He'd only recently moved here from Chattanooga and was already Gus's right-hand man.

"Okay, it looks good." Gus called, "Mac, I want you and Quentin to make two more exactly like that one."

Quentin looked bewildered. Tony wondered if he had a clue what he was supposed to do.

Mac saluted and grinned. Sweat darkened his sleeveless gray T-shirt. Removing his safety glasses for a moment, he dried them on his shirttail and nodded in Tony's direction. "You've got a visitor, boss."

Gus turned. His smile made Tony think today was going pretty well. "Hey there, little brother."

"Hey to you, too." The sounds of the air gun mingled with those of several other power tools. Tony wouldn't even know how to turn them on. If he did get the things turned on, he'd probably put a nail through his hand or eye. "I've got a favor to ask."

"You've got the gun. Shoot." Gus proceeded to laugh at his own joke.

"Can you coach Jamie's game tonight? I have to run up to Ohio." He watched as Gus studied him for a full minute. It looked as if he was trying to read Tony's mind and would like to ask a question. He forced himself not to, and Tony didn't volunteer anything.

"Yeah, I can do that. I'll call Catherine and have her come over. We'll do dinner and a baseball game."

"Thanks, I owe you."

"Damn straight." With a sharp nod of his head, Gus turned. His eyes went wide and he dashed after Kenny. "Kenny, stop!"

After a blissfully uneventful drive, Tony received a warm welcome in Cincinnati. The Cincinnati Police had been working the case while he traveled. He was ushered to the desk of Detective Jones, the man assigned as his liaison with the local police.

Detective Jones, a rangy black man with a shaved head, leaned forward, shook hands and immediately handed Tony a computer printout. "It didn't take us long to find out your ticket is one of three purchased together. The buyer paid cash, two weeks ago, at one of the ballpark ticket windows." His sharp expression displayed a quick wit and a fair amount of curiosity. "So how long do you think this plan has been in the works?"

"My guess, several months." Tony flipped through the photocopies of the news clippings he carried with him and handed them to Jones. "We are assuming these four people are all dead. Maybe more." He paused. "These deaths all occurred at the same general time so it's been someone's secret for twenty years."

"What brought them up now?" Jones looked carefully at each page, frowning at the stories he read.

"My wife found a skeletonized hand three months ago in a local park. According to the state lab, the bones could not have been in that spot for very long. Clearly, someone took the hand from its hiding place and dumped it in an area of new houses." Tony pushed aside the memory of Theo's distress when she found the bones behind her best friend Nina's house. Nina herself had not been able to shed any light on the grisly find.

"Our mysterious contact might or might not have been involved in the killing. It could be a witness. Someone who has waited and watched for years to see if the bodies would turn up or the killer would confess."

"All those new television shows about how cold cases are solved by DNA or new information might have stirred someone up. Either way, this is an ugly business." Detective Jones studied the clippings. "You ready to do this?"

Tony nodded, gratified the Cincinnati police were taking this seriously. Although they, like Tony, did not believe anything violent was likely to occur, they had a team of plainclothes cops in the club room. An undercover cop was operating the elevator.

The ballpark front office people were not happy. They didn't want any negative publicity or any fans getting caught in a crossfire. Short of closing off the area, however, they didn't have a better plan.

Tony would be lying to himself and everyone else if he said he wasn't nervous. He drove back to the Kentucky side of the Ohio River and parked according to his instructions. Adrenaline surged through his system as he climbed out of the car and began walking across the Purple People Bridge, the pedestrian bridge spanning the Ohio River.

Sitting on the edge of the river, the new ballpark beckoned to the baseball lover in him. The decorative smokestacks were ready to shoot off fireworks if one of the home team hit a homerun. The new ballpark was a sight he'd wanted to see but this wasn't quite the occasion he had in mind. He had thought the whole family would come up together. It would be a hot dog and pretzel kind of night. This game of cat and mouse could go south in a heartbeat. He didn't like being the mouse.

The cop in the elevator was a young woman with a bouncy ponytail. Industriously chewing a piece of gum, she looked about eighteen and bored to death. She checked his ticket and shuttled him and a young couple up to the club level. The instant the couple stepped out and moved away, her manner changed abruptly and she spoke softly.

"Sheriff, I've tried to check for anything that looked off, you know, but . . ." She kept her finger on the door-open button. "For what it's worth, there isn't a big crowd in there yet."

"Thanks." He pasted on his I'm-a-hick-and-I'm-happy-to-be-here expression. "None of us knows what to watch for tonight. Thanks just the same."

Three laughing men in their sixties approached the elevator. The overall effect of the trio dressed in red shirts and hats made them look like one overweight, three-headed tomato. Tony released his breath and stepped out of the elevator and headed for the club room.

The room was long and fairly empty at this hour. To his left, a glass wall separated the room from the ballpark seats. He could see a row of concession stations in the middle and to the right, rows of tables and chairs. Televisions suspended from the ceiling showed the pregame program. Ahead of him, he could see a full bar. Although not generally a big drinker, a shot of whiskey sounded pretty good right now. It would have to wait.

The tables to the right overlooked the street below and had no view of the ball field. Few people sat there. One, a thin old man wearing a red baseball cap struggled to his feet and beckoned to Tony.

He was more than thin; he was gaunt, Tony thought as he stepped in that direction. In his bright red T-shirt and worn jeans, the man looked harmless and very ill. His knees gave way and he sat down abruptly, collapsing onto his chair. Spreading his hands on the red tabletop, he smiled.

"I'll bet you don't remember me, Tony. I remember you."

Surprisingly deep, his voice was steady. "We went to school together."

Tempted to shake his head, Tony studied the face carefully. This man looked to be closer to sixty than thirty-eight. Sunken cheeks made the deep-set brown eyes seem too large for his face. The nose was slightly crooked. His steady gaze didn't waver. Tony could see nothing familiar in it.

"My name is Harrison Duff," he said. "You can tell your police friends I'm harmless." He lifted skeletal hands from the table in mock surrender.

The name rang a bell in Tony's mind and he nodded. "You lived in Silersville for only a few months. Yes, I do remember you. You arrived my senior year and created quite a stir with your city ways." Tony stared. That boy had been strong and handsome and had worn his thick hair in a ponytail.

"Yeah, I thought Silersville was the deep end of the dump. My folks were splitting up and I got sent to live there with my aunt." Harrison lifted one thin shoulder. "She was nice, I was not."

"Why the newspaper clippings and the mysterious stuff with the ticket?" Tony sat down across from Harrison but didn't suggest his police backup go home. His gut said it was safe. He also knew guts aren't very smart and sometimes dangerously inaccurate.

"I'm dying." A sickly grin holding only a hint of amusement crossed the sallow face. "I wanted to have a little fun and then clear my conscience. When I made my grand plan, I honestly had no idea it would cause so many people so much trouble. My priest seems to think a full confession is necessary for my soul."

"Cancer?" Tony would guess liver maybe. In truth, the man looked nearly dead already.

"AIDs."

"Sorry." Tony tilted his head slightly. "Do you want to confess here? At the police station? In Silersville?"

"Here's fine. I typed it all out and signed it and my priest witnessed it. I will happily answer any questions you have." As soon as he pushed the paper across the table, an expression of deep peace crossed his face. "Here he is now."

Tony took the offered paper. Harrison watched a portly priest with a florid complexion approach the table, carrying a tray of snacks and drinks. He circled around behind Harrison and sat down next to him. The priest didn't say a word to either of the men but simply stared at Harrison.

"I gave him the paper."

"Good." The priest looked at Tony and offered his hand. "I'm Father Neal. I'm a hospice volunteer. I have to say I do not approve of Harrison's method of getting you here. I told him he had to be creating a lot of work for you and your fellow officers."

Just then, an officer with a German shepherd strolled up to the table. The dog, trained to find explosives, sniffed under the table and each person in turn. He settled on his haunches, staring at Tony.

"Thanks guys," said Tony, glancing around at the police backup. "It looks like you got all dressed up for nothing."

"See?" Father Neal gently poked Harrison in the arm. "You have caused a lot of people extra work with your little fanfare. The game will be starting soon. If you want to see any of it, get on with your confession." He offered Tony a plate of nachos.

Chastised, Harrison began his tale. "I hated everybody and everything that spring except for the Ms and V. That is marijuana, moonshine and Vicky. I don't remember her last name. I might not have ever known it." He pulled a plastic cup of beer close to the edge of the table. His hands trembled too badly for him to lift the cup to his lips so he leaned forward and sucked the foam off the top. "Vicky was wild. I think she was two grades behind us. It might only have been one. She was fat and had black hair and this thumb that looked like it had been smashed in a car door, you know?" He raised his left thumb into the air.

Tony instantly knew whom he meant. The description, not the name, rang a bell. Like Harrison, Vicky arrived when he was in high school. Somewhat overweight, the girl had a pretty face and long black hair. She circled her bright blue eyes with too much makeup and dressed in tight T-shirts with low-cut necklines that exposed more of her ample breasts than they covered. Tony suspected most of the guys, like him, rarely pulled their eyes from her chest to her face. She made it clear forming friendships with either gender was not in her plan. About a month after she arrived, she left again. No one missed her, or, more accurately, no one was sorry when she left. Something of his feelings must have shown on his face.

"I can see you remember her. Vicky was really something, wasn't she? Anyway, I liked weed and booze. A couple of girls liked me. They said I was good-looking and had nice hair." He touched his bare scalp and grinned at Tony's baldness. "I guess we've both changed, huh? Well, anyway, this Vicky, she followed me around like a dog and would watch me with these other girls. I started putting on a show for her, sort of tying them up and showing off, you know."

Tony thought he could guess. "Did Vicky know it was a show?" He reached for a nacho.

"I really don't know."

Tony wondered if Harrison had escalated his game until someone died. That theory didn't quite fit. The bones Theo found belonged to a male. "What happened next?"

"Vicky decided we should go up into the national park and pick up a stranger. That was okay by me." A glimmer of a smile creased his ravaged face. "There weren't many girls in town who were willing, if you know what I mean."

"So what did you do?"

"We cruised around. Vicky drove and I sat there and smoked weed. We picked up a girl with a backpack. She was hitchhiking in Cades Cove." He slurped more beer. "Vicky said she could have a ride only if she'd be *real* nice to me, if you catch my drift."

Tony held up a hand to stop him and glanced through the document. The whole thing was spelled out. No recording would be more complete. "I haven't read you your rights."

"That's okay. I know them." Harrison coughed into a handkerchief. "I'll be dead soon anyway."

His words were spoken so matter-of-factly Tony paused for a moment. "So, you were a total stranger and this girl didn't mind?"

"Naw, it didn't mean nothin' to her. We pulled into a picnic area and Vicky stayed in the car. Watching. Next thing I know, Vicky's covering the girl's head in plastic bags. She had it wrapped tight in seconds." His prominent Adam's apple moved up and down in his throat. "It was awful scary. I tried to get her to stop. All the sudden she turned on me, pulling an old revolver. I figured she'd kill me, too."

Even though he'd probably heard the story before, Father Neal's cheeks lost their rosy glow.

"Go on." Tony wasn't sure he wanted to know what else happened that day.

"After I helped her put the girl in the trunk, Vicky handed me a fresh jar of shine and we took off again. I passed out. When I woke up, the car was stopped. I sat in the car and watched as she killed three more people. Two men and another woman." He drank half of the beer. "Afterwards, she made me help her load them into the trunk, and I kept drinking and smoking and hoping I was just having a really bad dream."

"What about the bodies?" Tony's heartburn forced him to stop eating. He reached into his pocket for a handful of antacids. "What did she do with those?"

"There was an old freezer in a shed at the back of her family farm." He made the sign of the cross. "God forgive me. I helped her wrap them in plastic bags, like so much garbage, and stick them in there. After that, I walked home and never saw Vicky again." He toyed with a soft pretzel, pulling it apart. He didn't raise any of it to his lips.

Tony forced his hands to remain still. "What makes you think we found one of those bodies?"

"The McMahons lived right next to Vicky's family. She talked about their daughter, Nina, a lot. What Vicky felt for Nina was worse than hatred. It was a real sicko obsession." A youthful smile crossed his face. "Nina was pretty and sweet and had gorgeous copper-red hair. I liked Nina even though she couldn't stand me."

Tony thought back. "The Parkers and the Teffetellers lived closest to the McMahons."

"Vicky Parker. That was her name." Harrison slurped some more beer. "Such an ordinary name for a murdering bitch. I wonder how I could have forgotten it."

"Do you happen to subscribe to the *Silersville Gazette*?"

"Yep. I signed up a few months ago." His sunken eyes twinkled in his gaunt face.

Tony guessed he knew the answer to his next question but asked it anyway. "Do you happen to have any idea how the body got out of the freezer and into the park behind Nina's yard?"

"Yep. I put it there." The twinkle vanished. "I hoped it would lead you to the others in the shed." He coughed again. "I swear, I didn't want to leave it near Nina's house but it about killed me to move it that far. I dragged it on an old tarp and that was as far as I could manage even though it wasn't more than bones. I couldn't drive up there." He raised a hand like he was swearing an oath. "If you'd arrested Nina, I would have called and confessed right away."

The truth glowed in Harrison's eyes. This man was ill and tired and praying for peace. Tony hoped the letter would be enough to get a search warrant for the shed. He doubted any court would convict Vicky Parker without additional evidence. Without it, assuming they could find her, she and her uncle could claim that if Harrison knew where the bodies were, it was because he had stashed them there himself.

The national anthem began. Everyone rose. Tony watched the priest support Harrison's emaciated body. When the song ended, the priest retrieved a wheelchair from where he'd left it against the wall.

"Can we go watch the game now?" asked Father Neal.

Tony nodded. The adrenaline left his system, leaving behind an odd exhaustion. Even as he watched the dying man smile, peace glowing in his eyes, Tony dialed Theo's phone. She answered on the first ring.

"Tony?"

He could hear the concern in her voice and that warmed him. "Everything's fine. It's quite a story, and not a pretty one. It will keep until I get home."

"You know I love a good story."

He wasn't sure if the sigh of relief came from her or from him.

"What will you do now?"

"I'll go over and take care of the cop stuff. Then, if I'm done quickly, I might come back and eat some chili and spaghetti and watch the end of the game. Hopefully I'll get some sleep and be home around noon."

"Good."

"Speaking of games, how is Jamie's game going? Did Gus get the team organized?" Having both the head coach and the assistant gone was unfair to the kids even though it was unavoidable. They just wanted to play.

"They're behind, six to one at the end of two innings, with one on second base." Her next words were drowned out by the sound of screaming. Theo's scream of excitement, not fear, added to the cacophony. Laughing and breathless, she returned to the call. "Make that six to three. Kimberly just hit a home run."

"Kimberly did?" Tony tried to visualize the scene and failed. The little girl weighed half as much as the next smallest player and could barely lift the bat off her shoulder to let it fall to the ground. No way would she be able to swing it.

Theo's laugh rang in his head. "Okay, so maybe the bat slipped off her shoulder and accidentally bumped the ball and it landed fair. We'll say Kimberly bunted, and after a series of errors, she crossed the plate. Hey! It still counts."

CHAPTER ELEVEN

Jarred from sleep by the insistent ringing of his cell phone, Tony felt disoriented and exhausted. His pillow smelled like stale cigar smoke and beer instead of Theo. Cincinnati. "Mmph." The glowing red letters on the hotel clock read four thirty-eight as he flipped open the tiny phone. "Sheriff." He held his breath hoping it was a wrong number.

"Sheriff?" Deputy J. B. Lewis's distinctive voice rumbled through the line. "I hate to wake you."

Tony jerked to an upright position. His gut twisted.

"Your family's fine, sir."

Hearing the problem had nothing to do with his family, Tony's tension eased. "What's wrong, J.B.?"

"I was driving my regular route and stopped at the new museum, you know, just to, you know."

"And?" Tony could hear the normally unflappable man breathing hard, making odd little rasping sounds. He squeezed the telephone hoping that would force J.B. to talk a little faster.

"The trailer your mom and aunt have turned into an office and storage area was broken in to, sir." J.B. released a deep breath into the phone. "The door was wide open when I came by so I went inside. The mayor's wife is in there. She's dead, sir. Murdered."

"You sure?"

"Oh, yeah." J.B. cleared his throat, several times. "There's this thing with a jillion spikes coming off it jammed into her throat. I don't know what it is but she sure didn't just fall on it."

"I know what it looks like." Tony remembered the vicious-looking tool he'd studied in the office/trailer. "Is she the only victim?"

"Yes, sir. Whoever did it tried to cover her up with an old quilt." He made an odd croaking sound. "There's dried blood all over it. I had to move it, sir."

"It can't be helped." Tony shrugged. "Are you alone out there?"

"Yes, sir, unless you count the deceased."

Tony smiled at the attempt at humor. J.B. would be okay. "Wake up Wade, Mike and Sheila. Have them take pictures and start collecting evidence. They know the drill." He turned the switch on the bedside lamp, flinching at the sudden brilliance. As they talked, Tony gathered his personal items. Maybe he could spare five minutes for a shower. "While you're calling them, I'll contact Doc Nash. Since he's our county's coroner he'll have to come out and declare her dead. I'll find someone else to do the autopsy."

"Why is that, sir?"

"Doc has so much personal animosity against Doreen, I don't want him doing more with the body than he has to. I'll probably arrange to send her to Knoxville."

"What about the mayor? Should I tell him?"

"Damn." Tony rolled his shoulders, releasing some of the stiffness, while he considered the situation. The man had to be told. Telling the family was the worst part of this job. "After the others get there, I want you to drive over to the house and tell him in person she died. Don't volunteer any information. Don't answer any questions. Don't let him near the body. I'll be there as soon as I can."

★ ★ ★ ★ ★

Tony made good time until he was just south of Richmond, Kentucky. Suddenly, the farther he drove, the harder it rained. Visibility on the highway reduced to about zero. The weak morning light mixed with gray rain and dark trees, producing a murky condition where everything from the sky to the pavement was the color of mildew.

He couldn't stop because someone behind him might plow into him. Creeping along, he eventually saw a sign for the turnoff to the rest stop and followed it. Cars and trucks all but filled the parking lot. The rain pounded harder on the roof of the Blazer, imprisoning him.

It seemed like a good time to call Theo. If he let someone else tell her about Doreen's death, she would never forgive him. She just didn't deal well with being blindsided by one of her customers. She answered on the second ring.

"I'm on my way back."

"Not sleeping in?" Her voice was warm, amused. "I thought you'd be out swapping cop stories all night."

"I was."

"What happened?" The tone of Theo's voice changed from warm to concerned. "Your contact go bad after all?"

"Nope. J.B. called." He paused. "Doreen's dead. Probably murdered."

There was nothing but stunned silence from Theo.

"No details are being released. Really, few are known, sweetheart. I wanted you to know just in case someone comes into your shop this morning with the news." He waited, knowing he'd awakened her. She would catch up in a second.

"Oh, my!" Theo exhaled loudly. "I'll keep track of all the rumors I hear."

"That's what I need you to do. I'll fill you in on my secret confessor when I can see your face." He told her about his rain-delayed travel and disconnected.

The rain grew even stronger, so he reclined the seat and closed his eyes. He fell asleep almost immediately. When he awakened, sunlight poured through the windows and he realized he was sweating, baking like a potato wrapped in foil. He'd slept for the better part of two hours.

The nap had done him good. After the ballpark excitement, Tony and some of the Cincinnati police chewed the fat. He owed them big-time. He hadn't been in bed more than a couple of hours when J.B. called. He didn't want to think about how long it might be before he would get to sleep again.

Mid-morning, Theo ran to the post office for a minute. When she returned, Vicky Parker was in the quilt shop, standing at the bottom of the stairs to Theo's studio. The first thing Theo noticed was that she didn't have her little boy with her and wondered if he was somewhere with his father. The next thing she noticed was Vicky's expression as she studied the items on a wall rack next to her. It held quilter's rulers, marking pens and other notions. Vicky seemed mesmerized by the razor-sharp rotary cutters. Something in her expression made Theo doubt that fabric would be what she wanted to cut.

"Good morning, Vicky," said Theo, pasting a smile on her face. "Can I help you find something?"

"No, I'm just admiring your store. I couldn't stay long the last time."

Her bright blue eyes focused on Theo's face, although Theo didn't see anything that looked like admiration. She didn't know how or why she felt like Vicky wasn't quite right. Mentally.

"What's up there?" Vicky pointed to the door of Theo's private space.

"Just my office."

"Can I see it?"

"Sorry, no visitors." Theo shifted, moving away from the stairs, hoping Vicky would follow her.

"I hear voices," said Vicky.

Theo didn't doubt that at all. Then she realized she heard voices, too. And the laughter of children. Chris and Jamie were up there playing with the cat. "My children."

"How old are they?"

It was not an unusual question. For some unknown reason, it spooked Theo. Tony's phone call from Kentucky to tell her Doreen had been murdered and he was delayed on the road home was likely the reason for her odd mood. Hearing that a killer roamed somewhere in their quiet community made her uneasy. She certainly didn't think Vicky was responsible. Finally, she managed a smile. "They're six and eight."

"Fun ages."

Theo nodded. Why was she having so much trouble being polite? "How old is your little boy?"

"One." She smiled proudly. "He's just starting to walk."

Theo searched for words to discourage an extended visit and edged closer to the counter. Gretchen stood behind it, chatting with a customer.

The front door flew open, slamming into the supporting wall. Startled, all eyes turned toward the sound. "The Queen is dead." Nellie Pearl Prigmore stalked into the shop, raised her arms high and shouted, "May she rot for eternity!"

Dead silence reigned in the large room, for a count of three. Theo should know. She started counting the instant Nellie Pearl fell silent. The tourists looked confused as every local shopper rushed toward the old woman, begging for information. Theo edged around Vicky and joined the group, wondering what Nellie Pearl would say.

It was early afternoon by the time Tony arrived in Silersville.

Convinced Doreen wouldn't get any deader and smelling a bit rank, he stopped by the house, took a thirty-second shower and put on a clean uniform.

Only Daisy witnessed his visit. The big dog wagged all over and attempted to get him to spend the rest of the afternoon scratching her ears.

Tony assumed Theo and the boys were at the shop.

He ate a peanut butter and banana sandwich as he drove to the museum site. Just as he arrived, an ambulance he assumed was bearing Queen Doreen to Knoxville pulled onto the road. Tony saw Doc Nash standing in the parking lot near his open car door. It looked like he was about to climb in. Tony waved, catching his eye and Doc closed the car door and walked toward the Blazer.

Doc Nash started talking before Tony could get out of the Blazer. "I came by intending to stay just long enough to declare her officially dead. As usual, I ended up staying to watch. I'm no better than the rest of the ghouls." Doc Nash nodded toward the clump of bystanders standing across the road and shook his head. "I'd have sent her to Knoxville anyway. It's going to take an expert to determine the actual cause of death, although I can promise you it was murder." His voice faltered.

"Can you tell me anything else?" Tony rarely saw any signs of uncertainty in Doc Nash.

"At a glance, it looked like a single massive blow to her throat with that vicious thing." Doc's brown eyes mirrored his disappointment in his fellow humans. "It would take a strong person or one in a rage to use it."

Doc's focus shifted to Wade, watching as the deputy emerged from the wall of vegetation near the highway and joined them.

Tony glanced at his deputy. Wade's face, predictably, was a shade of green that meant serious problems except when seen on a plant. His lopsided grin told the rest of the story. Wade's latest meal had reappeared and had probably been deposited behind one of the bushes. A dead body got him every time.

Wade began his report. "The Knox County Coroner will call when she's ready to perform the autopsy."

"So, what else have you learned?" Tony's gaze took in the yellow tape draped around the trailer/office and a fair amount of the real estate as well. At the far side of the yellow tape, the work crew, Quentin, Mac and Kenny, all stood with Gus, drinking coffee from steel thermos bottles. No one was joking around. Jane sat in a folding chair under a tulip tree near the road, holding hands with her sister. He was surprised how old his mother looked. A small crowd gathered on the far side of the road. Water filled every rut and depression. Tire tracks of all descriptions ran in every direction through the construction area.

"Someone used a crowbar or something like one to rip the hasp and plate right off the door." Wade pointed to the mutilated trailer. "I took lots of photos and then bagged the hasp and plate."

"Any obvious attempt to pick the lock?"

"Nothing I can see. Maybe if we send it off an expert can tell for sure."

"I doubt it would make any difference," Tony said. "Did you find the tool?"

"Nope. We've searched high and low. The killer must have taken it with him."

"Have you formed a theory about what happened?"

"I think Mrs. Cashdollar and her killer went inside. Not necessarily at the same time or in that order. Very little seemed disturbed in there. Your aunt checked for us and identified the murder weapon. It's a flax hackle. I guess it was used like a comb to separate the strands of flax or hemp, maybe even to card some wool. Evidently, they have a whole collection of them in different sizes." Wade's color worsened. "It is an evil-looking thing."

Tony agreed, nodding as he asked, "Any time frame?"

"Gus said things were locked up and tidy when he and the crew left at six in the evening. No one admits to being here until J.B. did his check at four-fifteen or so this morning."

Tony turned to the doctor. "I don't suppose you're prepared to take a wild guess about time of death?"

"Not really." Doc Nash frowned. "She'd most likely been dead for at least a couple of hours."

"Okay," said Tony, wishing for something exact. "So sometime between six P.M. and four A.M., she and whoever killed her are in the trailer. And what? This person picks up the hackle thingy and just shoves it into her throat?"

Wade frowned. "Don't you think she would have to be unconscious first? We bagged her hands, although they looked pretty clean. No defensive wounds that I could see. Nothing obvious like a broken fingernail or blood or dirt was on either of them."

"And then what do you think happened?" Tony studied the area, seeing nothing out of place.

"Then whoever did it covered up the body with a quilt and left. J.B. said if her feet hadn't been sticking out, he might not have even looked under it."

Tony said, "Did you find her car? I didn't see the Volvo when I drove up."

"Her car isn't here." Wade shook his head. "And I know it's not parked in the Cashdollar garage, either. I looked."

"Which means?" Tony didn't like the feel of the setup. He couldn't put his finger on what was bothering him. "Was killing Doreen the plan all along?"

"You think she drove the killer out here? Willingly? And then what?" Wade took off his hat. With the back of his fingers, he wiped the sweat up from his face and onto his closely cropped black hair. "Nothing makes any sense. They break into the office. Take nothing obvious. There isn't a knock-down drag-out fight and they don't throw things. Suddenly her partner kills her and drives off in her car? Why?"

"And who?" Tony looked at the muddy mess created by construction and rain. "Where did they park? I don't suppose there are footprints?"

"Not that we have matched. Her shoes had pretty high heels and yet they were clean. That tells me she didn't walk far in this area and it was definitely before this morning's little downpour."

Doc Nash cleared his throat. "Maybe the killer carried her from the car to the trailer."

Tony nodded. "Where's the whatsit? The flax hackle?"

"It went with the body." Wade paled. "Should I have kept it here?"

"No."

"How about her purse?"

"I haven't seen it." Wade looked around, his expression wary. "If anyone has found it, they haven't told me."

"Maybe it was the reason she was killed. Do you suppose she had something in her purse worth killing for besides her keys?" Tony tried not to make any guesses ahead of the evidence but couldn't help himself.

"Like what?"

"Like I don't know. Anything. Money? Blackmail pictures? Prescription drugs?"

"Even if she did," said Wade, "why come out here?"

CHAPTER TWELVE

At Theo's shop, Nellie Pearl's announcement about Doreen's death held the attention of the quilters for only a moment. It didn't take the women long to realize that more information would have to come from another source.

As one, they turned to face Theo. Their expressions showed hope that the sheriff's wife would be able to add to Nellie Pearl's information. She could only shrug. In truth, she knew little more than Nellie Pearl did.

Behind her, Theo heard the gossip sound level in the workroom rise. Doreen's name was on all lips. Still, each voice carried a tone of shock.

Susan, one of the newer residents, asked if Doreen was originally from Silersville.

"Not exactly." Nellie Pearl jumped back into the conversation. "Her people live a bit farther south. Her father is—was, I guess now—Sonny Cochran." She pronounced the name with tones of great reverence.

"Who's that?" Gretchen, pulled away from the counter by the gossip, moved to stand in the doorway.

Understanding the Indiana native would know little about local family histories, Theo explained. "They are old money and own a large farm, like a plantation, and are famous for the Tennessee Walking Horses they raise."

"The whole family is very uppity." Another woman tilted her head and looked down her nose at her neighbor. "Very left nostril, you know."

"Yes. I think they have always been in the horse business." One of the older quilters looked up from the frame and blinked. "I wonder if they'll have the funeral out there. I'm sure they have a cemetery on the property."

Theo noticed the mention of a funeral lowered many voices. Reality was setting in. As she wandered through the workroom, Theo picked up bits of different conversations. Maybe Doreen hadn't been popular. Shock that a murderer roamed their community kept down any excitement. No one except Nellie Pearl appeared to celebrate her death.

Instead, undertones of fear were woven in every word, every phrase. If the mayor's wife could be killed, couldn't any of them? Was her death random or personal?

Theo glanced around the room. Nellie Pearl and Icky Vicky Parker seemed to have vanished in the excitement about Doreen. That was fine with Theo. She felt once every twenty years was often enough for a visit from Icky. Now she'd had two in a short period.

Theo considered her own feelings about the mayor's late wife. She had never liked Doreen and most of the time she was irritated by her husband, Calvin. The mayor was unfailingly polite, to the point of insanity, and she considered him a cross between a cartoon and a pompous pain in the butt. His hair was a straight blond mop, usually in need of a good trim. It wasn't overgrown from a lack of funds. The mayor had more money than Croesus and sure didn't spend any of it on his clothes. Tall and gangly, he wore mail-order suits with too-short pants and sleeves that didn't reach his boney wrists.

Calvin might not be her favorite person, but his wife had been brutally murdered. Theo was at a loss about what to do next.

If Nellie Pearl was announcing Doreen's demise to all and

sundry, she felt like she could acknowledge the woman's death without spilling anything confidential. No details had been released, and she hadn't seen Tony since his return from Ohio.

Still, it seemed way too early to descend on Calvin with a casserole, so she called Nina. When her friend answered, Theo spoke without preamble.

"You should have been in the shop this morning. Nellie Pearl told us Doreen's been killed."

"No!"

Theo was satisfied by Nina's shocked gasp. The loop was complete.

"I'm on my way in to town now." Irreverent and irrepressible as usual, Nina's words came out in a torrent. "Take notes until I get there."

Before Theo disconnected, her own unruly thoughts bounced in another direction. Since Calvin was the local undertaker full-time and only the mayor part-time, would he prepare her body himself? "Hey, Nina," she said. "I just had a ghoulish thought. Do you suppose Calvin will embalm Doreen and then keep her on display in his office? You know, like Evita Peron?"

"That is awful." Nina laughed. "It would be easier to inciner-ate her and carry the ashes around in his car. I know for a fact they have some beautiful urns at Doreen's Gift Shoppe."

Tony needed to talk to Calvin. The mayor needed to account for his whereabouts. J.B. told him he had tried to deliver the news at five-thirty in the morning. No one answered the bell. Wade tried several times later with the same result. It wasn't until after nine, when the housekeeper arrived, that the news of Doreen's death had been delivered. Evidently, Pansy reluctantly ushered Wade into Calvin's home office and the mayor eventu-ally joined him.

According to Wade, when the mayor did arrive, his hair was

wet and he hadn't put on his tie. Although he hadn't managed to produce any tears, Calvin had honestly seemed stunned by Wade's news.

Tony turned the Blazer onto the mayor's long driveway and slowly drove toward the house, trying to marshal his thoughts. He needed to offer condolences and run an investigation at the same time.

The sight of Calvin wrestling a large cardboard box from the back of a gleaming white hearse distracted him. Tony pulled the Blazer to a stop and sat and watched.

The hearse was parked in the driveway just in front of the steps. Calvin clutched some smaller boxes with his left arm as he dragged the large box toward the front door with his right, letting it bump up the steps. Another box sat next to the door.

Tony eased the Blazer forward. Seeing the man's lips moving, Tony lowered his window to listen. Grief made people do peculiar things. Calvin was not acting like Calvin. For the first time Tony could remember, he had removed his suit coat and loosened his tie. As a rule, the mayor made no concession to the sweltering heat. That wasn't all that seemed out of character.

Calvin was singing, belting out a gospel hymn with verve and obvious joy. Pausing, he used a knee to thump the largest carton like he was playing the drums. The man had a nice voice.

Intrigued, Tony climbed out of his vehicle and approached him. "Can I help?"

Startled, Calvin's singing stopped mid-note, and he whirled around, releasing his hold on the large box. That sent him falling backwards over the fallen carton. When he crashed to the ground, the boxes he managed to hang on to flew from his arms and bounced on the sidewalk. One of them cracked Tony in the knee.

Tony bent over and massaged his wounded knee. The box was heavy cardboard, and the bump surprisingly painful.

Calvin climbed to his size-sixteen feet and began rubbing his wounded elbow. A welcoming smile illuminated his plain face.

Tony wasn't sure he'd ever seen Calvin's real smile before. Countless times he had witnessed the ceremonial stretching of his thin lips. This was a real smile, one that not only exposed Calvin's big, square, horse teeth, but one that put a sparkle in his eyes.

"Good morning, Sheriff."

"Mayor." Tony tossed the carton that had assaulted him on top of the growing pile. "What are the boxes for?"

"Just thought it would be a good time to pack up a few of Doreen's things. Give 'em to charity, you know."

The mayor's jovial attitude rendered Tony speechless. He was expecting, if not crippling grief, at least shock and numbness. Suspicion reared its ugly head.

"I have to ask you not to do that. In fact, I don't want you to touch any of her things. This is still a murder investigation, and Wade is on his way now with a warrant to search this house."

"Am I a suspect?" Calvin's cornflower blue eyes widened and his shoulders drooped like a child denied a carnival treat.

"You ought to know my job is to ask lots of questions in a case like this. It's nothing personal." He pulled out his notebook. "Would you mind answering a few questions for me now?"

"Ask away." Calvin's expression looked like a smirk. "I have nothing to hide."

Wade arrived, search warrant in hand.

"Excellent timing," said Tony.

Wade's proud grin was tempered by the solemn occasion. "What are all these boxes for?"

Irritation colored the mayor's voice. "They are for you to stack up right there." Calvin pointed out the designated area and dragged one more carton out of the hearse and added it to the collection.

"Okay, Mayor." Tony waved to the front door. "Why don't we go inside? I have several questions in need of serious answers."

Calvin nodded and led the way into the formal parlor.

Tony frowned at the mayor's back. "You didn't expect your wife to be home last night?"

"No." Calvin folded his long legs and more or less dropped into the chair, all signs of his previous enjoyment vanished. "She was supposed to be off on another of her buying trips. It's really not very unusual for her to be on the road."

"And you were where last night?" Tony made a couple of entries in his notebook. "Starting at five."

"Why, here, of course." Calvin turned his face toward Tony. He seemed very careful not to make eye contact. "Well, I got here at six. I was at the mortuary until then."

"And you were here all night?"

Calvin nodded.

Tony felt his stomach tighten. J.B. said he had been here at five-thirty in the morning, and Tony believed the deputy's story. The mayor was lying.

"So when I came by at six, seven and eight, where were you then?" Wade consulted his notes. "I rang the bell and dialed your telephone number each time."

"I must have been in the shower." Calvin steepled his fingers and leaned forward. His eyes showed no emotion. "I love to take showers."

Accepting the blatant lie for the moment, Tony and Wade made a cursory check of the house. Tony saw nothing obviously out of place. He learned more than he wanted to know. The mayor and his wife shared the huge house, not the bedroom.

Covering most of the second floor, Doreen's bedroom suite was the size of a cottage. It consisted of a sitting room, a sleeping room, a bathroom most deluxe hotels would envy and a walk-in closet the size of a double garage.

Nothing appeared to have been disturbed in the suite. If anything was missing, Calvin didn't seem to know about it. Tony would bet that Pansy, who doubtless spent hours each week cleaning in here, would be a better source of information.

She wasn't.

After their uninformative conversation with Pansy, Wade left.

Tony confronted Calvin again, sensing the man would talk more one-to-one. "Out with it."

Calvin twitched but didn't refute Tony's assumption. Finally, he reached into his wallet and removed a receipt for a room in a chain motel in nearby Pigeon Forge. Before he relinquished it, he looked directly into Tony's eyes, "I need you to swear you'll keep my secret, especially from your wife."

Unsurprised the man had secrets, Tony nodded.

"I was in Pigeon Forge until it was too late to safely drive home." Calvin's voice shook slightly. "It's not what you think, at least not this time." He cleared his throat several times.

Fascinated, Tony watched the mayor in silence.

"I am taking private quilting lessons from a woman over there."

"Why?" The word fell out of his mouth. He never would have guessed this secret.

"I want to finish some quilts my mother started." Calvin twitched again.

For a moment, Tony couldn't respond. He cleared his throat. "What I meant is why not have Theo teach you?"

"It's a matter of pride. I want to be accomplished before I ask if I can join her quilting group." His big hands flopped to his sides. "Your wife is my quilting goddess. I'm not fit to share the air she breathes."

Tony stared. Keeping this story from Theo might kill him. If she learned about it from someone else, she might kill him.

Either way, he hoped the mayor would call her soon.

On his way back to his office, Tony stopped at Doreen's Flower and Gift Shoppe. His hand barely touched the handle before it opened abruptly. His eyes dropped to the woman holding it open.

"Are you closing the shop?"

"No. Why would I close the shop?" Tony stared at Bernice Osborne's tired face and thought Doreen's only full-time employee fit the description of downtrodden, desperate, and impoverished. She raised eight, mostly normal, children with minimal support from their father, Slow.

Slow Osborne worked odd jobs, badly, and was usually hired because people felt sorry for his family. The local churches bore the brunt of his services.

"Then, why are you here?" Bernice's words jarred him back to the present.

"I thought I'd ask if you knew of anyone Doreen argued with lately."

Bernice stuck her fingers into her tight gray curls and closed her eyes. "There's Calvin, of course, Pansy, your aunt Martha, a few customers I ain't seen before." Her eyes widened behind the thick old-fashioned glasses she wore. "Can't honestly say I haven't wanted to kill her." Her tired eyes stared up into his. "But she pays regular and the checks don't bounce."

Tony accepted her claim. "I haven't seen Warren around lately." Bernice's youngest child was a familiar sight in the county jail, mostly for public intoxication.

"Warren?" The name rolled slowly off her tongue as she considered his statement. "Oh, you mean my boy Speedy. I forgot what I wrote on the birth papers."

She clearly expected he'd understand losing track of eight

names, so he nodded. "Okay, so bring me up to speed on Speedy."

Bernice didn't react to his play on words. "He's away."

"Where?"

Speedy picked that moment to let himself in through the back door. "Got you a burger, Ma." In contrast to his name, he moved gingerly through the shop, edging between displays as he clutched a go box from Ruby's Café. "I ate most of the fries on the way." He didn't notice Tony standing outside. "Now that the Queen is dead, is all this stuff yours now?" His homely face glowed with delight.

"No." Bernice took the food box.

"Why not? She's not going to need it anymore." Speedy's eyes moved across Tony's badge and he stopped smiling.

"It don't work like that. If Calvin don't want me to work here, I'm out a job."

Seeing there was little to learn from Bernice, Tony eased away, leaving mother and son discussing their future prospects, or lack thereof.

Chapter Thirteen

After a late dinner, Tony put the last of the clean dishes in the cabinet and turned to face Theo. She looked as tired as he felt. This was the first chance today they'd been able to talk without the boys and their portable antennae, also known as big ears, lurking around. Chris and Jamie had gone to get the dog's worn tennis ball, and Daisy's excited barking drowned out every other sound. As curious as he was about Doreen's apparent murder, the tale he'd heard in Cincinnati haunted him.

Theo poured herself a tall glass of sweet iced tea and strolled onto the front porch. He followed her, wondering how to ask his questions without alarming her.

They sat side-by-side on the top step and watched the boys playing ball with Daisy across the street in the park. It was almost dark. Decorative lights glowed along the walking path and the tiny brown bats began leaving their wooden homes for their insect hunting.

"Tell me what you remember about Vicky Parker."

"I don't know I can tell you much." Clearly curious, Theo didn't ask him to explain. "She and her father moved here for a little while. They lived with her uncle. You know him. Her uncle is Nelson Parker."

"Yes, I do know him, at least by sight. He's the old recluse who has the place up past Nina's. He comes into town about twice a year and never causes any trouble." Tony thought the man was maybe fifty-five. He looked a hundred. He had no visible teeth, and that made his lips and gums sink into his face like those on a dried apple doll. Tony pulled his lips over his teeth and smacked his fake gums together. Leaning closer to his wife, he panted softly. "Give us a kiss, pretty girl."

Theo dissolved into a fit of the giggles. "That's him, all right. However, he does wear his store-bought teeth on ceremonial occasions."

"I thought he lived alone up there." Tony's eyes drifted to the dark mass of the mountains.

"Well, he probably does now." Theo pushed her glasses up onto the bridge of her nose. "Vicky and her father didn't live there full-time. They would arrive for a few months and then be gone for several years. I don't think Vicky and her father stayed up there very often after you moved away."

"Any idea where they moved to? Or where they moved from, for that matter." Tony doubted his own choice of residence had any effect on the Parkers.

"No." Theo turned to face him. "You ought to ask your mom. Since they joined your dad's congregation, he might have learned that and passed the information on to her. I do remember Vicky liked you, a lot, and she spent quite a bit of time hanging out, watching you." She gave him a sparkling grin that made him feel warm and safe. Her next words spoiled that effect. "When you left for the Navy, she talked about you at Sunday school, you know, like the two of you were engaged. No one believed her. Not really."

Tony couldn't suppress a shiver and lifted his eyes to watch the boys. They took turns throwing the ball to each other and then for the dog, sending the big retriever diving into the shrubs. He hadn't told Theo what he'd learned from Harrison, but he would eventually. He also believed Harrison's version of events right down to the last words of the letter.

"When did you last see her?" Tony stole Theo's glass and

drained the last of the tea.

"This morning." As she retrieved her empty glass, Theo gave him a glare that could have melted an iceberg. "It's funny you should be asking about her. I saw her the other day for the first time in years." She pulled an ice cube out of the glass and rubbed it on the soles of her bare feet. "She came into the shop just a couple of days ago. We chatted for a little bit and I suggested lunch. She showed up this morning just before Nellie Pearl arrived with the news about Doreen."

Tony felt a chill, and the hair on his arms lifted. He hoped his voice would not betray his unease. "She was in your shop? Today? Has she moved back again?" He surged to his feet, preparing to call the boys home, and sat back down when he realized he was overreacting. The golden retriever only behaved like a clown. She was fiercely protective of the boys.

He hoped Theo hadn't noticed his bizarre behavior as he continued his interrogation.

Theo's eyes widened behind the lenses of her glasses. She had definitely noticed.

Her mouth opened. He rushed ahead, forestalling her inevitable curiosity. "Is she married?" In his horrified state, he realized he hadn't given Theo time to answer one question before he asked the next. He shut up.

"Maybe." Theo gave him a curious look. "She did have a little boy with her the first time. I think she said he's one year old. She didn't have the boy with her today." Theo held her arms protectively close to her chest. "I don't know why she makes me feel uneasy. When Nellie Pearl announced Doreen's death, she stayed for a little while and then left. I was glad. I don't want to eat with her."

Most days, Tony saw Theo for the woman she had grown up to be—confident but reserved, creative, energetic and full of love. Rarely now, he saw glimpses of the tiny little girl she'd been, looking out at a world she was forbidden to join. Growing up without television or other "lurid" entertainment, Theo hadn't become desensitized to violence of any kind.

"If it's all the same, I'd rather you two don't become chums."

Theo stared at him for a minute and then nodded.

Tony hoped he'd said the right thing. Vicky's killing spree, if true, took place almost twenty years ago and had yet to be proven. He could imagine what would happen if he told Theo about it. Her social skills didn't extend to acting. She'd make Vicky suspicious. Theo couldn't pretend she hadn't heard the weird story. Theo would end up staring at Vicky as if she was an exotic insect.

Tony shifted and wrapped an arm around her, pulling her close to his side. Even in the stifling heat, he welcomed the warmth of her pressed against him. He was not surprised to feel her tremble. Until he realized it was himself and not her who shivered.

Tony lay awake in the dark.

When he closed his eyes, he could still see the devastating wound the flax hackle had left in Doreen's throat. He hadn't seen the injury until he attended the autopsy that had taken place late in the afternoon.

Tony's stomach churned and he eased from the bed, searching for antacids. Doreen's throat had been pierced to the bone with the rows of spikes. Death was inevitable. The coroner doubted immediate medical attention could have done more than slow the process.

Tony's number-one suspect in the death of Doreen had to be Calvin. His obvious glee at his wife's demise was understandable, however politically incorrect. Dragging packing boxes into the house before setting the date of the funeral was not acceptable behavior. Surely, if the mayor wanted to look innocent, he would trot out the sackcloth and ashes instead of tap dancing up the sidewalk like Fred Astaire?

The whole scene of the crime out at the museum didn't look like a premeditated job. It looked angry, impulsive, like someone had grabbed the murder weapon from a shelf and used it. It might even have been self-defense.

So suspect number two had to be? His mother? Fabulous. His aunt? Excellent. His own wife. Better and better. If his list expanded to include everyone who ever had a skirmish with the woman and drew back a bloody stub, it would be a roster of the whole county.

His thoughts shifted to the problem of getting a search warrant for the Nelson property. That dispelled the last possibility of sleep, so he wandered downstairs to his miniature office where he distracted himself by scribbling ideas for his Western in a worn spiral notebook. Questions about Doreen's death and Icky Vicky continued to plague him.

Tony awoke with a start.

He realized he still held his pen and the notebook had shifted into the space between his leg and the recliner's armrest. Although he dozed in his chair, he found little comfort anywhere. He might as well go to work. He needed to organize his rioting thoughts. Every question that popped into his head led to six more.

A quick shower revived him a bit, so he felt reasonably alert when he arrived in his office.

He found a pink phone message slip on the center of his desk. Deciphering the night dispatcher's handwriting, he learned Doreen's beige Volvo had turned up in a long-term parking lot near Maghee Tyson Airport, the airport serving Knoxville and the surrounding area.

When had the car been left? By whom? More questions

circled in his head and Tony hoped the parking ticket would be inside the Volvo and might provide some lead.

Tony didn't know what to think. Had the killer driven the car to the airport or had Doreen? It was too early to phone Calvin. He left his office and drove, searching for inspiration.

Drawn to the museum site, he couldn't shake the feeling he was missing something important.

He parked the Blazer at the entrance, rolled down the window and simply sat. At this time of day everything remained in semidarkness, awaiting full morning light. It was already hot and muggy. The promise of a storm hovered in the air.

A rooster crowed. The way sound bounced through the hills, it could have come from anywhere. If Doreen had screamed, that sound would have been distorted as well.

"What was Doreen doing out here?" If he could answer that question, Tony believed all of the other answers would fall into place like a key opening a lock.

He closed his eyes, thinking. An educated guess would be that Doreen went into the trailer because of the quilt. She might have decided against lending it. Did she surprise a thief? Before he finished that line of thought, another scenario presented itself. Maybe Doreen and her killer arrived together, had an argument and things got nasty. And then what? The killer drove out to the airport and abandoned Doreen's car?

Either way, he suspected those quilts were at the center of the events.

Gus should arrive soon.

Tony settled in to wait for his brother. The scent of warm earth mixed with the soft sounds of birds and insects lulled him to sleep.

The *k-chunk, k-chunk* sound of a nail gun awakened him. He checked his watch, surprised to find an hour had passed. In full light it was easy to see that where the previous day's red mud had dried, it now looked like alligator skin.

A quick call to the mayor produced nothing new. The man was useless as far as information about his wife's travels. He didn't know when she planned to leave. He didn't know when she was due back. He didn't know where she was going. He didn't know if she might leave her car at the airport and drive somewhere with someone else. He promised to look for the extra set of keys.

The foundation and framing showed the new part of the museum was moving rapidly. Tony watched as Mac and Gus worked high off the ground, nailing plywood on the pitched roof. Below them, skinny Quentin and tiny Kenny wrestled a sheet of plywood over to the wall and then shoved it up until Mac and Gus could lean over, grab it and lay it in place. The idea of being up there and leaning over the side made Tony feel a little queasy.

He looked away.

Yellow police tape still sealed off the trailer and the surrounding area. Steam rose from the deeper puddles. Heavy equipment sat idle, parked between the new structure and the kudzu-covered hillside. At this time of year, you could practically see the stuff growing, twining itself around everything in its path. A noxious experiment had gone awry like some science-fiction monster, kudzu had been imported to lessen erosion. It thrived on the poor soil and climbed telephone poles and buildings with equal enthusiasm. It was a cosmic joke.

His mother and aunt arrived and met him as he lowered himself from the Blazer. The women looked tired. He doubted either of them managed even as much sleep as he did.

"Did you want us to go inside with you?"

"We'll wait for Wade." Tony frowned at his mother's disheveled state. Her hair looked uncombed. Not at all Jane's style. "I need you to look around and tell me if you notice anything out of place or different in any way."

Wade arrived and pulled his camera out of its case.

Tony nodded and escorted them toward the trailer. The broken hasp and hardware had been bagged as evidence. The laboratory technician who had taken his call assured him that if presented with a tool, they would be able to confirm or eliminate it as the item used to pry it off.

A new, stronger hasp had been bolted to the trailer door and wall about a foot below the original. The size and strength of it displayed Gus's workmanship. His first construction job had been a birdhouse in Cub Scouts. It would last a hundred years.

Gus loved to build things to last.

His brother Gus was a gentle soul, the least violent of all his siblings. That was enough information to keep him off the serious suspect list. Finding it inconceivable wasn't enough to eliminate him.

Suspicion nagged at Tony. Gus and Doreen had an unpleasant history. Last he knew, Doreen still hadn't paid Gus for some carpentry work in her shop. And he was one of the last to leave the site. And it would be child's play for him to break into the trailer. And he would easily have the strength to wield the flax hackle.

Tony could only positively eliminate himself as a suspect. That left the field wide for possibilities. He could even come up with a scenario in which any of the women in his life would want to kill Doreen; however, none of them would have tossed an antique quilt onto her.

His mother sagged against him. Although she wasn't young, she wasn't old, and her energy level was remarkable. Not today. Today as she looked around the items in the trailer, she appeared pale and smaller than usual. Of course, stepping over the chalked outline of Doreen's body was enough to make anyone quiet.

"I just don't understand. What are we looking for?" Jane's fingers caressed the items on the shelves. "There is nothing here with any monetary value. It's all family stuff or something with regional history."

"No one's donated the original Magna Carta?" Tony teased, trying unsuccessfully to get a rise out of either of the women.

His aunt pointed to a clear glass cookie jar. Even from across the room, it was easy to see coins and bills inside. "I'd take that if I broke in, and it's only got maybe a hundred dollars in it."

"You don't think Gus did it, do you?" Jane's sudden statement looked like it took her by surprise.

Tony swung around to look into her face. "Do you?"

"No." Her response was emphatic. Her eyes remained uncertain. "I can't imagine him doing such a thing, can you?"

"No." With the word came total belief, and he knew what he said was true. "Not Gus."

CHAPTER FOURTEEN

Theo sat in the corner of the shop classroom working on a wall quilt. The room buzzed with chatter as quilters worked on the charity quilt or a project they'd brought along. Theo's current quilt had informed her it wanted beads added to it. As usual, she accepted the notion that arguing with fabric was a waste of time. Either projects held real opinions, or the subconscious was smarter than the conscious. It didn't matter. She would sew beads. Concentrating on placing the beads and keeping up with the various conversations in the room was becoming difficult.

From what she could tell, the general consensus among the quilters gathered in the room was, although Doreen had not been anyone's favorite, hers was a terrible way to die. There was a certain amount of speculation among the older ladies about whether or not the murder quilt had played a role. Maybe it carried a curse.

As titillating as the idea of a voodoo quilt might be, the truth was much sadder.

"What do you know about the murder quilt, Theo?"

Theo looked over at the small group working on a charity quilt. The sweetly voiced question came from an unexpected source. Louise Gormet, co-owner of the new Gormet Coffee Shop next door, was a newbie to quilting.

"Doreen gave us a brief history." Theo frowned, remembering Doreen would not be able to give them the full one now. The family might even decide to remove it from the museum.

She hoped not. "Do you know there are two quilts?"

Louise nodded.

"As I understand it, the engagement quilt was pieced by her father's family. It was made to celebrate Abigail's engagement to the son of a state senator." Theo set aside her project. "All accounts are that Abigail didn't want to marry the young man her father had more or less selected for her. He put his foot down when he learned Abigail was with child. The father of the unborn baby was never disclosed. The assumption is he was already married or he simply abandoned her."

"So why did she agree to the engagement?"

"It was an arrangement by the families, more or less." She glanced around the room. "Women weren't so independent then, you know. Having a fatherless child was beyond shocking."

"Did you say there was a second quilt?"

"Yes," said Theo. "Apparently, Abigail made it all by herself to give to the young man she loved and was pregnant by." The room seemed filled by Abigail's sorrow. "I don't have many facts. I understand Abigail finished the quilt about the same time her groom realized she was pregnant and he killed her, wrapped her body in her lover's quilt, and left town, never to be heard from again. The murder fueled stories for the next generations, but her lover's name was never spoken."

"Was the man arrested?"

Theo shrugged. "I don't think anyone knows what happened to him. If you've got the nerve, you could always ask Bathsheba. She was Abigail's sister."

Everyone suddenly seemed fascinated by their projects.

As if summoned by a witch's spell, Bathsheba descended on Theo. She wished it was winter, the season Bathsheba spent in Florida. The tiny old woman's blue-veined hands clutched her cane with the strength of hickory. In her cataract-clouded eyes burned the hatred of the generations.

"You tell your lazy husband I know it was her husband who killed her. If he wants to keep his job, I suggest he make an arrest. Today."

Theo blinked and returned to the present. Bathsheba was talking about Doreen and Calvin, not Abigail and the unwanted fiancé.

Tony stopped by Ruby's Café for lunch. When Ruby brought him the menu, a flash of light on her left hand caught his attention. The diamond ring was new. He grinned. "You're finally going to put Mike out of his misery?"

Tony—and everyone else in town—knew Deputy Mike Ott had been asking Ruby to marry him for months. It was almost a running gag. Several informal bets had been made on the date she would finally accept his proposal. A tinge of rose crept onto her cheeks, brightening her flawless olive complexion. Her deep brown eyes glowed. Happiness transformed the most beautiful woman in the county into the most beautiful woman in the state. Tony grinned.

Ruby gave him a mock salute. "Yes. I thought I'd wait until he presented me with a petition signed by the majority of the county residents."

Tony laughed. "I'll bet almost every signature was female."

"It was your vote that pushed it onto the yes side." Ruby leaned closer and dropped her voice. "Actually, it's because Mike and Dammit are inseparable and I've decided I can't live any longer without dog drool on my furniture."

"I'm happy for both of you." Tony opened the menu with studied casualness. "Does Theo know you've decided to officially adopt a bloodhound and his owner?"

"Not yet." Ruby's blush deepened. "You're the first person I've seen since I said yes."

Tony's grin widened. "You mean if I hurry over to her shop, I can deliver the latest news?"

Ruby laughed. "I'll even give you a head start."

The door into the kitchen swung open and then closed, sending the aroma of warm apples wafting from the kitchen. Tony's stomach rumbled and his mouth watered. "First, I need a slice of pie and a glass of milk for lunch."

When he had a chunk of the pie on his fork, he hesitated, half afraid the pie would not live up to his expectations. As usual, the flavors took his breath away. Whatever Blossom used for a secret ingredient was fantastic. Try as he might, he had never figured it out. Not that it really mattered. He wasn't going to fix one and Theo would probably just call and order a pie rather than cook it herself. His wife was brilliant and creative and not much of a cook.

On his way out, he went into the kitchen to talk to Blossom. She must have fallen into the flour bin. Covered with a large, spotless white apron and the cloud of flour, she looked like a snow figure. One with improbably orange hair.

Blossom cast him an adoring glance.

Tony stayed close to the door. "The pie was as delicious as ever."

"Thank you." Her eyelids fluttered.

He cleared his throat. "You and Doreen have never gotten along very well, have you?"

"Nope." The welcoming glow disappeared from her bulbous eyes. Her little lips stuck out in a pout.

"Are you satisfied she didn't steal your lawn ornament?" Tony had lost count of the number of purloined gnomes and the like. The epidemic raged on. He had neither clues nor the manpower to track them down.

"Yep." Blossom traced a pattern in fallen flour with the tip of her big toe. Finally she looked up at him. It looked like she had tears in her eyes. "I didn't kill her."

"I know you didn't." Even if she had wanted to do it, Tony couldn't imagine how a woman of Blossom's considerable bulk would have been able to squeeze into the space where the killing occurred, much less be able to wield the flax hackle with those child-sized hands. He thought, not for the first time, Calvin's large, long-fingered hands would have been able to wield it with ease.

Blossom smiled and waggled her fingers at him.

As he paid for his pie, he wondered if he needed to drive to Theo's shop with lights and siren on in order to be the first with news about the engagement.

He found his wife in the community workroom instead of in her office. When he announced the news about Ruby and Mike to the quilters, a cheer of delight was followed closely by the beginning of a discussion about making the couple a wedding quilt.

After all, Ruby was one of them.

NIGHT ON THE MOUNTAIN
CLUE #2

Construction A.

On the reverse side of each of 12, Light #2—4 1/4" squares, draw a diagonal line from corner to corner. Place it right side facing down on the right side of 4 1/4" square of Medium #2. Using the drawn line as a guide, sew a line of stitching 1/4" on both sides of the line. Cut on the line. Open and press to the darker fabric. Trim the resulting squares to measure 3 3/4". You should have 24 half-square triangle squares. Set aside.

Contruction B.

On the reverse side of each of 24 squares of Light #1—2 1/8" squares, draw a diagonal line from corner to corner. Place one right side facing down the right side of 3 3/4" square of Medium #2. Line up edges even with one corner of medium—the drawn line should travel across the corner of Medium #2. Sew *on* the drawn line.

Press to corner.

You should have 24 squares with a light triangle on one corner.

CHAPTER FIFTEEN

In a good mood, Tony returned to the law enforcement center.

Ruth Ann must have been watching for him, because he didn't have his outside door closed before she arrived at his inside door. As she handed him a sheaf of phone messages, he couldn't avoid noticing her latest nail polish. He hadn't seen this shade before. Her fingernails glinted with a hint of pink glitter embedded in bright blue polish. "New color?"

Ruth Ann nodded as she continued to force him to accept the stack of notes.

He frowned even as his fingers closed around them. "I don't want these."

"They are all for you." Ruth Ann held a pink palm up to stop him from handing them back. "I really think you'll be intrigued by the one from the Park Service. You've got a believer who would like to call in the FBI."

He felt a flash of relief. The cold case involving Vicky Parker and the soon-to-be-deceased Harrison Duff would require incredible man-hours. Even if they wanted to follow up, his small staff was stretched to the limits.

"Are the Feds claiming jurisdiction?" If he could get this albatross off his neck, he'd be happy.

"Not exactly," said Ruth Ann. "They are making sounds like they might be willing to look into it. That is, if you can find some evidence to support your guy's story. The bones Theo found are not enough because they could have come from anywhere."

Tony's surge of excitement vanished. He couldn't imagine any judge issuing a search warrant on the uncle's private land just because a terminally ill man claimed there were bodies in a freezer.

Having heard from Harrison what they'd put in the freezer made him consider a long trip. The lazy part of Tony hoped the freezer was gone. If Harrison's story proved out and there were bodies in it, the investigation would be a nightmare. Even if the Feds did take over, he would still have to keep track of what they were doing in his county.

The greater part of him was driven to protect the innocent and punish the guilty. It won. He recognized the same fire in Ruth Ann's eyes.

"I'll drive out there and see if Mr. Parker will let me look around his place." The idea of tramping around in the exceptional heat and stifling humidity held little appeal. He fanned himself with the papers. "First, though, I'll go through these and reread the confession."

Even he recognized this as a stalling technique. He continued, "Tell Wade to give me fifteen minutes to digest my lunch and he's going with me."

Ruth Ann nodded and turned away.

"Oh, by the way, Ruby agreed to marry Mike and she's wearing a new diamond ring."

Ruth Ann turned back, a wide grin lighting her face. "Well, it's about time."

For a quarter of an hour, he lounged in his desk chair, leaning back with his legs comfortably crossed on the open lower drawer of his desk. He tried concentrating on the warm pie. That didn't work. Maybe thinking about the book he was writing would get his mind off his job. Unfortunately, writing about an imaginary lawman of the eighteen hundreds only circled his brain back to the problems at hand.

Unless someone confessed to the murder of Doreen Cash-dollar, he might be in professional trouble. There were only vague suspects. Calvin was way too obvious. He was smart enough to have hauled out the sackcloth and ashes if he'd killed her. Right now it looked like he would hire a defense attorney for anyone suspected of killing his wife.

Tony didn't like coincidence. He considered Vicky Parker being in town to be stronger than coincidence. What had brought her back after all these years?

"Sheriff?" Wade stood in the doorway.

Tony waved him in and moved his feet to the floor. The expression on Wade's face told him the deputy didn't have news that would help.

"I checked the Volvo. If anyone besides Doreen has been in the car, it was long enough ago that even her mechanic's prints are gone." Wade frowned and pretended to read his notes. "The ones on the door handle and trunk lid were not smudged and they were definitely hers. And the parking ticket was stamped four hours before she could have possibly died."

"That tells us something we didn't know before."

"Sir?" Wade didn't seem so certain.

Tony reached for his antacids. "It tells us Doreen did not deliver herself to the museum, doesn't it? To me, it looks like she arrived with the killer."

Wade sat down on a chair facing him. "So she knew and trusted him."

"Him?"

Wade nodded. "I'd say her killer was most likely male."

Tony agreed. "Why do you think it's a man?"

"It seems simple." Wade shifted forward on the chair. "To start with, the hackle whatsit is big enough that not too many women I've met could hold it and lash out with any kind of force." He flexed one of his own hands. "Prudence Sligar might be able to. She arm wrestles and her hands are big enough. Doreen is her cash cow."

Tony nodded. He considered Prudence. "She just had her latest baby and hasn't lost the weight. I'd be surprised if she could fit into the trailer."

"True," said Wade. "It also seems unlikely Doreen would go out there with any woman she's not related to—you know, like her mother." He paused. A hint of mischief sparkled in his eyes. "She never seemed to care much for other women."

Tony thought that was a masterful piece of understatement.

Tony rode up to Parker's farm with Wade because Wade's vehicle had better air-conditioning.

The ozone and particulate haze over the Smokies hung thick and gray in the air. It made the dark mountains mysterious and foreboding, like giant creatures growing in the heat. These ancient mountains looked strikingly different from the mountains of the western states. Tony remembered his first view of the Beartooth Mountains, rising abruptly from the land. There was no vegetation to soften the tallest peaks, and snow still clung to them in early May.

A pair of pollen-laden insects splattered on the windshield like little water balloons. Studying them distracted his thoughts. In his personal rating systems of color, size and juice, he scored the bugs a nine out of a perfect ten.

"Damn." Wade slunk lower in his seat. "I'm almost driving blind." He squirted the insect blobs with windshield washer fluid. The windshield wipers came on automatically, smearing the mess.

"Maybe old-man Parker will loan you a bucket of water and a rag."

Wade's eyebrows raised and he shook his head. "As far as I can tell, we'll be lucky if he doesn't give us a double barrel load of buckshot. He's not exactly warm and fuzzy."

Tony silently agreed. He considered this a fool's errand. Still, they had to try. The Parker property was just around the curve in the narrow road, and Wade slowed the vehicle, stopping in front of the driveway.

A gate constructed of bits of wire and tree branches closed twin ruts to visitors. The ruts curved past a pitiful garden of weeds, tobacco and corn. Beyond the garden sat the house. Weathered to silver, the small building looked as it had always looked. Twin windows flanked the open front door. The house had no eaves. The way tree branches came over the roof from the back, the leaves looked like hair on a large gray face.

A double-barreled shotgun came through the doorway, and then Nelson Parker emerged. He held the butt of the gun pressed to his shoulder. In spite of the heat, he wore a long-sleeved plaid shirt under worn overalls. A battered straw hat shaded most of his face. Toothless gums parted. "Hold!"

Tony froze. "I'm not on your property, Mr. Parker."

"Lucky for you."

Tackling the subject of searching for dead bodies with a shotgun aimed at him strained Tony's power of persuasion. He tried a smile. "How are you today, Mr. Parker?"

A sharp nod was the answer.

"Do you suppose you could lower the shotgun?"

A single shake of the head answered the question.

Tony didn't move. His chocolate-brown uniform shirt collected sunlight and turned the vest under it into a sauna. Sweat slid down his face and neck. The barest movement of air carried the smell of something sweet and rotten.

Parker stood in the shade and waited.

Nelson Parker had never been an easy man to deal with.

Tony decided against asking about the freezer. If it was there, any interest on his part would have Parker destroying the evidence.

He cast about in his brain for an excuse for their visit. "I haven't seen you in town lately. We just wanted to make sure you hadn't died of the heat up here."

Parker gave one more shake of his head before turning and walking back into his house.

Giving up the freezer project for the moment, Tony and Wade climbed back into the car.

Tony slammed the car door. "We need a warrant."

Wade cranked the air conditioner up to full blast. He turned to face his boss. "I could come up here tonight and just look around. No one would ever know I was here."

For a moment, Tony considered it. The Marines had trained Wade well. He could turn into a shadow. "No. Let's do it right."

Theo needed some chocolate. Now. She opened the bottom drawer in her desk. Nothing. There had to be some in this office. She could almost taste it. Almost feel the slide of warm chocolate on her tongue.

"Dammit, who stole my chocolate?" The emergency stash in the bathroom cupboard, behind the extra toilet paper, was gone. Unthinkable. Heads would roll for this.

She opened the miniscule freezer on the pint-sized refrigerator and pulled out the ice cube tray. Wedged into the space between the tray and the back wall was a tiny candy bar. Life was good. Theo tore the wrapper off with her teeth as she scribbled herself a note. It was a simple code. A capital C with three lines underneath signaled it was the first thing she needed to put in her grocery cart at the Food City.

Tony opened the autopsy report. The official photograph made

117

him wince. It showed Doreen's throat once the hackle had been removed. He guessed if she had been savaged by a wild animal, it wouldn't look much different. Torn to shreds.

According to the pathologist, Doreen had not died instantly. The cause of death was a combination of loss of oxygen and loss of blood. It was deemed doubtful that even with immediate medical attention she could have survived such horrific wounds. Time of death was narrowed to a four-hour window between six and ten.

The manner of death was absolutely murder. The other choices were natural, accidental, suicide, and undetermined.

Tony worked on his list of people who were known to spend time at the museum site. First and most frequent were his mother and her sister, followed by his brother, his brother's wife, Catherine, and Theo. Gus employed three men on a full-time basis: Quentin, Mac and Kenny. Other subcontractors came and went.

Doreen herself. According to all sources, Queen Doreen spent part of each day out there, issuing royal directives with no authority and generally making herself a royal pain.

Who kills someone for being a pain?

Tony eliminated his wife, his mother and his aunt on emotional grounds. Just because he couldn't imagine it, didn't mean it couldn't happen. He crossed Gus and his wife off the list for the same unscientific reason.

After asking Wade to meet him there, Tony headed over to the museum site to have a little chat with Gus and his regular workers.

CHAPTER SIXTEEN

As Tony approached the museum site, he wondered why he and all of his siblings tried so hard to please Jane. Their mother wasn't demanding. She didn't whine or ask for any special favors but received them just the same. Tony didn't think he and his siblings were still competing for the position of favorite child. Maybe they were. Certainly they took turns with the major efforts.

A year ago, his sister Callie reluctantly accompanied Jane on a cruise, in spite of a lifelong tendency toward motion sickness. Calpurnia, as his mother insisted on calling her, suffered ten days of horrendous seasickness while Jane blithely sailed along and had a wonderful time. The last time he'd talked to Callie about the trip, she claimed she still got sick looking at water in the bathtub.

This summer it was Gus's turn to bang his head against a wall. Being Jane's virtual slave at the museum site kept him from several lucrative jobs. Jane paid him less than he was worth.

So far, brother Tiberias let his contribution consist of free dental work. If Tony knew Berry, bigger and more expensive plans were in the works.

Ruefully acknowledging his own efforts to replace the appellation of baby with the title of favorite, Tony stopped near the driveway and watched the construction crew at work.

Quentin and Kenny marched across the ruts carrying a long beam. Because of the difference in their heights, they looked like a greyhound and a bulldog.

Kenny's compact body possessed most of the energy and strength of the pair. Although he was only five foot five, Gus said he could outwork two bigger men.

Tall, thin and twitchy, Quentin's bout with meth had been short-lived but intense. He certainly suffered some emotional problems that could be attributed to his detoxification. Surly, cranky and bad-tempered were some of the kinder descriptions. Gus mentioned once the normally kind Quentin had developed a volatile temper. When aroused, he threw hammers, pliers, boards or anything else he could pick up. So far, he hadn't been known to throw them toward anyone.

Had he gotten into an argument with Doreen and popped his cork? He swore not. He claimed he and Mac were at the Okay Bar and Bait Shop after work. When he left the Okay, he had gone home and Mac had gone to see his girlfriend.

It didn't surprise Tony to learn Mac had been in town for only a short time and already had a steady girlfriend. Single men over thirty with jobs and halfway decent social skills were scarce in Park County.

Kenny was a single father. Tony believed his alibi. After all, Theo provided it. She sat next to him when his daughter Kimberly hit the home run bunt while he was in Cincinnati. When the team went on to win, he took everyone for celebratory pizza.

Kenny's extra vigilance as a father had a lot to do with his untrustworthy ex-wife. The last thing he was likely to do was risk her gaining custody of their two little girls.

Tony called and talked to Mom Proffitt, owner of the Okay Bar and Bait Shop. She remembered Mac and Quentin came in and had a couple of beers. They ate some potato skins and shot a little pool. Nothing unusual. Just two guys who worked together, cooling down after a sweltering day at an outdoor job.

When asked, Quentin's neighbor, Nellie Pearl, said she saw Quentin's flashy black truck headed up the hill to his place. To get there when she said, he had to have driven directly there after he left the Okay. To pay for the information, Sheila carried yet more stacks of boxes up and down the stairs for almost an hour.

Mac's girlfriend, Allison Babb, invited Tony and Wade into her living room. She smiled pleasantly at Tony then turned her full-wattage smile on his handsome deputy. It was lovely, although it exposed the myriad fine lines on her face. Allison was fighting for youth and losing.

"I understand you are seeing Mac socially." Tony folded his long legs and sat down on the teal leather sofa. He sank into the soft cushions.

Allison nodded. "Is there a problem?"

"No." Tony opened his notebook. "We just have to verify where everyone was when Mrs. Cashdollar was killed."

"He was here, Sheriff. All night." A tinge of pink crept up her neck and brightened her face. Her eyes drifted to Wade and her shoulders lifted just a bit. "We've been dating for a couple of months."

"How did you two meet?"

"I ran into his cart at Food City." She smiled. "It was almost an accident."

Tony let the statement pass. "Does he mention his work?"

Allison's head moved up and down. "He likes your brother a lot. I think he is interested in the new museum, too." She gave a soft laugh. "I'm not ready to pick out china or anything, but I think he might stay here. Permanently."

Tony was sure he had seen a flash of anger in her eyes. "No problems?"

"Nothing serious." Her fingers tapped the arm of the pink wingback chair.

Tony tried to imagine Mac living in this pink and teal room with the white carpet and flowery curtains. It didn't work. Mac belonged in a big leather recliner with a beer cooler in one armrest and a universal remote in the other.

He smiled. "There is a problem?"

The anger in her eyes vanished and was replaced by something harder to define. Maybe fear. "He knows I hate it when he comes here still stinky and dirty."

The tenseness of her throat told Tony she was more than a little miffed that Mac had shown up without stopping for a shower. Theo nagged whenever Tony or the boys tracked mud and dirt into the house. Never did she look this angry about it. It seemed unlikely a construction worker would arrive home smelling like the perfumed air in this room.

Tony wasn't always clean, yet Theo hadn't thrown him out. Gus sweated like crazy and his wife loved him anyway. "So he arrived dirty?"

"Yes." She met his eyes. "He took a shower and changed into some clothes he leaves here, and we drove into Maryville for dinner."

"And?" Tony could see there was more.

"I forgave him. His manners aren't great but I think he can be trained." She began rearranging the magazines on the coffee table. When neither Tony nor Wade said anything, she sat back. "Let's face it, I'm not getting any younger and there aren't many single men in the area. Still, I'm not quite ready to give him a key. You know what I mean?"

Tony did. She was definitely afraid. She feared Mac might be the man she would settle for and was also afraid she couldn't mold him into her idea of a well-trained husband.

Wade leaned forward. "Have you been to his place?"

"You're kidding. Right?" Allison jumped as if a cockroach had run up her leg. "He rents a room in Roscoe Morris's trailer.

I would never go there."

Feeling like he had wasted his time, Tony returned to his of-fice.

A full-size sheet of stationery lay on his desk along with an official report. With all the deputies overworked, he'd sent Ruth Ann to check on the most recent yard-art thefts. He studied the theft reports and drawings. Ruth Ann's dearth of artistic skills could not be worse than the actual appearance of the two latest victims of the garden art thief. Each crude drawing sported ar-rows and descriptive highlights.

A three-foot-tall elf wearing a purple and red jacket was stolen in town. According to the owner, it did not wear pants. Ruth Ann's comments on a sticky note suggested it be arrested for indecent exposure.

The second report claimed a bright blue toadstool support-ing a pink and green toad vanished from a yard about five miles away. The sticky note on the report claimed overuse of the word "toad."

Tony wondered how much more, if anything, Ruth Ann knew about the ornament thefts than he did.

Theo's office pipeline to the details of Queen Doreen's upcom-ing funeral was Gretchen. Her employee, a member of the church choir, continued to cut fabric and put away the bolts as she updated Theo. The event was set for later in the day. No customers were in the shop yet, so it was a good time for her to finish filling the day's Internet orders.

"You know it's set for two o'clock at the First Baptist Church. I suggest you get there early." Gretchen studied the order form she held and began pulling the bolts she'd need to fill it. "If the choir didn't have special seating, I'd be getting there about noon."

That surprised Theo. Queen Doreen was not at all popular,

and the Baptist Church was large enough that it routinely had several empty pews. "Really?"

"Oh yes. It promises to be a gala affair." Gretchen flashed a smile. "Our choir has been practicing for three days. We'll sing a series of upbeat gospel hymns." Her smile dimmed only slightly. "We'll have to make do without our best bass voice."

Theo felt her eyebrows rise.

"Calvin came to choir practice last night. He told us he took Doreen's favorite dress up to the funeral home in Knoxville and they did a real nice job fixing her up." Gretchen swallowed hard. "From what I heard, it couldn't have been easy to do."

"Is he singing with you?"

"No. We'll miss Calvin's voice. He has to sit on the front pew with the rest of the family."

"That makes sense." Theo reached for a sheet of paper and a marker. "I guess I'll put a sign on the door saying we'll be closed today starting at noon."

She dialed Tony and got his voice mail. "I'm going to the funeral at noon and I'll save you a seat."

CHAPTER SEVENTEEN

Even with Gretchen's warning, Theo was surprised by the size of the crowd. She sat directly behind the family, next to her mother-in-law and Martha. Her efforts to save Tony a seat almost failed. The reserved space was smaller than hoped for when Tony squeezed in next to her just before the service began.

Sardines had more space in a can than she did on the pew. Crammed up against Tony's side the way she was, his holstered sidearm dug into her waist. The portly, unfamiliar man on the other side of her seemed to be expanding. And sweating.

Theo felt trapped.

When she glanced down and saw mud on the knees of Tony's khaki pants, her eyes widened in surprise. It wasn't like him to arrive in a church in uniform, much less a dirty one.

"I didn't have a chance to change." Tony's softly spoken words reached her ears. Theo nodded. She just hoped he wouldn't have to leave during the service. She couldn't see how he would be able to stand up without making everyone else on the pew rise.

Her lips twitched as she considered what would happen if her husband created such a scene. Queen Doreen might throw back the lid of the coffin, sit up and read them all the riot act if her service was interrupted.

A blanket of pink carnations covered every inch of the casket. Baskets of flowers flanked it. Theo thought the effect was simple and tasteful.

Calvin sat with Doreen's parents and her paternal grandmother, Bathsheba. The four mourners looked tired but dry-
eyed. Theo guessed they had cried out all of their grief.

The temperature in the church rose quickly in spite of extra
fans gently moving the air. With the outside door closed and the
interior doors left open to allow overflow seating in the vestibule,
there was simply no way the air-conditioning could prevent it
from progressing from hot to hellish. The heavy, sweet scent of
the carnations mixed with the aromas of a variety of deodorants
and body powders. Someone seated nearby must have showered
in heavy perfume. Theo swallowed hard against a wave of
nausea. One after another, beads of sweat rolled between her
breasts and pooled on her belly.

She couldn't breathe.

The service was moving into the final hymn by the choir.
Gretchen's classically trained contralto voice soared above the
rest. Her eyes closed in rapture as she belted out an upbeat
hymn. Just as she hit the high notes on "Dear Jesus," the front
door crashed into the wall as if hit by a bus. Another member of
the choir screamed, a bloodcurdling noise sending shivers down
Theo's spine.

Dark spots danced before her eyes and something seemed to
be muting the sounds around her as she lost consciousness.

Propelled by instinct, Tony surged upward at the startling *thud*
produced by the wooden front doors opening wide and crashing
into the church's exterior wall. Every head turned to face the
back of the church. From his half-upright stance, Tony had a
clear view of the doorway.

The sound of the impact produced a muffled shriek from one
elderly member of the congregation, awakened from a nap.

"She's alive!" Horror laced each syllable that fell from the
organist's lips before she fainted, falling forward, her face crash-

ing onto the keys. The instrument heaved a minor chord that continued, echoing through the sanctuary.

Tony glanced at Theo. He wouldn't have known his wife had fainted if he hadn't seen her eyes. As she began to fall sideways, he pulled her into his arms, lifting her so she could get some air.

A member of the choir dragged the organist from her bench, silencing the instrument.

Absolute calm held for a moment.

The whisper of tiny footsteps on carpet made Tony's skin crawl. He didn't want to believe his eyes. Striding down the blue carpet path between the rows of pews was none other than Doreen Cashdollar.

A furious Doreen Cashdollar.

Tony felt stunned, like someone had slammed his face into a steel hatch. He heard, more than witnessed, Calvin fall. From the corner of his eye, he saw the mayor go down like a shallow-rooted tree in a high wind, crashing onto the altar steps.

The congregation erupted into a cacophony of screams and maniacal laughter.

Stretched out next to the floral arrangements surrounding his wife's coffin, Calvin sobbed uncontrollably, his face buried against a broken spray of bloodred gladiolas.

Immediately on the heels of his shock, Tony felt a mixture of anger and confusion. His thoughts slammed together and bounced in all directions like the brightly colored balls on a billiard table.

If that was Doreen striding toward them wearing a stunning blue dress and matching very high-heeled sandals, then whose autopsy had taken place? Why had a stranger been in the museum office? Did the killer know it wasn't Doreen?

Most importantly, whose body were they about to bury?

Without realizing he had moved, he found himself in front of

Doreen bending forward. She was a good foot shorter than him. With her high-heeled shoes and his attitude, they stood almost nose to nose.

"Where the hell have you been?"

The moment he opened his mouth, silence fell on the congregation and his softly spoken words carried to the farthest corners of the church. A couple of ladies on the second row, semi-professional funeral attendees, gasped with shock. Tony's fleeting glance at the avid expressions on their lined faces convinced him it was a sham. They were not offended by his language; they were thrilled to be present.

Doreen Cashdollar managed to look down her nose at him from her disadvantaged height. "Not that it's any of your business, I've been on a little trip to San Francisco."

"Who? Who?" Calvin stuttered owlishly from his position in the flowers. "Who?" A bony index finger pointed at the casket.

"An excellent question, Mayor." Tony hadn't taken his eyes away from Doreen. Almost forgetting he still held Theo in his arms, he tightened his grip on his wife. "We had your car towed."

"So that's what happened to it." Doreen stamped her tiny foot and pointed toward the back of the church. "I started filling out a police report at the airport and then the next thing I know, this baby-faced cop is driving me here. He kept mumbling something about my being murdered and today being my funeral."

She whirled and stomped back up the aisle and grasped part of the cop's arm as if she planned to lead him somewhere. It was only then she appeared to notice where she was and what was going on. Reality hit her, and she turned slowly and faced the pulpit. Her eyes focused on the flower-bedecked mahogany casket for the first time. Her lip curled.

"Pink carnations! That's simply hideous, Calvin. You know I hate pink carnations."

Turning her back to the sight, she dragged her oversized police escort and left the church, slamming the heavy door behind her.

Dead silence lasted four long seconds. Then the babbling and laughing by the members of the congregation began. Above it all, the continuous, heart-wrenching sound of Calvin sobbing. The commotion threatened to remove the roof from the building. No one turned to follow Doreen.

Tony took a breath, torn between going after her and opening the coffin.

Before he could move, the door swung open again and all heads turned. The cacophony stopped in mid-breath. Silence reigned. Fascinated, Tony, like the rest of the congregation, watched Doreen stride toward Calvin and the casket.

She swept aside the offending blanket of carnations and unlatched the coffin.

No one moved. Tony couldn't even feel his own heart beating. The sweet scent of the discarded flowers wafted in the warm air.

If she were a taller woman, Doreen might have been able to open the coffin with a flourish. As it was she staggered slightly, teetering on her high heels as she lifted the lid.

As one, the congregation leaned forward, trying to see over her shoulder.

Tony had the advantage of both his height and the fact he was standing. He could see the deceased clearly. Even allowing for the subtle facial changes accompanying death, it looked like Doreen in the box to him.

Doreen studied the body for only a moment before she let out a shriek any self-respecting banshee would envy. She slammed the lid even harder than she had slammed the front door.

Tony thought even her fiercest enemies would be sympathetic

to a woman seeing herself at her own funeral. It would be just so damned disturbing.

His considerate thought vanished in a heartbeat when Doreen rounded on her husband. Calvin struggled and managed to pull himself into a more-or-less standing position by using the pulpit as a support. His narrow chest heaved with sobs and he wiped his nose on a large, white handkerchief.

"How dare you!" Doreen advanced on the hapless man.

The congregation settled back onto the pews like a well-behaved group at the theater. All eyes were glued to the action on the stage. Hands pressed together in excitement rather than in prayer. If the first two acts set up the action, Act Three promised to be a real barnburner.

Abandoning the handkerchief, Calvin wrapped his long arms around the pulpit and lowered his face to the slanted surface and moaned. The pitiful sound raised goose bumps on the back of Tony's neck.

"My favorite dress!" Doreen pulled back her leg as if to deliver a kick. "How dare you give this little tart my favorite dress!"

Theo wiggled, reminding Tony he still held her in his arms. She whispered his name. Tony tilted his head to listen to her without removing his eyes from the melodrama.

"She knows who it is."

Tony nodded. Mesmerized by the action, he studied the expressions on the Cashdollars' faces. Doreen's was full of fury and disgust. Calvin sobbed, his face contorted with grief and terror.

Theo whispered again. "I don't think Doreen's sorry the woman's dead, either."

"I guess I'd better go up there." Tony suspected his voice lacked conviction. In truth, he didn't want to miss any of the show.

Before he could move a muscle, all hell broke loose.

Sonny Cochran leapt from his spot between his wife and mother and charged the tableau.

"Daddy?" Doreen's arms opened wide to greet him. "Help me."

He slipped past her screaming, "My baby! You've killed my baby!"

Still seated on the pew, Bathsheba sobbed. Her tears fell faster, now that Doreen had returned from the dead.

The Queen Mother, Mrs. Sonny Cochran, rose to her feet and followed her husband to the aisle. The moment her feet touched the royal blue carpeting, she turned sharply to the right and marched toward the rear of the church with the same speed and determination her daughter had exhibited minutes earlier when she entered. If her expression meant anything, Sonny was in deep, deep trouble at home.

Clearly bewildered, Calvin straightened but did not release his hold on the pulpit, clinging to it like a lifeline. Tears streamed down his homely face as he watched his furious wife and his distraught father-in-law screaming and wailing over the casket.

Tony thought a look of such confusion could not be feigned and felt somewhat relieved at least one other person in the congregation was as confused as he was himself.

Theo poked his shoulder. "You can put me down."

Her words snapped him out of his paralysis. He looked into her face. She still looked a bit pale, but her eyes were clear and focused. "You fainted."

"It's over a hundred degrees in here. I couldn't breathe."

He set her on her feet and made his way to the pulpit and held up a hand for silence. It took a minute to stop the voices.

"Mike? Wade?"

The deputies moved forward. Tony said, "I want everyone except the immediate family to go with Mike."

"Where should I take them?"

"Why not let them have the planned refreshments?" Tony glanced around. "Make a list of who's here and then let them go home. Wade, I want you to bring Doreen's mother back in here. Hog-tie her if you have to. But get her."

Wade vanished in an instant.

It took Mike a bit longer to get the attendees on their feet and out the door. Like a well-trained sheep dog, Theo helped the deputy herd them through the doorway and onto the lawn. Some of the "mourners" required more pressure than others.

Tony considered this obvious reluctance on the part of the congregation to be absolutely understandable. He wouldn't have wanted to leave, either. Tony simply stood and watched until all except the family exited the sanctuary and Wade returned with Doreen's mother.

Tony arranged the bereaved family in the front row. He had lots of questions. He decided to start with the most important. "Who is in the coffin?"

CHAPTER EIGHTEEN

The overwhelming problem to Tony was one he couldn't ask and none of them would likely have an answer to. "Was Doreen the intended victim or was she?"

Calvin looked bereft. If he thought he had killed his wife, only to find her still alive and bitchier than ever, he might confess just so he could go to prison. Somehow Tony doubted Doreen's mood would improve when she discovered Calvin had boxed her belongings for a charity.

Sonny was in tears.

Bathsheba was in tears.

Doreen was pissed. Her obvious fury would not abate any time soon. Tony didn't want to talk to her. The display she had made over the selection of flowers was just the tip of this angry iceberg. He didn't want the family members talking to each other.

Actually, he thought, that didn't look like a problem.

Lined up on the front pews like first-time flyers, none of them looked at the others. No one touched another. Doreen and Calvin sat at opposite ends of the left pew. Bathsheba and Sonny sat on the front pew on the right side. Mrs. Sonny, having been forcibly returned to the church, sat behind mother and son. Her expression threatened to ignite the oak furnishings.

Wade stood slightly behind them to prevent anyone from leaving.

Facing the unhappy group, Tony stood in front of the closed

coffin and it felt like the weight of it rested squarely on his shoulders. Calvin sat, twisting his hands together, and Tony couldn't help wondering if it would be long before one hand came completely off.

"Who is she?" Tony moved to face Sonny, ignoring the rest of the merry band for the moment and pointed toward the coffin. "You seemed to recognize her."

Sonny's face showed the effects of true grief. The man had been crying continually since his stricken outburst. He took a shuddering breath and looked into Tony's face. "She's my daughter Patti. Patti Yager."

Tony frowned. "I was under the impression Doreen is an only child. Isn't that what you told me the last time we talked?"

"Well, yes." Sonny seemed fascinated by the pattern he was creating by rubbing his toes across the worn carpeting.

"Officially," Mrs. Sonny spoke. The woman looked like she wouldn't mind if her husband fell through the floor and into a tank of starving piranhas. Her collagen-perfect lips curled back from her beautifully capped teeth. "My husband," she said, her hissed words sending droplets of spittle through the air. "My husband has several extra children."

Sonny swiveled to face his wife and then turned back as if he realized nothing he could say would make it worth his opening his mouth. His head bobbed up and down as if it was attached to his body by a spring and not the usual selection of bones, tendons and muscle. "I'll admit I'm a weak man."

Weak and fertile, thought Tony. He viewed them with the fascination of a tabloid journalist. "Do your children all know each other?"

"No." Sonny pulled a handkerchief from his pocket and wiped at the steady stream of tears. "Doreen and Patti knew of each other, mostly by sight."

As Tony watched them, sitting there, angry and mournful, he

noticed Doreen was a much smaller and definitely female version of Sonny. Patti, too, had been a carbon copy. There were few signs that Doreen's mother had contributed many genes to her appearance, except maybe the shopping gene. The nose, eyes, chin and even the ears were Sonny's.

"And do they all resemble you, too?" Tony could only imagine the complications that could arise if a third half sister with the same face strolled through the doorway. An icy chill went down his spine at the thought. If his suspect pool had just doubled, a third sister would send it into the stratosphere.

Sonny's eyes opened wide as he turned to look at Doreen. "I never realized." His head moved slowly from side to side. "No. Only the two girls look alike."

The frown contorting Mrs. Sonny's face suggested the conversation would be better held outside her spitting distance. Tony escorted Sonny to the back of the church. Wade joined them, standing in the aisle where he could keep an eye on the rest of the players in the melodrama. "Tell me about Patti."

"She lives in Chattanooga and has all her life. If it matters."

"Married?"

"Widowed." Sonny smoothed his silver hair and then stuck his shaking hands into his pants pockets and hunched his shoulders. "Her husband died maybe six months ago in a car accident. They never had children." The tears fell more rapidly. "She really wanted children."

Interviewing grieving people always seemed cruel to him. It was necessary. Tony needed a bit more information. "Did you have any idea Patti would be in Silersville at this time?"

Sony just shook his head.

"Did she visit Doreen very often?"

"Hell, no." Sonny snapped to attention. "Doreen knew Patti, slightly, and wouldn't give her the time of day. Patti was a sweet girl. Maybe she wasn't super bright but she was a good person, much nicer than Doreen. Her mother did a good job raising her."

"Where is her mother?" Tony became aware of the spicy, sweet scent of carnations wafting toward them. Somewhere in the church, a door or window must have just been opened or closed. He watched Doreen's expression. The way her face tightened, he knew the aroma had not gone unnoticed by her. Queen Doreen looked ready to kill.

"Vivian—that is, Patti's mother—died several years back. Breast cancer." Sonny resumed his slumped posture. "Poor Patti. I was a lousy father, she had no kids, and lost her mother and husband too soon. And now," he mumbled and waved toward the casket. "And now, the poor girl didn't even get her own damned funeral."

"When was the last time you saw Patti?" Wade asked.

Sonny looked thoughtful for a moment. "She came to my birthday party in April. It was a big celebration I threw for myself over in Asheville. Doreen and her mother went shopping in London. Cost me a fortune. Still, I figured it would be the only way I could see most of my kids."

Tony followed Sonny's gaze and saw Mrs. Sonny tapping her well-manicured fingers on the end of the pew. If anything, her expression had become even more malevolent. Some unshared thought brought on a sudden tightening of the woman's flaw-less lips.

Extracting a pair of antacid tablets from his pocket, Tony slipped them both into his mouth. He might not like Sonny, but he certainly didn't envy the man. He had a wretched family life. Sitting down to a family dinner must be like dining with jackals. "Who inherits when you die?"

Sonny stumbled slightly. For the first time, he looked up, meeting Tony's eyes. "I'm not going to lie to you and tell you I'm a good man, however, I do love all of my children. I'm leaving half to my wife. The rest will be evenly divided among all the kids."

Tony nodded and made a note to find out later just how many kids would be involved in the division of Sonny's estate and if one wanted a bigger cut than the others. One of the oldest motives in the world was greed, and one of the greediest families he could think of offhand was the Cochran clan. "You can go sit down."

Sonny shuffled down the aisle and collapsed onto the pew next to his mother.

Bathsheba handed him a pile of lemon drops she pulled from her purse. "I guess we don't get fed." Her sour expression didn't seem to have any connection to the candy.

"Mom," said Sonny, "how can you think of food at a time like this?"

"I'm a-grieving, just like you." The old lady shrugged. "I still lost a granddaughter. I'm just hungry, that's all. You know Blossom Flowers always brings pecan caramel coffee cake to the funerals here. I had my heart set on it."

Once Sonny was resettled on his end of the pew, Tony glanced at Doreen. Her eyes were bright and clear, her makeup flawless, the shining cap of white-blond hair seemed identical to her sister's. He found it odd they should share a hairstyle when they appeared not to share their lives.

With a gesture, he invited her to join him and Wade in the back of the church. She flounced up the aisle like a sullen teenager and stood before him, her fists on her hips as she stared at his badge.

Tony pulled himself to his full height and waited.

Finally she looked up into his face.

"How long have you worn your hair in this style, Doreen?"

She fluffed her bangs. Diamonds and rubies sparkled on the hand arranging her hair. Tony noticed even more diamonds sparkling on her ears. He didn't recall seeing any jewelry on the deceased. Of course, the only time he saw Patti was at the autopsy and moments ago in the casket.

"I had it cut like this just over a week ago."

Her response surprised him because his thoughts had moved elsewhere. He had better pay strict attention to this group. "I don't suppose you had it done in Chattanooga?"

Her lip curled, giving the impression she'd prefer to have a slug dropped down her blouse than be associated in any way with her half sister.

"If you mean do I share a stylist with her?" Doreen tipped her head very slightly in the direction of Patti's coffin. "No. Prudence Sligar cuts my hair. I shop local when I can, and when she's not messing with her pack of kids or telling fortunes, she is very capable." She managed to make the compliment without choking.

Kids. He remembered a notation in the autopsy report he hadn't wanted to ask Calvin about. Clearly, he should have. According to the report, the deceased had recently had a miscarriage. Tony had believed it would go beyond the bounds of callousness to ask a grieving husband about another grief. Doreen had to be about forty-five. Tony assumed the woman waited to conceive, whether by design or not. It was none of his business. At least not until now.

"When was the last time you saw your sister, Doreen?" Tony wasn't surprised when his question was met with silence. "I can stand here as long as you can, maybe longer, because my shoes are comfortable."

She glared at him. If he hadn't already lost his hair, Doreen's expression would have singed it right off. "I saw her about a month ago. I was down at the farm visiting Daddy. She left almost immediately, but I saw her checking me out." The jewels twinkled again.

"Did you have this haircut?"

Doreen looked surprised, then confused. "No. I haven't seen her since my hair was cut."

Tony ushered Doreen back to her seat and beckoned to Calvin.

The mayor lurched to his feet and seemed to stagger as he plodded up the aisle to the front. "As God is my witness, Sheriff, I had no idea it wasn't Doreen." His voice lowered. "When you're through with us here, is there any chance you can give me a head start? It would only take me a few minutes to put her things away. I didn't pack much."

A moment of irritation vanished, and Tony released him. He just couldn't believe Calvin would kill the wrong woman. Or if he had, he would have realized it as soon as he checked the body. No way would he have packed her belongings with such open glee. Tony thought it was probably saving a life to send the mayor home early. "I can't promise you more than twenty minutes. Someone from my office will drive Doreen home."

"You're the finest sheriff this county ever had." Calvin jerked forward. The mayor looked like he wanted to fling himself to the floor and kiss Tony's feet. He managed to right himself and bolted through the front doors as fast as his size-sixteen feet would carry him.

Once the door closed behind the tortured man, Tony beckoned for Doreen's mother to join him and Wade.

Talking to Mrs. Sonny was a treat. He learned she did have a first name, Louise, a name too lyrical for the woman she'd grown to be. She was quite a piece of work. Tony found himself pitying Doreen and understanding Sonny's wandering eye. Living with this woman had to be hell on earth. Doreen had had two choices growing up, total rebellion or total conformity.

Doreen chose to conform.

This woman couldn't see any world beyond her own mirror.

She, like her daughter, had bamboozled a man whom she could manipulate and who could afford to support her in the manner, or manor, she desired. Tony entertained himself with his pun for a moment before he realized the woman's bright blue eyes focused on him. Her gaze could cut like a laser. He thought she could do surgery with a mere glance. Killing her husband's extra children might be her entertainment.

"I don't know why you people are making us stay here." Mrs. Sonny's words carried the whip of authority.

Tony didn't respond to the challenge. "When was the last time you saw Doreen?"

"Sometime last week. I came up when she donated those family quilts to that silly little upstart museum." She sniffed. "After all, they were only Cochran quilts. If they were quilts from my side of the family, I know she would have insisted on donating them to a finer museum."

Like mud on her shoe, she dismissed his aunt and mother and their "upstart" museum. It took a lot of his reserves to keep from yelling and reminding her just who those women were. Just before he did anything rash, he decided she wasn't worth his breath and tamped down his soaring temper. "And Patti?"

The Queen Mother's spine straightened even more. She managed to look down her nose at him as if she'd stepped in something unpleasant. "I don't socialize with her."

"I don't care if you socialize with her. I want to know when you last saw her." Tony jabbed the air in front of her with his index finger. "I understand she comes out to the farm."

"When she comes, I stay in my suite." She spat her answer and didn't wait to see if he had more questions before she spun away from him and stalked down the aisle. Barely slowing, she snatched her purse off the pew and sailed past Tony and Wade, slamming the door as she left the church.

Tony had to admire the quality of the doors and hinges the

Baptists used. In spite of their ill treatment, the doors hadn't cracked or fallen off. They were taking a boatload of abuse. He frowned at the paneled door. Mrs. Sonny hadn't exactly answered his question. He wrote himself a note, detailing her evasiveness and lack of cooperation. She would have to talk to him.

So who did he have for suspects? Calvin, the husband who thought his marital problems were at an end. Mrs. Sonny, a proud woman whose husband continued to humiliate her and who was also a mother who hated what her daughter's half sister stood for. Embarrassment. Doreen, the half sister who despised the victim. Bathsheba, a grandmother who was strong and feisty and who preferred the deceased granddaughter. Sonny, the father who preferred the illegitimate daughter.

Shakespeare could probably make something out of this group. As far as Tony was concerned, the sheriff of a county too small to have a town big enough to maintain a separate police force needed more to work with.

Wade stared at Mrs. Sonny's departing back. "You want me to bring her back?"

Tony just shook his head.

CHAPTER NINETEEN

Still half sick from the heat inside the church, Theo stood on the church lawn next to her mother-in-law and Martha. She watched Mike write the names of the attendees in his notebook. Like Theo, Mike would know everyone by name, if not better.

Theo struggled to suppress a giggle. Doreen might not be well liked but she couldn't complain about attendance at her funeral.

It looked to her like the congregation had divided into two camps. One group talked about going home. The other half talked about going into the fellowship hall for the food. No sense letting a good ham and multiple side dishes go to waste.

From her post near the front doors, Theo watched Calvin fly from the church, dash to the street and jump into the gleaming white hearse. Half a second later, he made the first turn on two wheels. The hearse was almost airborne.

Not long after Calvin left, the Queen Mother stalked out, looking neither left nor right, and drove away in her Mercedes. She drove only slightly more slowly than Calvin.

Theo wished she could be a fly on the wall inside the church. Simple curiosity was eating her alive.

"You want anything to eat, Sugar?" Drawing her attention, Martha shifted the handle on her purse up higher on her shoulder. "I could use a tall sweet tea and a ham sandwich myself."

"I'm not hungry right now. Go ahead. I'll join you in a bit."

Theo took a deep breath, pushing away the last vestiges of faint-ness.

Theo watched Martha stride toward the door into the church hall. At least half of the congregation fell in behind her, follow-ing her like a flock of sparrows, too hungry to leave and too nervous to approach a new bird feeder without a leader. The sight of Parker Nelson dressed in his grubby overalls, holding the door for the equally casually garbed Nellie Pearl made Theo realize the food was the big draw at this funeral.

Not having to sit through the service obviously pleased the attendees.

Nina strolled across the lawn, joining Theo and Jane. Her copper hair bounced in the midday sun, shooting off sparks of gold. "Have you ever seen anything like that?" Exuberant as ever, Nina's laugh echoed between buildings. "I swear I thought Doreen was about to molest a corpse. Strip her bare in her own coffin and to hell with the witnesses."

"No kidding. I think she would have if she hadn't realized she'd probably never want to wear her favorite dress again. Can you imagine wearing the dress you were almost buried in?" Theo started to giggle and soon others were laughing as well. Half of the regular patrons of her quilt shop gravitated in their direction.

An impromptu survey of her customers confirmed that none of them knew who was in the coffin.

"Let's go eat." Nina led the way, and Theo was swept along in the crowd.

Once they had filled their plates with food, most of the Thursday night bowlers settled in at one of the long tables. The women ate for a while in satisfied silence, punctuated by moans of delight.

Martha still had her hands wrapped around a thick ham sandwich when she looked at Theo. "Tony hustled us out of there so fast it about made my head spin."

Theo might have replied when Jane launched herself into the conversation. "Sonny sure was carrying on about 'his baby.' " Jane emptied a pair of sugar packets into a short glass of iced tea. "Which one of Sonny's girlfriends do you reckon is the mother of that poor girl?"

No one seemed to have an answer to the question. The majority knew Sonny sowed his wild oats liberally, although not in Silersville or the immediate vicinity. At least not so far.

"Do you suppose any of the items Doreen and Bathsheba donated to the museum were hers? You know, the body's?" Jane looked up from her heavily laden plate and glanced around.

"No." Martha jumped as if she'd been hit with a bolt of electricity. "When they brought those quilts in to me, they swore since there were no other Cochran women, no one would object to our displaying the quilts." Martha waved her fork, making her nearest neighbor lean away. "They said it like only women are interested in family heirlooms. Do you know how many men are really into genealogy?"

"Did you know I was invited to Sonny's farm one time?" As a topic switch, it was powerful enough to quiet the group. The speaker, elderly little Caro, waited until she had all their attention. Sliding forward until she perched on the edge of her chair, she arranged her silverware with arthritis-gnarled fingers. Her faded eyes twinkled. A born storyteller, she knew how to pull an audience to the edge of their seats.

"When was this?" Theo asked.

"Oh, it was years ago. My husband still loved to ride those Tennessee Walking Horses of his in shows across the country. Sonny invited us to a luncheon out there to celebrate a big prize he'd won. Sonny, that is. While my husband and Sonny had some discussion about the horses, I mostly looked around. Sonny's mother, Bathsheba, was there and so was her husband.

He was still alive at the time." Caro giggled.

"And of course Sonny's wife wore a dress that would cost a year's wages." Caro smiled a dreamy little smile. "The farm was the most beautiful place I've ever been. All of the buildings were painted with fresh white paint and the trim was red. I remember it like it was yesterday. Miles of white board fences contrasted with the beautiful green grass. It made those black Walking Horses of Sonny's look like they were part of a painting."

"What was the Queen Mother like then?" Nina leaned closer.

Caro lifted her napkin close to her face, covering her nose and mouth.

Theo thought she heard the elderly woman make a snorting sound. She discounted it as a figment of an overactive imagination.

"She was very gracious, but cold. Isn't it funny that no one ever uses her first name?"

"What is it?" One of the newer quilters leaned close.

Caro's shoulders rose and fell. With a slight shake of her head, she returned to her story. "I did feel like I was in the presence of royalty. Even though we ate outside, the table was covered with a heavy linen cloth and lots of silver and crystal. It was the prettiest table I ever did see." Her gnarled fingers smoothed the vinyl tablecloth next to her plate. "Nobody in my family ever had anything to speak of. In the summer we ate lots of greens, and corn in the winter. It seemed like there was never any meat except pork on the table." She took a dainty bite of the slab of ham on her plate. "Sure tastes better when someone else does the slopping and curing and cooking."

Theo could tell something else had happened that day. She suspected the others felt the same, because no one interrupted or changed the subject. They all quietly watched Caro eat while they enjoyed their own piles of food.

Finally Caro picked up the threads of her story. "A young woman came while we were there. She was a pretty girl, small and blond and looked like the painting of Doreen that hangs over the fireplace. I thought she was Doreen at first until Mrs. Sonny—don't you think it's odd she doesn't use any other name?—anyway she just stood up from the table without so much as a word and stalked off."

Jane looked appalled. "What did the girl do?"

"She apologized very sweetly for interrupting our lunch. Then she whispered something to Sonny and he excused himself for a moment, and they talked down by the stable for a little while and then she left. I don't know where she came from or where she went. Sonny came back after a bit and picked up his fork and we continued with lunch. He didn't introduce her and he didn't say a word about his wife's departure." Caro pulled a piece of sticky bun apart with her fingers. "I do remember noticing our luncheon was more fun after the Queen Mother left. What is her first name anyway?"

Tony stared at the unburied coffin. He'd sent the family away, mostly because he was at a loss for words.

Equally silent, Wade sat across the aisle, his eyes trained on the blanket of pink carnations now strewn in an untidy heap on the floor.

Tony's eyes moved over upended floral displays and back to the deceased. What were they supposed to do with Patti's body? He mentally ran through his vocabulary, looking for a word to describe his mental condition. Flummoxed. Although not a word he used daily, it about covered his thought process. He had no idea what happened. How had everything gotten so screwed up? He could understand how and why the misidentification had occurred, although the melodrama created in the church turned it into a topic that would be discussed and

146

explored for the next forty years. He could even understand why Doreen's return hadn't exactly created the kind of happy excitement that might be expected after such a miracle.

Would the gossip hurt Doreen's feelings?

Did she have feelings? She must, even if she wasn't exactly Mrs. Warmth on a good day.

Tony's thoughts circled again. Why was Patti Yager in the museum office trailer? Why did Patti come to Silersville at all? How did she get to the museum site? The easiest solution was sometimes the best. In this case, the simplest answer would have the killer drive her out there. But, who? Why? Was there a possibility Doreen herself did it? She could have killed her half sister and driven off in Patti's vehicle.

He jotted down a series of notes to himself. He needed to find out if Patti had a car and, if so, what make it was. Where did she work and when was the last time she was seen there? How long had she been in town before she died? Tony didn't want to make a trip to Chattanooga. He would anyway.

He flinched when he heard the front door of the church open again. What now?

A half turn of his head and a quick glance revealed the mayor's lanky form. Blocking the afternoon sun, he clung to the knob on the door. Sweat rolled like tears down his lean face. His eyebrows rose in a silent question.

"Come in." Tony leaned back on the pew.

Calvin tiptoed down the carpeted aisle and stopped in front of Tony. "Thank you, Sheriff. I swear I will never mention the word 'impeach' again, I'll vote for you and endorse everything you stand for."

"Did you get all of Doreen's things put away?" Tony noticed the mayor's complexion looked less healthy than the body in the box, his pallor tinged with green.

Tony guessed the man must have broken every speed limit in the county.

"No, but enough to save my life." Tears welled in Calvin's eyes. "She's at home, fussing about the mess I made while picking out a dress." He turned to look at Patti's coffin and placed his right hand over his heart. "I had no idea. I swear that I didn't know."

Dignified and determined, the preacher walked in and stood, hands clasped, near the casket. He stared at the three men. As a hint, it was subtle as well as effective. Without speaking, he simply waited without moving until Tony spoke to him.

"I suppose you would like Calvin to take Patti's body back to the mortuary," said Tony.

"Thank you, yes," said the preacher, releasing a heartfelt sigh. "We certainly can't just leave her here."

Calvin's expression went beyond mournful. He looked like he was about to throw himself over the mahogany lid and sob like a broken man. In spite of the mayor's heartfelt thanks, Tony could only imagine Doreen's return to her home had been a disaster. Not for the first time did Tony wonder why the couple stayed together. It certainly wasn't for the children. There weren't any. He supposed the example set by Sonny and the Queen Mother had a great deal to do with it.

"What will happen to her now?" Wade finally found his tongue.

Calvin said, "I spoke briefly to her father and understand she'll be buried next to her husband in Chattanooga. Sonny said that he'll make the arrangements and then we'll transport her." He gently latched the coffin lid and lifted the broken blanket of pink carnations from the floor and spread it over the top. A fair number of crushed blossoms fell off, sending a wave of scent through the room. "Sonny's in shock right now, so I doubt it will be very soon. He said something about contacting the rest of his children. He was whispering so softly I couldn't catch everything he said."

Tony found himself fascinated by the tabloid-style family and had to rein in his impulse to ask for unrelated details. His own family had been the dullest imaginable. His father, a Methodist minister, had married a Latin teacher and they had raised four exceptionally dull children. The most interesting thing about any of them was their mother's penchant for christening them with names harkening back to the world of ancient Rome. As children, it had been embarrassing when the teachers seemed to delight in using their full names. They had lived through it.

Tony watched Calvin. "You never met Patti? You knew about her, didn't you?"

"Not exactly. Doreen and her mother were adamant about keeping Sonny's indiscretions away from me and everyone possible. I knew he had other children, but with such a cold reception, why would anyone want to visit?" He pushed the shock of wheat-colored hair out of his eyes and looked directly into Tony's. "I swear I had no idea that it wasn't Doreen, and furthermore, I swear I had nothing to do with this woman's death."

Tony believed him. Why would someone make up such a ridiculous story?

Only minutes later, the mayor and preacher wheeled the coffin down the aisle. Their softly spoken words held only respect for the dead. As soon as they passed through the doorway, leaving the sanctuary to the two lawmen, Tony turned to Wade. "Did you see anyone at the service who seemed out of place? Anyone who surprised you?"

"Oh, yeah." Wade's dark blue eyes sparkled with mischief. "Queen Doreen." The moment the name passed his lips, he started to laugh and the more he laughed, the funnier he seemed to find his joke.

A long-suppressed rumble of laughter finally escaped Tony's own chest and soon he and his deputy were howling with merriment. "Did you ever see an expression like D-Doreen's when she l-l-looked into the c-coffin?"

"Calvin's when he saw her coming toward him." Wade's nose began to drip and his whole body shook with mirth as he pulled out his handkerchief and wiped his eyes and nose. "I never felt so sorry for anyone in my whole life. I thought he was going to pee in his pants." Unable to control himself, he surrendered to another bout of hysteria.

If Tony could have stopped laughing himself, he would have agreed with his deputy. As it was, all he could do was double up, overcome by the situation, until he was almost ill. At last, he stood bent over with his hands braced on his thighs and gasped for breath.

Another few minutes passed while they purged their inappropriate responses and regained their equilibrium.

Side by side, the two men strode up the aisle. Other than a telltale gleam of amusement, he was sure they had been unable to remove, Tony felt certain that the pair of them looked like men on a mission. He turned to face Wade as he pushed the door open. "We need to find out why Patti was in town and how she got out to the museum."

"Why do you think she was out there?" Wade's expression reflected his own curiosity. "I could understand why Doreen might go, since she donated a bunch of stuff, but her half sister?"

"I haven't had much time to think about it, either, although it does seem odd. I guess not really much odder than the idea it was Doreen out there. It never made any sense that Doreen would go there after hours." Tony stared across the yard and saw a few well-fed, would-be funeral attendees leaving the fellowship hall.

A couple of teenage girls strolled toward them. Putting an

extra swing in their hips, they smiled at Wade.

Wade kept his eyes forward.

Tony laughed. "At least I know that my mom and aunt didn't kill her."

"How's that?"

"Because they would never risk getting blood on an antique quilt," said Tony.

"That probably eliminates your wife as well." Wade adjusted the bill of his cap. "I'd have to say it also eliminates a fair number of the quilt shop customers."

"At least we get to eliminate someone. It's a start." Tony grinned as he slipped an antacid tablet into his mouth. "I'm going to the office."

"I'm going to see if any of the food is left." Wade patted his flat stomach. "Maybe someone in the hall will look suspicious."

Tony's stomach rumbled. "If there is any pie left, bring me a slice, would you?"

"Sure, boss."

CHAPTER TWENTY

Orvan Lundy was waiting for him when Tony got back to his office. Standing in front of the wall quilt Theo made, the little man seemed even smaller than usual. Stooped and gnarled and still tough as hickory, Orvan liked to make confessions. After the last confession, and hoping to keep him out of the office, Tony had suggested to Orvan perhaps he might look into converting to Catholicism. Not only could he make his confession, he might even find the penance to redeem himself.

Old Orvan probably hadn't seen the inside of any church in the last sixty years, but the Baptist in him was still too strong to accept the idea of conversion. His expression suggested Tony had taken leave of his senses.

Tony needed one of Orvan's confessions today like he needed more work. He knew all too well delaying the inevitable took longer than getting it over with right away. It was a lot like ripping a bandage off instead of peeling it slowly away from a cut. "Take a seat." Reluctantly, he waved his visitor to one of the heavy vinyl chairs facing his desk.

Orvan took his time. He adjusted his bib overalls and tugged at his shirt sleeves before sitting down. It looked like he planned to stay for a while. Even in this heat, the elderly man wore a long-sleeved flannel shirt over a long-sleeved thermal undershirt. His only concession to the vile heat had been to leave the collar button on the outer shirt undone and rolled up the sleeves a couple of inches above his bony wrists.

Tony felt tiny beads of sweat forming on his scalp. Just looking at Orvan's costume made his temperature rise. He adjusted the thermostat accordingly.

"I suppose you went to the funeral today." Orvan launched into his topic without wasting time on any of the preliminaries. "Quite a sight, I hear."

When Tony failed to rise to the bait, Orvan cast his hook again. "Shoulda been fun watchin' Her Majesty peerin' into her own coffin."

A sudden wheezing sound came from the old man and alarmed Tony. At least until he realized the sound was laughter. He'd never heard the old guy laugh before. He couldn't suppress his own grin. "You heard about the mix-up pretty fast. Were you there?"

"Nossir, I wasn't. I guess there ain't nothin' wrong with my ears, though. Even the bees were a-talkin' about the confusion and spread the story across the mountains."

Gossip always traveled like lightning. Tony had never suspected the bees were responsible for the speed at which it spread. "Bees, huh?"

"Yessir. They done came to me whilst I was caning a chair and told me I must come in and explain how it was I killed the wrong woman. I am powerful sorry about that." Tears welled in Orvan's rheumy eyes and his slumped shoulders almost met over his chest.

Tony mentally shrugged, admitting defeat. He knew Orvan would not leave until he finished his story. Tony lowered himself onto his desk chair and sat with his head resting on one hand, shielding his expression, his elbow on his desk. With the other hand, he reached for a pen and paper. Theo would kill him if he left out any details of Orvan's latest confession. "What happened?"

Orvan wiggled his scrawny butt on the seat until he was

almost falling off the front of the chair. "It were an honest mistake. I got the feeling in the middle of the night. I needed to kill her. Don't know why it were any different that night. I awoke knowing what I had to do. I grabbed up my old shotgun and lit out. It took me nigh on to three hours to hike my way to her place. I was plumb tuckered out when I got there." He stopped, a pitiful expression pinching his wizened face. The shoe polish darkening his hair was melting, sliding into the deep wrinkles of his permanently weathered neck. He panted softly.

Tony understood. He reached for the intercom button. "Ruth Ann, I'd like you to come in here, and would you bring Mr. Lundy a bottle of cold water."

Ruth Ann appeared so quickly Tony knew his secretary had been lurking near the door, waiting for a reason to come in. Her customary preoccupation with her fingernails was no competition for hearing one of Orvan's confessions. She handed Orvan the bottle and plopped down on the other chair. Her dark eyes glowed with satisfaction.

It would take a stick of dynamite to dislodge Ruth Ann now.

"So where did you go, exactly?" Tony smiled at the little man.

"Don't you know, Sheriff? I swear I don't know why the county pays you to look into things." He frowned at Tony then turned to address Ruth Ann. "He ain't any sharper than my cousin Sid, is he?"

Tony worked to keep the smile pasted on his face. He knew being compared to Sid Lundy was like being accused of having a brain like a cabbage. Actually, a cabbage would score higher on any IQ test. Tony tamped down the urge to defend himself.

Orvan cast an adoring expression in Ruth Ann's direction. He might have reached over to pat her knee if he could reach far enough without falling off his chair. Luckily for him, he didn't, because Ruth Ann would not put up with behavior like that. Orvan did wag a finger in the air, making a scolding sign. "I kin remember when I come in here and drew the sheriff a map to old Matthew's still and darned if he did anything about it."

Tony wasn't about to tell Orvan he had already known the location of the still and had passed the information along to the ATF. There was more going on up on the mountain than a simple moonshine business, and Tony felt lucky to be well out of it.

In fact, he was determined not to become involved. If the Feds wanted to clear out a nest of homegrown terrorists for him. Good. More power to them.

Orvan dragged a few more details of what he considered inefficiency on Tony's part into the conversation.

"Stop." Tony's sharp word brought a sharp halt to the recitation. It looked like Orvan was settling in to detail everything he considered Tony had done wrong and everything he felt the county had been responsible for. Tony wasn't in the mood to let Orvan sit in his office and insult him. "Just tell us the details."

"Okay, okay." Forgetting he held anything, Orvan waved his hands and water sloshed out of the top of the bottle and soaked the bib of his overalls. The cold shower seemed to shock his mouth into action. "I went to bed, same as usual, after having my evening dose of cure-all. Long about three in the morning, I got the call, if you know what I mean, and I was headed to the privy when it come clear I needed to get my old shotgun and take care of that moaning, whistling banshee for once and forever." He paused and took a rather theatrical swig of water. "I was guided by this here old hoot owl. He led me down to town and over to this house I ain't never seed before. All this time, the old owl was a-screechin' and the banshee was a-wailing, I thought my poor old head would plumb explode."

"You were in town?"

"Didn't I just say so?" Orvan stuck his lower lip out.

Since neither the museum nor the Cashdollar residence was within the town itself, Tony tried to imagine what Orvan might have been shooting. Tony took down the confession in his scrawled handwriting, suspecting the cure-all was moonshine and the banshees wailing were the result of overimbibing. On the other hand, confusing Queen Doreen for a banshee wouldn't be much of a stretch. He didn't say so, just nodded for Orvan to continue.

"Well, sir, I seed it coming toward me, through the rhododendron and I lifted my old shotgun and held my ground. It was a-screechin' even louder, and I could see it had red eyes like the devil. Then I looked again and saw it had four eyes, two red and two little white ones. I let go with both barrels and I knowed I killed it because them eyes stopped starin'."

"Excuse me a moment, Orvan, while I go check something." Tony hurried out of his office before he started to laugh. Only a few long strides took him to dispatcher Rex Satterfield's desk.

Unflappable as ever, Rex looked at him. "Sheriff?"

"Can you check to see if anyone reported having their taillights shot out in the past couple of weeks?"

"Taillights?" Rex mumbled to himself. "Probably happened on the night shift, huh?" His fingers flew over the keyboard of his computer. All the time he typed, he continued to monitor the locations of the deputies. "Here we go. Four nights ago, we got a call claiming someone shot Roscoe's truck with a shotgun, knocking out all of his taillights. J. B. Lewis stopped him and took his report." He stared at Tony. "How did you know?"

"Orvan just confessed."

"Why'd he shoot Roscoe's truck?"

"He thinks he killed a banshee, the mayor's wife."

"Better luck next time." Rex cackled. "I heard about the funeral and the theatrical melodrama."

Tony rolled his eyes. "At least we can say we solved one major crime today. I wish I could get my brain wrapped around the idea of Doreen having a double. It was weird. They even had the same hairstyle."

Rex's eyebrows flew up. "That is weird. The Queen changes her hair more often than my wife buys groceries."

Tony nodded. Theo had made a couple of major changes in her hair in the ten years they'd been married, but usually her blond curls varied in length by only several inches. "It is very odd."

Only half of his thoughts dealt with Doreen's hair. The other half were busily involved with needing to find a way for Orvan, who had nothing, to repay Roscoe, who also had nothing. He felt compelled to find a solution even though it wasn't strictly speaking part of his job.

Roscoe Morris was as nice a man as ever lived. Unfortunately, Tony recalled a local wag once mentioning Roscoe's load had shifted and he didn't always think things through. Any man in love with a vending machine couldn't be reality based.

By the time Tony reached his office, he came to a decision. Even though Orvan couldn't afford to pay for the taillights, he could make Roscoe a pair of ladder-back chairs. Tony wouldn't offer the plan to Orvan just yet. He needed to talk to Roscoe first.

Orvan was still perched on his chair, although he had gone from confession to flirtation. He batted his eyes and leered at Ruth Ann in a most determined fashion. For her part, Ruth Ann was busy keeping him at arm's length. She did look somewhat relieved when Tony returned.

"I'm disappointed in you, Orvan." Tony frowned and placed his fisted hands on his hips. His stance in front of the wizened old guy brought Orvan back to attention. It was all Tony could do to keep a straight face. Orvan had evidently run his hand over his melting hair darkener and then wiped the same hand across his mouth. Smudges of black shoe polish coated a quarter of his face. It did not make him look like a killer, even though Tony had long suspected Orvan might have killed someone in his younger days.

"Go home, Orvan." Tony sat and began pawing through one of his desk drawers. "I'll get back to you on what your punishment is going to be."

The little man didn't hesitate. As eager as he always seemed to make his confession, it certainly didn't take him long to scuttle his skinny butt out the door afterwards. This time he didn't even take the time for his customary last leer at Ruth Ann.

"Is it my imagination or did he actually shoot something?" Ruth Ann turned, curiosity burning in her expression.

Tony nodded. "He shot the taillights out of Roscoe's truck."

"Poor Roscoe. How's he going to get the money to fix it?"

"You really want to know how he can afford to make payments on Dora and afford new lights, don't you?" Tony tried to squelch his grin. Poor Roscoe had fallen in love with a vending machine named Dora, and the only way he could keep her was to make weekly payments to the Riverview Motel. "What do you think about having Orvan make some chairs for him?"

"As restitution?" Ruth Ann ran her little finger back and forth across her lower lip as she gave the matter some serious thought. "Unless he sells them, it still won't solve the problem. He can't drive a truck without lights. Maybe the chairs should go to the Thomas Brothers Garage instead."

"Excellent idea. Why don't you use your law school training to work out the negotiations and clear this mess up? I've got a couple of other fires to put out." Tony leaned forward and rested his hands on the cluttered surface of the desk. "Oh, and while you're at it, see if you can make the deal include fixing Roscoe's fan belt or whatever causes that god-awful screeching noise. It's enough to set my teeth on edge every time I hear it."

Nodding her agreement, Ruth Ann strolled out, leaving the door open.

The next time Tony looked up, Wade stood in the doorway, a worried expression pulling down the corners of his mouth. "What's wrong?" Even as Tony asked the question, he was reaching for the omnipresent antacids.

"They were out of apple pie." Creases now wrinkled Wade's forehead.

"I doubt it's a reason to be concerned." Tony felt a chill. "Is it?"

"Blossom's on her way to fix a special pie, just for you. She'll be here soon."

War broke out. Tony's mouth and stomach wanted pie and his brain screamed. Dealing with Blossom and the funeral fiasco seemed too much for one day. "She's probably coming to check on our progress with her case. We still don't know what happened to her yard ornament." He lifted one of the files on his desk and waved it at Wade. "What's the latest count of missing gnomes and garden things?"

"Fourteen." Wade tapped the copies of the police reports. "A few people lost two items in one night."

Ruth Ann's voice came to them through the intercom. "Sheriff. Mr. Sonny Cochran is currently at his daughter Doreen's house and would like to talk to you. Should he come in or will you go there?"

"I'll be there in just a few minutes." Tony shut the gnome file and smiled as he rose to his feet. "With any luck we won't be back when Blossom arrives."

Wade laughed and followed him. "Yeah, so you get the pie without the baker."

"Blossom needs a boyfriend to fatten up." The last thing Tony needed was a groupie.

CHAPTER TWENTY-ONE

On the way back to the shop from the almost-funeral, Theo stopped at Ruby's Café for a cup of coffee and a chat with Ruby herself. She knew Ruby hadn't been at the church and guessed now would be a quiet time in the café. Theo had been assigned to learn something about the bride-to-be's color preferences for the wedding quilt the bowlers planned to make. Theo wasn't much of a spy or a diplomat and hoped she wouldn't give the whole thing away.

After greeting her friend, she went into the ladies' restroom. The changes in the little room were startling. The last time she was in there a pretty wreath of dried flowers hung on the wall next to the sink. It was gone; only the pitifully bare brass hook remained. The same thing with a striking watercolor painting of flowers, once hanging over the toilet, now vanished. Both items were part of Ruby's campaign to make the restroom more pleasant and inviting. Clearly her notions had taken a drastic change of direction. Not that Theo thought either item would supply any clues about Ruby's personal color preferences, since a public powder room rarely resembled the decorations in a master bedroom.

Poor Mike had spent so much time getting Ruby to the point of accepting his proposal, Theo would bet he'd agree to sleep in a pink and lavender boudoir with swags of tulle and lace. Her lips twitched. Dammit the bloodhound would look charming with his huge head and droopy skin falling over a delicate, heart-shaped pink satin pillow.

She assumed a more dignified expression before returning to her table. Ruby sat waiting for her.

"Why did you decide to change your decorating scheme? I thought it was pretty." Theo poured cream into her mug. She almost had the fragrant brew to her lips when she heard Ruby growl.

Startled, she looked up into her friend's face. Ruby looked as angry as she'd ever seen her.

"I didn't take anything out of there. Nellie Pearl took the decorations." Her dark eyes flashed and her hand tightened on the coffeepot's handle.

"No way." Theo's response was strictly ceremonial. In truth, she wasn't surprised the crotchety old lady was a thief. Still, ripping the decorations off restroom walls was extreme, even for her.

"I know. It surprised me, too." Ruby poured herself a cup of coffee and sat the pot on the table. "I saw her go in there, carrying that nasty canvas bag of hers. You know the one."

Theo nodded. The bag in question was faded and stained, in addition to being huge. "She could smuggle a small car in it and still have room for groceries."

A twinkle crept into Ruby's dark eyes. "That's no joke."

"So, you went in after she came out and the decorations were gone?"

"Exactly." Ruby took a sip of coffee. "I told Mike, and he said he would write up a report even though he seriously doubted Nellie Pearl would admit to any wrongdoing. If we found them, my name wasn't on anything."

"No fair." Theo's protest was partially fueled by her frustration with shoplifters herself. Since the beginning of tourist season, several times she had found empty cardboard centers hidden behind a row of fabric filled bolts.

"You don't suppose she carries around one of Blossom's yard ornaments in there, do you?" Ruby's mischievous smile put the twinkle back in her eyes. "Imagine if we solved the case."

"Well . . ." Theo paused. "The bag is certainly big enough to hold one. Still, didn't she have one snatched as well?"

"Details, details." Ruby waved the statement away. "She probably hid hers in order to throw everyone off the scent."

Theo considered their proposed scenario. It seemed unlikely but certainly not improbable. Would the old lady work that hard for a prank? Maybe. If not a prank, what could the motive be? "Do you think she could lift it?"

"I'm a morally weak man, Sheriff." Sonny sat on an elegant brocade wing chair in Doreen's immaculate parlor, his face shaded by his fingers buried in his thick silver hair.

There seemed to be no immediate response to such a statement so Tony let it hang in the air between them while he studied the room. Most houses these days didn't really have a parlor, at least not the ones Tony spent much time in. The closest thing his aging house had to a parlor was the small room in the front. A combination of home office and dog house. Their old worn love seat by the window was Daisy's favorite spot when the family was away. Since Tony thought of a parlor as a room no one enjoyed, it didn't qualify.

No one used this room, Tony thought as he glanced around. There were no impressions on the chair seats to show where someone had been sitting. The three men, Tony, Wade and Sonny, were likely the only people ever to sit in here. He doubted if either Doreen or Calvin knew how to play the harpsichord occupying the place of honor by the window. A fringed scarf of red silk covered the top. An arrangement of fresh flowers sat on the scarf.

Tony felt somewhat surprised Sonny was allowed back in the

same house with his daughter, Queen Doreen and his wife, the Queen Mother. Those were not women he would expect to deal well with humiliation and embarrassment, and there had been plenty of both at the funeral.

Sonny finally looked up. Tony saw nothing but raw pain in his tear-reddened eyes. Whatever his weaknesses, Sonny Cochran was a grieving father and deserved compassion and any answers his office could supply.

Tony held his notebook up. "I'm sorry to have to ask you these same questions about another daughter. Is there anything special you can tell me about Patti's life? Any detail that might help me?"

"I'm ashamed to say this, Patti was my favorite." Sonny wiped his eyes and glanced over his shoulder at the empty doorway. He spoke softly, "I know it's wrong to have a favorite, but I can't help it. She was always a happy, laughing child. When I'd come to visit, she'd run to me and throw her arms around me."

"And as she grew up?" Tony sensed she had changed.

Sonny's face reflected his unease. "It was only natural she would feel slighted. I tried to visit as much as possible and had her out to the farm when the wife was away. It's not the same as living in the same house, is it?" He shrugged. "When she was a teenager, she would beg to see pictures of Doreen. She copied her hairstyle and the clothes she wore."

"Did that bother you?" Tony thought it sounded like an unhealthy business, but he was not an expert.

"Oh, yes." Sonny scrubbed the tears from his cheeks with the heels of his hands. "I thought it was, well, kind of sick. I was thankful when she outgrew the phase and turned into an independent, sweet woman. Her late husband was a good man and she was happy with him. Unlike myself, he was faithful and kind. They liked to go to the NASCAR races and every summer they drove over to Myrtle Beach for a week."

"When did he die?" Wade looked up from his notes.

"About six months ago. It was tragic. One of those freak things, you know. He was headed home when the car in front of him just stopped cold. Had some kind of malfunction. His car plowed into the back of it and a tanker truck behind him turned him into a seat belt statistic." Sonny jumped to his feet and began pacing, leaving footprints in the thick pile of the carpet. "The insurance money she received was pretty good so Patti was okay financially. Her husband's death just took the heart right out of her." He paused, breathing hard, as if he'd been running, his chest heaving.

Watching carefully, Tony saw something shift in Sonny's face. He knew it was important. "What changed?"

"She met a new man." Sonny stopped right in front of Tony, his hands spread. "I don't know where she met him or anything about him. She said he made her feel alive. She said he was wonderful. It bothered me."

"Why?"

"It was too soon. It had only been a short time since her husband's passing." He looked at Tony and laughed in a quiet, self-deprecating way. "I am not a moral person. She was."

Tony hated his next question. "Did she tell you she was pregnant? And she miscarried?"

"No." The word seemed to suck the air from his lungs and Sonny stopped pacing and collapsed back into his chair. "How bittersweet for her. To have a baby at long last, you know. She and her husband tried for years to have one." He stared sightlessly out the window. A tear traced unnoticed down his cheek. "Whose baby was it? Her husband's or the boyfriend's?"

"Most likely her boyfriend's." Tony felt truly sorry for the pain this man suffered. In only hours, he had lost a beloved daughter and now a grandchild. The pain had to be unimaginable. Theo had miscarried, a little girl, when Jamie was two, and the sorrow lingered. The loss of any child was every parent's worst nightmare. Tony cleared his throat, wondering the best way to phrase his next statement. "The autopsy showed it was a recent loss."

"Poor Patti." Tears overflowed Sonny's eyes and he reached into his pocket for a handkerchief. Too overcome to continue, he cried quietly for a time. At length, he blew his nose and sat up straighter. "What can I do to help?"

"Just tell us what you can. Do you know why she was here when she died?"

"No."

"Do you have any idea when she last came to Silersville?"

"Not really." Sonny frowned. "I know she came sometimes to spy on Doreen. Her marriage was the only thing she preferred to Doreen's life."

"What kind of car did she drive?" The image of this lost and grieving woman stalking her half sister, copying her clothes and hair, was disturbing and tragic.

"It's a dark green Chevy. It's not new and it's not falling apart, either."

"Do you have keys to her house?"

Sonny nodded. A half second later, he looked stricken. The reality of what had happened to his daughter couldn't be pushed away any longer. He understood. "You want to go through her house?"

"Yes."

With shaking hands, Sonny pulled an overloaded keychain from his pocket as he dictated her address to Wade. He flipped through the keys, finally removing one and handing it to Tony. "When you're done, I'd like it back."

"Of course." Holding the key in his fist, Tony rose. "I just need to ask you one more question for now. Where did she work?"

"Some insurance company in downtown Chattanooga. I can't remember the name of it just now. I can give you the phone number." Sonny scribbled the number on the back of a gasoline receipt and shoved it into Tony's hand.

Tony looked at Wade. His deputy's expression reflected his own concern. Sonny was on the verge of collapse. The grieving father needed some time and space.

"Thank you, sir," said Tony as he rose to his feet. "I appreciate you taking the time to meet with us."

Sonny started to stand but his legs did not support him and he fell back, threatening to tip the chair over backwards. Wade pressed a hand onto the older man's shoulder, stabilizing him. "We'll let ourselves out."

Tony paused at the doorway and glanced over his shoulder. From there he could see Sonny, his face buried in his handkerchief. His entire body shuddered, his visitors already forgotten.

Somewhere in that house, Tony guessed, the less-well-loved daughter must be busy unpacking her possessions.

He felt sorry for Doreen.

Carrying the receipt with Patti's work number written on it, Tony went back to his office, thinking maybe he was in the wrong line of work. Maybe he'd be happier building something, like Gus, rather than cleaning up the messes others made. His contemplation lasted until he remembered that his skill with a hammer made carpentry an impractical solution at best.

Plus, he loved the thrill of catching the bad guy. It always gave him a rush. Well, almost always. Sometimes his sympathies lay with the person who did the wrong thing for the right reason, yet he couldn't twist the law to suit himself.

Theo often teased him, saying he was a vigilante at heart. Maybe she was right. He did feel like hanging someone. But who?

He settled into his chair and sat quietly, staring at the cluttered surface of his desk without really seeing it. Notes and printouts from his own and other law enforcement agencies littered the surface. A baby had been abducted from a mall in Charlotte, Virginia. A suspected arsonist was running amok in the Johnson City area. The U.S. Marshals Service moved another escaped felon onto their list.

Tony found it all depressing to consider. Surely there was good somewhere. Maybe inspiration would strike.

He waited for a long time letting random bits of information run through his mind. No clear pattern emerged.

Without thinking about what he was doing, he rubbed his head with both hands as if stimulation would organize his thoughts. An idea did occur to him, although it had nothing to do with this case. If he had hair, he would have massaged it away by now. The notion made him smile, though, easing the tension coiling his gut.

He reached for the jar of antacids on his desk. Maybe if he ate more of them and kept his hands off his scalp he'd have a thick, glossy head of hair like Wade's.

Finally, he picked up his phone and punched in the number for the Chattanooga police department.

Only a minute later his call was forwarded, and he found himself chatting with a Detective Zeller. Tony thought that Zeller sounded interested, helpful and about sixteen years old.

"I guess it would take me about two hours to drive down there and find the place," said Tony. He hoped that Zeller would offer to do all the leg work and send a report. "Maybe, you could . . ."

He didn't get to finish his suggestion before Zeller interrupted. "Sounds good, I'll meet you at your victim's house about ten-thirty in the morning. We can poke around there for a bit and then head down to her office."

"Sure, that's fine." With a marked lack of enthusiasm, Tony wrote himself a note. He felt as if he had too much on his plate already and didn't want to make another trip out of town. Oh well, at least he'd be traveling around in air-conditioning.

Zeller continued, "In the meanwhile, I'll see what I can learn about your woman and her husband. This is a nice community and still not too big to mind other people's business."

Tony felt guilty and petty for wanting Zeller to do his work. Zeller was already doing more than he needed to. Tony mustered more enthusiasm. "Thanks, I appreciate all your help."

With a perky, "Look forward to meeting y'all tomorrow," Zeller ended the call.

Feeling not the least bit perky, Tony decided against calling the insurance agency where Patti worked. If one of her coworkers was involved with her personally, which was possible, he saw no sense in letting them know he was on the way. What if one of them drove Patti to the museum and killed her? The drive would be easy. The motive for killing her and doing it in such a spectacularly bizarre location, baffled him.

Maybe it was a good thing Zeller hadn't volunteered to investigate. The puzzle kept changing, like a jigsaw puzzle he'd worked on once that was reversible. The pieces looked right, when in fact, they were upside down.

Like killing Patti instead of Doreen, who was the real intended victim?

Tony hit the intercom and spoke to Wade. "Meet me here at eight-thirty tomorrow. We're going on a road trip to Chattanooga."

"Yes, sir."

Ignoring the stack of papers and files waiting for his attention, Tony cross-checked the insurance agency phone number and wrote the address in his pocket notebook. He looked up the address on the Internet before he reached for his worn atlas.

Technology was all very convenient; still, he preferred paper maps. They had an almost magical quality, he thought as he ran his finger across the small map of Chattanooga.

The office would be easy to find.

He sighed.

With the true identity of their victim established, maybe solving Patti's murder would be simple. Nothing would please him more than being able to bring her killer to justice. How many true enemies could the woman have? Arresting someone for her murder wouldn't return Patti to her grieving father and grandmother. It would be better than twenty years of lingering questions like his cold case.

He went home dragging with him other people's grief. At least he had something fun to look forward to; Jamie's game would start soon. What could be more fun than watching six-year-olds play baseball?

CHAPTER TWENTY-TWO

As Theo left Ruby's Café through the back door, she glanced across the overflow parking lot and spotted Nellie Pearl. This time the crotchety old woman was on the path that zigzagged up and over the hill separating downtown Silersville from the highway and Ruby's. Everyone used the shortcut, even tourists. Something about the old bat's stance attracted Theo's attention.

Nellie Pearl stood motionless, her hands like claws reaching toward someone dressed in loose-fitting denim overalls and a long-sleeved brown shirt. Clad in her usual layers of flannel, the old woman glared at her companion, her expression hostile at best.

Theo thought that wearing flannel in a heat wave would make anyone hostile. Nellie Pearl enjoyed her argumentative attitude and could pick a fight with anyone. Still, Theo had no way of knowing if the two had encountered each other on the path or if they were companions.

Was the disagreement their normal conversational style or was there an actual problem?

The other person stood in the shadow of a small tree, its dappled shade distorting the figure standing under it. Frustrated, Theo tried to identify the person and couldn't even be sure of the gender. Lots of the older generation still wore overalls to town. A couple even wore them to church.

The younger residents, which meant anyone under sixty,

171

were rarely seen in them.

"Overalls" suddenly lashed out, striking the flannel-clad woman with a stick or cane. It might have hit Nellie Pearl's arm. It certainly didn't keep the old woman from lunging forward, fingers reaching for her companion's eyes.

"Stop!" Theo sprinted across the parking lot, headed for the beginning of the path. As she ran, she watched the pair and fumbled in her purse, feeling for her cell phone. The two started pushing and shoving each other in earnest. The only voice Theo could hear was Nellie Pearl's. It sounded like she was saying "won't" or maybe "don't."

In Theo's opinion, Overalls seemed to be winning the fight. Nellie Pearl never backed away from anything or anyone. She was moving away now, bent forward, her arms crossed in front, protecting her face. Overalls gave the old woman one last shove and Nellie Pearl fell sideways to the ground and landed in a heap.

Theo scrambled up the dirt trail as fast as she could. By the time she reached the old woman, Overalls had vanished over the ridge of the hill. Even if she ran, whoever it was would be long gone before she got there.

"Are you okay?" Theo stopped at Nellie Pearl's side, her cell phone in her hand. "I'll call for help."

"I'm fine." Huddled against a shrub, Nellie Pearl glared at her as if Theo was the reason she was on the ground. "Put that dang phone away." Only the faint tremor in her voice indicated a problem.

"I guess that means you're not hurt." With a sigh, Theo slipped the phone into her purse and frowned as she bent over to check on Nellie Pearl's condition. "Who was that?"

Leaves and twigs had become snagged in the old woman's tangled gray hair and a fresh layer of dirt clung to the outermost flannel shirt. Cradling her left arm, she narrowed her eyes at

Theo as if shooting her with laser vision. "Who was what?"

Theo pointed up the empty path. "Your attacker."

"I wasn't attacked, you stupid child. Since you're here, be of some use and help me up."

Still panting from the run across the pavement and uphill, Theo sighed, extending a hand. Had she really expected the old bat to cooperate or express any sense of gratitude?

Reaching her right hand forward, Nellie Pearl sank her chipped, yellowish fingernails into the flesh of Theo's forearm and pulled hard, almost yanking the smaller woman onto her. Theo grabbed with her free hand and leaned back, finally hauling the older woman upright.

As soon as Nellie Pearl was on her feet, Theo released her and pried her arm free of the clutching hand. She glanced down at her arm. A row of half moon–shaped cuts seeped blood. She wanted to hurry to the shop and clean them with peroxide or something stronger. As dirty as Nellie Pearl's fingernails looked, Theo was afraid of blood poisoning. Even so, she wanted some answers.

"I thought I saw you with Nelson Parker this morning at Doreen's funeral," said Theo. It made sense. She knew Nelson was one of the dedicated overall wearers in Silersville, and he was about the same age as Nellie Pearl.

"Did you?" Nellie Pearl's expression gave nothing away as she dusted herself off with one hand, keeping her left arm pressed against her chest. "Spying on me?"

"No." Theo stared at the prickly old woman, feeling childish. A wave of irritation washed through her and she hoped the old bat's arm was broken. "If not Nelson, who?"

"Who indeed?" Without a word of thanks, Nellie Pearl retrieved her oversized canvas tote bag from a mountain laurel growing next to the path and stalked down the hill dragging it behind her. Something bulky and obviously heavy thumped with each step, crushing the tiny purple wildflowers in its path.

Theo wondered if the bag contained Ruby's powder room decorations or a yard ornament.

Then she wondered if Tony could arrest Nellie Pearl for attempting to murder his wife with dirt.

Tony delivered Jamie to the ball field and watched his son walk over to join his teammates. In contrast to Jamie's usual eager trot, today the little boy plodded across the grass. His shoulders slumped forward and he let his glove drag on the ground.

Although Tony was concerned, Jamie's lack of enthusiasm wasn't really a surprise. Tonight's baseball game would pit Jamie's team, Ruby's Café Reds, against their arch rivals the Riverview Motel Tigers. In the previous two meetings, the Tigers had put enough points on the board to invoke the mercy rule.

"Dreadful" pretty much described the games. Error after error produced what had to be a pair of the most lopsided baseball scores since Abner Doubleday or Alexander Cartwright thought up the game.

The expression on Jamie's face reflected those of his teammates. If something didn't change, Tony thought, they were whipped before they started to warm up. The twelve little boys and girls looked like they'd rather sprawl in the grass and chase bugs than face the Tigers.

Head coach Marjorie McKenzie charged toward the team, carrying a five-gallon bucket of baseballs and a bulging equipment bag. Tony knew better than to offer to help; he was only the assistant and Marjorie had opinions as strong as her arms. Trailing behind her was her son, Arthur, nicknamed Pug for some unexplained reason.

Pug usually had one finger up his nose.

Pug played shortstop. The boy handled a glove like a wizard. He could catch any ball coming his way. Unfortunately, he couldn't throw accurately for more than three feet. At the last meeting with the Tigers, he had single-handedly cost them the game. The Tigers must have hit a hundred ground balls to the shortstop. Pug fielded each of them cleanly. Then, in spite of instructions to hand-carry the ball to second base, he threw it away. Not a single ball made it to any plate before the runner. Every ball he tried to throw either dropped from his hand and landed at his own feet or sailed six feet above the first baseman's glove and into the dugout.

That game had felt like the longest two hours in the history of the game of baseball.

Tony thought Pug would make a great catcher and suggested a change. Marjorie ran the team. Generally competent, she knew baseball and did a good job of teaching the other kids the skills they needed. She had a blind spot where Pug was concerned. She wanted her son to be a shortstop and all conversation ended there.

Like most of the team, Jamie would be happy to win, more importantly he really wanted to play. It just about killed him when it was his rotation on the pine bench.

Leaning against the fence, Tony listened while Marjorie read out the starting lineup. Tonight Jamie would play shortstop and Pug would sit on the bench. Tony felt a glimmer of hope. Maybe they wouldn't win. At least now, they had a good chance of playing all the innings.

Theo took Chris to his baseball team's practice. She had a couple of small things to finish up before she would go watch Jamie play his game. Returning to the shop, she parked in the front instead of taking her customary space in the back. Barely out of the van, she didn't even make it to the sidewalk before she found herself cornered by Nellie Pearl. It seemed like every time she turned around, the old bat was there swooping into her personal space. It couldn't have been much over an hour since their encounter on the path.

Hoping for patience, Theo sucked in a deep breath, instantly regretting it.

If the old lady's concession to the heat was to wear fewer layers of flannel, evidently it didn't mean she washed the ones she wore. Nellie Pearl's sour breath and body odor seemed worse than before. The scent of camphor swirled in the air. Why she didn't collapse from the heat was a mystery of great proportion.

Theo tried to back away and gain some fresher air. The old woman pressed closer, trapping her against the scorching hot car door. "Please give me some room."

Nellie Pearl ignored her and leaned in. "I wanted to ask you about church."

Theo stilled, confused. As far as she knew, Nellie Pearl would no more go into a church, except for funerals, or wear a dress than Theo herself would strip off her clothes and dance on the bar at the Okay Bar and Bait Shop.

"What about church?" Theo eyed the huge canvas bag on the ground at her feet. It looked fuller than before. Once again she was tempted to ask the old woman about her theft of Ruby's decorations.

"I saw you this morning." Nellie Pearl's eyes met hers and moved away like she wasn't quite focusing on anything. "Have you no shame at all? You brazen hussy."

"Will you please back off?" Goaded beyond all patience, Theo reached up and pushed against the woman's shoulders. Finally Nellie Pearl stepped back. Most of Theo's irritation with her came from their past. As a child, Theo had been on the receiving end of too many insults to reconsider her opinion just because she was now grown up. Nellie Pearl always took delight in pointing out the anomalies of growing children, frequently drawing attention to oversized teeth or ears. She had made fun of Theo when she was just a timid little girl with thick glasses and a lisp. Now she managed to make it sound like being seen at church was on the same level as being seen going into a triple-x-rated movie.

"I guess you've recovered from your fall," said Theo.

Nellie Pearl narrowed her eyes. "I never fall."

"Okay, you were pushed. Will you tell me what happened?" Maybe she could learn who Overalls was. Unfortunately, it was like talking to a wall. The blank expression on the old woman's face could not be feigned. Nellie Pearl did not remember the incident on the hill.

Theo wondered what that meant.

"Can you believe the excitement at the Queen's burial?" As if she hadn't just insulted Theo and then not responded to the discussion of her fall, Nellie Pearl cackled and clapped her hands together. "Everyone in the state must have heard about it by now."

"Word does travel." Theo managed to say the most cordial thing she could. She edged toward the sidewalk, hoping to run into the shop for a few minutes and still get to Jamie's game before the first pitch.

Nellie Pearl stepped into her path and held her ground, blocking Theo's way. "You suppose your husband's aunt knew which one she was killing?"

"Martha had nothing to do with this." Too shocked by the accusation to think clearly, Theo stopped and stared at Nellie Pearl.

"Of course she did," said Nellie Pearl. "Who else could—or would, for that matter? Everybody knew Martha would do it someday. It was just a matter of time."

Theo bit the inside of her mouth to keep herself quiet. A couple of curious bystanders were blatantly eavesdropping. As much as she couldn't help being curious about the woman's statement, she would strangle on her own tongue before she asked a single question. She edged to the left, hoping to get around her.

"You don't know, do you?" Nellie Pearl moved directly into her path and began to cackle. Theo thought she sounded just like a grade-B movie witch. All she needed was a pointed black hat, green makeup and a broom. Then she would look as if she'd just stepped out of central casting. She shook her index finger right in Theo's face. Theo was appalled by the filthy fingernail hovering inches from her eye. She was sure the dark stains were her own blood. The hand stank.

The moment she got to the shop after the incident on the path, Theo cleaned the bleeding wounds on her arm. Now she considered pouring bleach all over them. It would probably sting like crazy but who knew what was under those fingernails?

"Mark my words. It was only a matter of time. Ask anyone." Nellie Pearl waved her arms, sending a wave of toxic body odor into Theo's face. "Martha stood right in the middle of Main Street and swore someday she would kill Doreen." Still cackling, she ambled along the sidewalk, headed toward the creek.

Theo breathed deeply, waiting for some cleaner air to dispel the faint nausea inspired by the old woman's stench. It had been a long, smelly day, and she had Nellie Pearl to thank for most of it.

Popcorn. She needed popcorn. Thank goodness they had it at the concession stand. It didn't matter that the concession stand was the trunk of a volunteer's car.

She changed her mind about going into the shop and headed to the ball game. Work could wait.

CHAPTER TWENTY-THREE

Ruby's Reds won. Theo guessed it was a combination of factors. Three of the Tiger's best players were ill and Pug sat on the bench. It didn't matter, Jamie's team won and the kids were happy.

The celebration began with ice cream for the whole team. The family continued celebrating in the Abernathy kitchen. Theo pulled a fresh package of chocolate-chip cookies from her hiding spot inside the broom closet.

Cookie crumbs and milk flew from the boys as if they hadn't had food or treats for weeks. Within seconds, Theo thought it looked like cookie-eating piranhas had been at the table. The boys bolted, excused, leaving their parents sitting among the wreckage.

Theo watched as Chris and Jamie settled down in front of the television to play video games. Although the distance from table to controller was only five feet, the boys moved into another world. Car racing replaced baseball.

"Can you think of any reason why your aunt would want to kill Doreen?" Speaking softly so only Tony could hear her, Theo posed the question raised by Nellie Pearl.

In the process of pouring himself a tall glass of milk, Tony's eyebrows flew up and his arm jerked. He missed the glass and ended up chasing runaway milk with the dishtowel. "What?"

"That's what Nellie Pearl suggested this afternoon." Theo handed him a damp cloth. The expression on her husband's face told her he was reassuringly shocked.

"Why would Nellie Pearl tell you something so bizarre?"

"I don't know. The old bat and I haven't got a great history. Still it seems out of character for her to make unfounded accusations." Theo sighed and lifted her shoulders toward her ears before dropping them again. The movement released some of the tension she felt in her back. "She usually delights in telling painful truths in the most public way possible."

"Still mad about the four-eyes jokes?" Tony dunked a cookie in his milk and then popped the whole thing into his mouth. Damp crumbs clung to the corners of his mouth.

"No madder than you were about the hair-loss jokes." Not really hungry, Theo stole one of his cookies and nibbled on the edge.

Tony lifted his glass in a silent salute. "You are absolutely right, sweetheart. She is an old bat."

"There was something else weird." Theo wondered if he'd be amused by the idea of Nellie Pearl stealing yard ornaments. The powder room decorations were not up for conjecture. She told him about her day.

"She does seem weirder than ever." Responding to her description of dirty fingernails cutting into her arm, Tony examined the crescent-shaped cuts on her arm before he kissed each mark. There was no trace of humor in his face.

Theo felt gratified by his obvious anger. "I don't think she remembers doing it, or even that she was on the path this afternoon."

Tony's eyebrows pulled together as his frown deepened. "I should think Blossom's donkey ornament would be too heavy for her to move without help." He did smile then. "The idea of her asking for help is way beyond weird. Still, stranger things have happened, so I'll see what I can find out."

His cell phone rang interrupting them. Tony pressed the green button and mostly listened. "Yes, I guess so. Tell him to be at my office at eight-thirty."

Theo knew who called before he said it.

"Dispatch." Tony pressed DISCONNECT and reached for another cookie. "Don't worry. I'm not going out."

Theo waited, thinking he suddenly looked exhausted.

"Sonny wants to go to Chattanooga with Wade and me tomorrow. I don't like it but couldn't think of a good reason why he couldn't go." Tony popped the cookie into his mouth and chewed. "After all, Patti was his daughter. Maybe he can help clear things up somehow."

Tony needed to get some work done before his Chattanooga trip and went in to his office early.

Judging from the stack of notes and files, it looked like his desk was covered with loose ends. Now he could add Nellie Pearl's accusation against his aunt. He would start by learning the truth of the old woman's statement. Although he didn't believe his aunt did it, he had to follow every lead.

Sighing heavily, he turned his back on the messy desk. He could talk to his aunt and be back in only a few minutes. If nothing else, he would feel he'd accomplished one little thing in the day.

Martha lived only a couple of minutes from his office and was an early riser. He parked in the street in front of her house. Like everyone who knew her well, Tony bypassed the front door and went directly to the kitchen door of his aunt's house. He could hear her belting out a song, singing a duet with Shania Twain. At fifty, Martha's voice still sounded young and fresh. Tony loved to listen to her sing. For a fleeting moment, he considered that if Martha and his mom had gone on with their musical summer plans instead of starting the museum, he wouldn't be standing at her back door wondering if there was a chance she was a murderess.

He wished he knew for sure who the killer wanted dead, Patti or Doreen.

Tony remembered another time he'd stood on Martha's back porch, watching her through the old screen door and wondering if he'd have to arrest her. At that time she'd been a suspect in the murder of her husband, Frank.

Since that day, the rickety screen door had been replaced with a new, sturdy white storm door. It was only one of many changes in her home, and like most of the improvements on her house and lifestyle, the money had come from Frank's estate. The old crook had squirreled away millions.

As Frank's wife, Martha inherited the money. Even after she paid the overdue taxes on it, Martha was left with much more than a tidy nest egg.

The bulk of it became the foundation for their museum.

"Hey, Tony, come on in." Martha answered the door when he knocked on the frame. "You're out early." She crossed the kitchen and turned down the radio hanging over a miniature desk. The maple cabinets were new, as were the hardwood floor and the granite countertops. A new table with white tiles set into the surface had replaced the old card table, and four ladder-back chairs were set around it.

Gus had done the remodeling and produced his usual perfect work.

"Does my brother work for you full time or is he allowed other jobs?" Tony ran his hand across the smooth wood on one of the doors and wondered if Theo would like new cabinets in their ancient, atmospheric kitchen.

"Oh, I let him take the occasional odd job, as long as it doesn't interfere with my plans." Without asking, she poured coffee into a beige stoneware cup with a robin's-egg blue interior and handed it to him. "Sit."

Tony obliged. The new chairs were surprisingly comfortable. He placed his notebook and pen on the white-tiled table and swallowed some of the coffee.

As she slipped onto her own chair, Martha's eyes widened, staring at the notebook. "Is this an official visit, Tony?"

"In a way. I didn't bring Wade." He liked to have a second person with him when he did official questioning. "We'll just call this a fact-finding mission. If at any time you decide you want a lawyer, we'll stop."

"That sounds ominous." The smile left her face.

"I hope it's easily explained." He fidgeted, turning his cup around on the table and then finally looked up. "I don't believe in rumors or gossip."

"But?" Martha prompted him. "But what?"

Tony reached into his shirt pocket for a couple of antacids. He chewed them slowly, gathering his thoughts. "Sometimes the line between gossip and fact is a narrow one."

"Spit it out, Tony. What do you want to know?"

"Did you ever threaten to kill Doreen?" Tony sat back, prepared for her denial. It didn't come.

After a considerable pause, she answered, "Yes, I did." His aunt folded her hands on the table and stared directly into his eyes. "It was a long time ago, and I wouldn't exactly call it my proudest moment. How'd you hear about it?"

With a slight shake of his head, Tony ignored her question. "What happened?"

Martha stared at him for a full minute before looking into her cup. A faint touch of red climbed the sides of her neck and made her cheeks rosy. He had never in his whole life seen his aunt blush.

Fascinating. Utterly fascinating. Tony felt himself becoming sucked in to this story the same way Chris did when playing video games. If the house caught on fire, Tony doubted Chris would notice. Mesmerized, Tony waited for his aunt to speak.

"I try to treat all of my students the same," said Martha. "Occasionally there is one I just can't like no matter how hard I try to or one I like more than the others."

Tony's eyebrows lifted. There were enough cases in the television news of teachers behaving inappropriately with students to give him chills. He stared at his aunt.

"No! Not like that, you nitwit." Martha jumped to her feet and retrieved the coffeepot. "I would never, could never. Don't you believe me?"

"Yes." Tony did believe her. "So what did happen?"

"This student worked two jobs to help out at home. One of the jobs was working for Queen Doreen at the Gift Shoppe." Martha frowned and rubbed the bridge of her nose. "You know the way the place is packed with merchandise?"

Tony nodded. Floor space was nonexistent. Gewgaws and gimcracks filled the shelves, hung from rafters and were stacked on the floor. He'd seen jars of jam, gift baskets filled with everything from soap to biscuit mix and many items he couldn't identify.

"Well, I was in there and the girl turned and barely bumped into a stack of stuff. A porcelain swan fell to the floor and broke. Doreen went ballistic." Martha frowned. "I tried to pay for it hoping to end the tantrum. Doreen wouldn't take my money. Nothing would satisfy her. She wanted the girl out of there immediately. Even though she eventually rehired the girl, our feud has only gotten worse."

"Worse, how?" Although it was still early, a breeze carried the scent of warm grass and honeysuckle into the kitchen mingling with the rich coffee aroma. He relaxed, sensing Martha's story had nothing to do with current events.

"I went out of my way to antagonize the Queen and she did the same, always threatening to have the girl arrested for shoplifting or stealing from the till.

"It came to a head in the middle of the street one morning." Martha squeezed her hands together. That seemed to make them shake harder. "I pulled Frank's gun out of my purse and pointed it at her and told her that she would cease tormenting the girl or I'd see that she did."

"That was it?"

"Not exactly." Martha turned her face away. "Harvey Winston locked me up in the jail. At least he never charged me with anything. I apologized for waving the gun, and Doreen finally agreed to let it rest."

Tony couldn't believe this. Nothing mildly interesting happened when he was growing up here. The minute he left, all hell must have broken loose. In recent days he'd learned about four murders, a feud and even that his aunt had threatened Doreen— with a gun. "Why all of a sudden are events of twenty years ago coming to light?"

"What do you mean?" Clearly confused, his aunt stared at him.

He thought her confusion was understandable. The suddenly un-cold case involving Vicky Parker was not available for public scrutiny and dissection. "Nothing. I'm just talking to myself."

He left her still sitting at the table and headed for the trailer park where Roscoe Morris lived with Dora-the-vending machine. As early as it was, the air-conditioning in the Blazer was barely keeping up.

CHAPTER TWENTY-FOUR

Tony approached the highway turnoff to the Oak Lawn Trailer Courts. At one time there had been a decorative sign pointing the way. Now, however, there was just a slab of weather-beaten plywood with crudely painted letters that read "Oak Trail Cour".

With a name sounding to his ears like a cross between a cemetery and a motel, the trailer park sat on the edge of town. Thirty years previously, it opened as retirement living. It boasted manicured lawns, a community center with an indoor meeting room and a weight room, plus outdoor amenities including a swimming pool, horseshoe pits and covered picnic area, it was beautiful.

Now, after years of neglect, garbage and kudzu, it was little better than an open cesspool. By all accounts, Roscoe loved it there. His trailer home had once been white with red trim and decorative red shutters. Tony stared at it as he turned toward it. It had definitely passed its glory years.

Roscoe's ancient pickup was parked in front.

Tony stared at the back end of the truck. The taillights were shattered. Newly exposed spots of primer gave the tailgate a speckled appearance. There were shallow dents in the finish. Tony wondered if he needed to talk to old Orvan again. The man must have loaded some pretty big shot to do this kind of damage. If he used it on a bird, nothing would be left. Maybe he'd been standing closer than he claimed. Either scenario was possible.

In a three-way trade set up by Ruth Ann, the Thomas brothers promised to fix Roscoe's taillights in exchange for the ladder-back chairs built by Orvan. The old pickup sat next to the dilapidated trailer that Roscoe called home. There was no sign of Dora-the-vending machine. Maybe she watched morning talk shows.

Joe Thomas, the brawnier of the mechanic brothers, squatted in the dirt replacing the pickup's light bulbs and covers. He would soon have the truck put back together. It would never be pretty, but it would be safe to drive.

Joe grinned as he worked and listened to a running commentary from Roscoe, whose knowledge of baseball was encyclopedic. Roscoe waxed eloquent, giving an almost play-by-play account of the last game he'd umpired.

Tony stayed long enough to see that everything was under control. Neither Joe nor Roscoe seemed to notice either Tony's arrival or his departure. He checked the dashboard clock as he pulled into his official parking space. He was back in plenty of time to meet Wade and Sonny.

From the corner of his eye, he spied Blossom carrying a pie pan, hoofing it toward him. As much as he wanted the pie, he wasn't in the mood to deal with Blossom and her adoring gazes. He sighed, looking for a way to escape. There was none.

"Yoo hoo, Sheriff." Blossom managed to balance the pie pan on one hand as she waved, setting the loose flesh of her bare arms in motion.

"Blossom." Tony paused, assailed by guilt. Her face was beet red and her breath came in great gasps. "Slow down. It's already too hot this morning to be charging around like that."

"I know. I know." She followed him into his office.

Disappointed that neither Sonny nor Wade was waiting for him, he stood hoping she would get to the point.

"I wanted to bring you this 'cause we ran out of pie yesterday.

Wasn't it something? I was there when the mayor's missus came back to life, so to speak. You think she's a vampire or something?" A sparkle of mischief glowed in her bulbous eyes. "I'll bet Calvin about dumped in his pants."

Tony gulped and bit his lip. If he'd had anything to say to that outrageous comment, it would be hard to get a word in edgewise. Blossom's color was returning to normal. The little tufts of her orange hair stuck to her sweaty scalp and she was in full-bore excitement.

"Pansy told me the mayor was crying something fierce last night. Relief, I guess he'd say, but I'm not so sure."

Waiting near his office door, Tony watched as Blossom rearranged the papers on his desk and then set the pie in the very center with a theatrical flourish. He didn't comment. His stomach growled as he eyed the delicious concoction of apples, spices and the secret family ingredient. Blossom's words flowed over him like water.

"So didja?" Blossom squeezed her hands together and looked anxious.

"I'm sorry, Blossom. I was enjoying the aroma of the pie. Did I what?"

"Find my lawn decoration. You know, the donkey?" She reached into her pocket and retrieved a handful of candy-coated chocolates. The bright-colored candies formed a small mountain in the palm of her hand. In one practiced movement, she sucked the whole pile into her mouth and began to chew. Her mouth remained open just far enough for him to see the different colors passing by. The sight was as mesmerizing as watching clothes through the glass of a front-loading washing machine. Her bulbous eyes bore a startling similarity to those belonging to his cousin's pug dog. She swallowed, leaving just a slight chocolate ring around her lips. "I read somewhere if a crime is not solved right away it never gets solved."

The specter of the unidentified bones moved into his head. "Not always, Blossom. Some cases just take a bit longer."

He didn't try to convince her that missing lawn ornaments weren't in the same category as murder. To Blossom, the loss of her beloved item was more important. She didn't like Doreen and didn't know Patti. She would have been a child when the murders Harrison Duff claimed to have committed with Vicky had taken place.

"That's good. Still, I wanted you to have the pie." She dug in her pockets and came up empty. "And to tell you your dead lady drove past Ruby's in an old beater. Of course at the time, I thought it was the Queen and it about knocked me over to see her driving such a wreck. She's kind of persnickety about her stuff, you know, always actin' like she's better than God."

When she paused to inhale, Tony interrupted her tirade. "Can you tell me what kind of car it was or the color?"

"It was dark green." Blossom pursed her lips and wrinkled her forehead into her practiced "thinking" mode. "And it looked really ordinary, which is why I noticed."

"Two doors or four?"

Blossom tapped her top chin with her index finger. Her face brightened. "Four. And it had a reddish door behind the driver."

Tony felt a real smile lift the corners of his mouth. "Reddish like paint or rust?"

"Like paint." She checked her watch, lifting it out of the fold of flesh surrounding it. "Oops, gotta go. Miss Ruby needed me to come in and bake some extra brownies for something." Without another word, she turned and swished out the door, nearly flattening the arriving Ruth Ann in the process.

Tony smiled at her back. Blossom's description of the car, although poor, was better than Sonny's reference to a green Chevy. Obtaining the license plate number along with the year, the make and model was easy. The detail about the primer wouldn't be in the computer.

When Ruth Ann made it inside the office, he smiled and told her about the car, knowing that a few taps from her now-purple fingernails on her computer keys would produce all the details he needed.

Tony wrote himself a note, adding a few questions to ask Sonny and Patti's employer.

When he glanced up, Wade and Sonny stood in his office doorway. Wade looked rested and alert. Sonny looked like death.

Time to go.

CHAPTER TWENTY-FIVE

As they neared Chattanooga on the interstate, billboards for Ruby Falls, the Incline Railroad and Rock City Gardens guided them toward Lookout Mountain. The mountain directions seemed unnecessary because the distinctive promontory dominated the skyline, almost pointing to the city on the bank of the Tennessee River.

For a while Sonny roused himself from his silence in the back seat and managed to give Tony and Wade a brief commentary about the changes to the landscape in recent years, especially to the riverfront area near the Tennessee Aquarium.

Tony didn't need the guided tour. Out of sympathy, he let Sonny chatter on, still thinking they should have left him behind. They would have, except he might be able to spot something out of place or out of the ordinary in Patti's home.

Sonny seemed to be imploding.

Tony thought the man must have lost ten pounds since they first announced Doreen's death, and now his skin looked grayer than his hair. The loss of a beloved child was too horrible for Tony to contemplate, so he turned his conjecture toward the hell on earth he'd consider living with Mrs. Sonny, the Queen Mother, to be. Even on a good day, life would have to be bad. Tony half wondered if Sonny got to use her first name in private, if he had to call her ma'am, or if they spoke at all.

"Turn left here," said Sonny, distracting him from his meandering thoughts. "It's the second house on the right."

The house Sonny directed them to was built on the west slope of Missionary Ridge and blessed with a good view of Lookout Mountain. Maybe the smallest house in the neighborhood, Patti's cottage appeared well-kept. Red brick and shaped like a box, it sat in the center of a postage stamp–sized lot landscaped with a manicured lawn and carefully shaped mature trees. A detached garage looked like a miniature version of the house. Everything appeared measured and symmetrical, as if the yard and garden were expected to conform.

Wade parked in the empty driveway and the three men climbed out in silence.

"Abernathy?" A man spoke through the open window of a dark blue sedan parked on the street.

"Zeller?" At the answering nod, Tony suppressed a grin and watched the Chattanooga cop unfold from the driver's seat and amble up the sidewalk. This was no sixteen-year-old. The perky voice and phone manner belonged to a veteran cop on the verge of retirement. Tall and slender, with just a touch of a paunch, Zeller wore his thick white hair cropped into an old-fashioned flattop. Alert brown eyes seemed to miss nothing as he joined the three men.

They all headed toward the front porch.

Handshakes and introductions took minimal time. Tony immediately realized how private the front door was. Only the neighbor directly across the street would have any chance to see who went in or out of the house.

"Did y'all bring the key?" The lanky detective looked at Sonny.

Tony thought Zeller's voice held more of the rich cadences of Georgia than Appalachia, which was not surprising since the city sat on the Tennessee–Georgia border.

Realizing the men were waiting for him, Sonny nodded and reached into his pocket. His hand shook badly and it took him several attempts before he eventually managed to insert the key in the lock. The instant the door swung inward, a gray-striped cat shot past them and dashed away.

"Muffin!" Sonny lunged after the cat, leaving the key in the lock. Muffin leaped over the fence and dashed up the street. Only the stench of an overfilled litter box remained.

The inside of the house looked as rigidly ordered as the exterior. The compact living room had two beige chairs arranged to face a beige love seat across a blond wooden coffee table. The walls were a slightly lighter shade of beige. Nothing hung on the walls. Even the most generic motel room would look gaudy in comparison.

Tony had lived with the colorful Theo too long to not be affected by her penchant for hanging things, usually quilts, on the walls, sofas and tables. Her choice of colors and patterns did not always "go together." If anyone mentioned their opinion to her, she invariably would laughingly agree with the assessment and ignore the criticism.

Theo's heart did the decorating. If she loved something, it was included, just like the different people in her life. There were times when Tony thought she'd overdone the colorful mix. Gazing around this barren room, he swore to himself he would never think that again. This room gave him the creeps.

"It's like no one lives here." Wade walked around the room studying the minimal furnishings and freshly painted walls. "Was she preparing to move?"

"No." Staring at the sea of beige, Sonny stood frozen at the doorway. "I never really noticed this room before. Patti was always my focus."

The other rooms were nearly as bad. No personal touches. No knickknacks. Order reigned in the kitchen; not even a coffeemaker sat out on the counter. Only the reeking litter box in the laundry area and a photograph in the bedroom gave any sign that this was a home. A small photo in a tarnished silver frame sat on the blond wood dresser. It showed Patti and her husband on their wedding day, laughing at the photographer.

"I took the picture," said Sonny.

"They looked very happy," said Wade.

"I believe they were." Sonny couldn't seem to pull his eyes away from the photograph. "At least they were at first. The longer they tried to have children, the more she began to resent their life. I'm afraid she treated her husband like a second-rate citizen after learning he would never be able to father a child."

"What about adoption?" Tony stared at the photograph. "Do you know if they discussed either that or artificial insemination?"

"I offered to give her money for either one. She refused and didn't say why." Sonny's shoulders began to shake. They left him sitting on the edge of a chair while they continued the search.

Zeller pulled Tony and Wade to one side. "I've talked to lots of neighbors."

"And?"

"And nothing. Everyone says the same. Patti was pleasant. Her husband was pleasant. No one knew them well. They didn't make noise, mow the yard too early in the morning, get drunk and have fights on the sidewalk. Nothing. Occasionally they had visitors. Pretty ordinary stuff."

"Thanks anyway," said Tony.

In the bedroom closet they found a small metal box containing her car title, house papers and a simple will. Everything was to be sold and the money donated to the Red Cross. No motive there. Charities were hungry, not murderous.

Zeller volunteered to stay with them or call for the forensic unit. There seemed to be no need. This was not the crime scene.

Patti had died in Silersville, in the museum trailer.

Even more subdued than before, Sonny directed them downtown.

Wade found a space on the street, parking near the office building where Patti had worked.

Sonny led the way as the three men walked into the reception area. A young woman behind the front desk wore a headset and seemed focused on the note she wrote in a book of phone messages, the kind that made pressure copies. She looked about twenty, with a magenta streak across the top of her black hair. A tight, low-cut aqua blouse displayed a fair amount of freckled chest and lacy black bra.

When she finished writing her note, she glanced up. The way her green eyes filled with tears as she jumped to her feet told Tony that Patti's father was not an unfamiliar visitor, and she knew Patti had died.

"Mr. Cochran. I'm so sorry about Patti." She trotted around her desk and threw her arms around the man. "We were all so concerned."

Tony felt a twinge of disappointment. He had hoped to break the news himself and see how her coworkers responded. He cleared his throat twice before he was able to gain her attention. She finally released the stranglehold she had on Sonny's neck.

"How did you find out?" asked Tony.

"I called Mr. Cochran last night. Patti hasn't been to work for several days." The receptionist looked from man to man to man. "Is it supposed to be a secret?"

"Not if you already know about it." Wade gave the girl a faint grin and was rewarded with a glowing one in return. "And your name is?"

"Hi, I'm Ann. Ann Bancroft, you know, like the actress." She rolled her shoulders forward and the blouse slipped a little lower in the front.

Tony thought she looked at Wade with the same expression of avid anticipation displayed by his golden retriever when she looked at a tennis ball. Daisy would start salivating the moment she spotted a ball and after chasing it for a while, would hide it under a bed. It made Tony wonder if his deputy was about to be attacked on the receptionist's desk or carried off to some dark corner.

Sonny's shoulders sagged. He glanced toward the outside door and then met Tony's eyes. "If you don't mind, Sheriff, I believe I'll take a cab and go back to the house and stay there until I can catch Muffin. When I get her, I'll rent a car to drive back home. I thought I could help, but I can't, I just can't stay." His voice cracked. "I need to leave now."

Seeing the glint of tears, Tony nodded. As soon as the older man left the office, the receptionist led the way, hips swaying in an exaggerated manner, down the hall to Patti's desk. There was little to see. It looked like a cross between a cubicle and a real office. It had walls and a door but little space inside. Two bucket chairs faced the functional faux-wood desk. A coat tree stood in one corner and a large fake plant filled another.

"Mr. Lyle, he's the owner, removed the office papers when she didn't come into work and didn't call. We were all worried." Ann rested her hands on the desktop and gave Wade a brave-but-sad smile. A tear, maybe real, sparkled on her cheek. "She's been depressed a lot lately, you know, what with her husband dying and then with breaking up with her boyfriend. Mr. Lyle went out to her house to make sure she wasn't, you know, wasn't . . . ."

"Yes, I do know," said Tony.

"Does he have a key to her house?" Wade asked.

Ann's mouth fell open and a scarlet blush climbed her freckled chest, moved up the sides of her neck and over her cheeks to her scalp. "Heavens, no!"

Tony smiled, watching her flustered response that seemed at odds with her lascivious smiles at Wade. In a blushing competition, she could out redden his aunt Martha. Maybe she was what his mother would call "forward." In any event, he thought this girl couldn't lie about the time of day. "Then how did he know she wasn't inside?"

For a moment Ann seemed totally bewildered. Then she gave a soft laugh and her eyes flooded with relief. "For a moment there, you had me wondering, too. He said that he looked through the windows in the garage door and her car was gone."

Tony's amusement ended as quickly as it arrived. At least her coworkers were concerned enough to find out the car was gone and the house was apparently empty.

The receptionist's eyes kept flickering past Tony and lingering on Wade. She studied his hands and her warm smile returned. Tony guessed it was the lack of a wedding ring that fueled her happy expression. "Take all the time you need. Don't forget, my name's Ann. I'd be happy to help you." Moving toward her desk, she left the door ajar.

Tony closed it.

It would probably take the pair of them about three seconds to check out Patti's office. It had as much personality as her house.

They gleaned nothing from their cursory examination of the office. Tony decided to send Wade out to the receptionist's desk while he made sure they hadn't missed anything. He wasn't above using Wade's movie-star looks to get information. "I believe if you happen to wander over near Ann's desk and give her your second-best smile, she'll tell you everything she knows about Patti—in private, of course."

"Of course." Wade flashed Tony a knowing grin. "Little details like who the boyfriend might be, or at least who fathered her baby."

"And any recent discussions about family members." Tony slapped him on the shoulder. "Especially chats including information about her half sister. Maybe she'll even know why Patti might want to drive up to Silersville to visit an unfinished museum after work had shut down for the day."

Wade ran a hand over his close-cropped black hair. "And you think I can accomplish that with only my second-best smile?"

Tony nodded. "Save your best one for your sweetheart." He didn't know who Wade was dating, he only guessed she supplied the recent addition of a small gold cross and medallion with some saint's face on it he'd seen dangling from a chain around Wade's neck. One thing was certain. Wade wasn't dating anyone in Park County. Ruth Ann would have learned about it the morning after their first date and posted the news on the bulletin board.

Wade didn't deny Tony's assumption. He didn't even try to pretend his looks didn't open doors or open the mouths of female witnesses. "Ann did look pretty desperate." A twinkle flashed in the deep blue, almost black, eyes. "Do I get hazardous duty pay?"

"Sure thing." Tony would give Wade anything he wanted if he could learn anything that shed some light on the case. "Next time Blossom bakes a pie for me, you get half."

Wade rolled his shoulders and flexed the muscles in his arms. "It's a deal."

CHAPTER TWENTY-SIX

Tony sat in Patti's chair and dug through her desk drawers. They were disappointing at best. There were no magazines, menus, scraps of paper with phone numbers. Not even an emergency chocolate stash. Did the woman have no interests, no life outside of watching her sister? So far, he hadn't found anything more personal than a few makeup items and a business card for the cat's veterinarian. He found no letters, no photographs, no souvenirs of any kind. His own desk drawers held the clutter of life, always needing to be cleaned out and sorted through. At least he had a life. He wasn't sure Patti'd had one.

What a waste.

He wondered briefly if Sonny had managed to catch the cat yet. The poor thing had to be hungry and anxious. Would it be welcomed into the Cochran house? Tony doubted it. Mrs. Sonny didn't strike Tony as the kind of woman who would welcome any further reminder of her husband's infidelities.

Tony sat in Patti's desk chair and stared at the polished surface as he waited for Wade's return. What had he expected to learn here?

Fifteen minutes passed. No Wade.

Finally, a half hour after he'd gone out to question Ann, Wade sauntered into the office and placed a paper bag on the desk. The fingers of his left hand pressed it against the glass surface. "I deserve a reward for hazardous duty. I want the whole pie."

"What did you have to do?" Tony tilted his head, trying to peek into the sack. He knew Wade hadn't done anything improper or immoral. His fingers itched to pull open the bag. He didn't. Wade had earned the right to tease him.

"I gave Ann my very best smile." A hint of mischief passed over Wade's face. "At least twice. Then I listened to her talk. And listened, and listened." He rolled his eyes. "She sure can talk."

"What do you have there?" Tony could feel his pulse race. If the expression on Wade's face could be trusted at all, he would gladly kiss the pie good-bye and much more.

"My new best friend Ann said she pulled this out of Patti's trash over a month ago. It seems Patti didn't mourn her late husband too long before she developed the boyfriend."

"No pie for no news." Tony narrowed his eyes. "Her pregnancy pretty much established that, wouldn't you say?"

"True." Wade waved aside Tony's statement. His eyes sparkled with excitement. "What we didn't know is the boyfriend dumped her before she miscarried. He didn't want any baby. He packed up and left town, claiming it probably wasn't even his."

"Was it?"

"Almost certainly. Ann claims that Patti only went out with the one guy. It was a grief/rebound relationship and it sounds like Ann and Patti were confidantes. Ann says the boyfriend dumped Patti over lunch on his way out of town. Patti ran into the office, crying and tossed his picture, frame and all, into the trash. After she left, Ann retrieved it and put it in the paper bag and stored it in her desk."

"Why?" Tony felt a surge of satisfaction and anticipation. He didn't need ESP. Wade's body language told him this would blow the case wide open.

"Ann said it was in case Patti changed her mind about him." A somber expression darkened Wade's face. "Before Ann could ask much, Patti miscarried."

"Oh, wow," said Tony.

"Exactly." Wade lifted his fingers from the bag. "Ann wanted to wait and see. If the boyfriend came back, she could return the picture to her friend, and if not, it was still a nice frame and she could always use it. At home."

"I presume said picture and frame are in there." Tony pointed to the bag.

"I haven't peeked." Without another word, Wade tipped the contents onto the desktop. A picture frame, made of cherry wood and constructed with simple clean lines, slid onto the desk.

The photograph inside the frame took their breath away. Smiling up at them from the desk was Patti and her boyfriend. A five-by-seven color picture captured not only Patti's radiant expression but also the face of the man standing with her. Tony recognized the smiling man whose arms were wrapped around her waist. Behind them was a sign welcoming visitors to Chickamauga Civil War Battlefield.

"Well, now, I'd say that changes everything we know about this case, wouldn't you?" said Tony.

Wade grinned as if he held the winning lottery ticket.

Tony suspected the expression on Wade's face wasn't because he had earned an apple pie baked by an expert. His bigger prize was the knowledge that he had cracked their investigation wide open, with a pair of smiles.

Of course, he did have to use his very best smiles.

NIGHT ON THE MOUNTAIN

CLUE #3

Construction A.

Place a 3 3/4″ square of Light #2 right side up on a flat surface. Arrange 4 of the Half Square triangles created in Clue #2 around it, placing a raw edge of the light triangle against the center square. Place a medium #2 square in each of the 4 corners. You should have a four-pointed star. It does not matter if the star turns right or left but be sure the star has four points before you sew the block together using 1/4″ seam. Look at it carefully—if any two points form a straight line, it's wrong.

Make six.

Construction B.

Place a 3 3/4″ square of Light #1, right side up on a flat surface. Arrange 4 of the squares with a light triangle corner constructed in Clue #2 around it, placing the raw edges of the light triangle against the center square. As above, place a Medium #2 square in each corner. Again, make sure your star has four points before sewing the block together.

Make six.

CHAPTER TWENTY-SEVEN

Theo stood with Jane and Martha at the museum site, a fine trickle of sweat tracing a line from the back of her neck to her waist. She stared at the cordoned trailer/office and wondered what the ladies hoped to accomplish today.

Work on their new museum stopped the day Patti's body was found and restarted after several days. Gus and crew stayed as far from the trailer/crime scene as they could. The framework for the reconstructed barn was finally complete and the men toiled, nailing the original boards onto the new skeleton. It required several pairs of hands to set each one properly. The trailer remained unusable, crime scene tape and seals keeping it off limits. The last time they'd asked him, Tony'd said he didn't know when they could get inside.

Until he made an arrest and Archie Campbell, the county prosecutor, and whoever the defense attorney would be, had a chance to go through all the evidence, the place would remain locked.

Determined to continue their project and unable to get into the trailer/office until some unknown date, the older women were forced to work from an even more makeshift office—the back seat of Martha's car. A friend offered them the use of her RV. Unfortunately, they wouldn't get it until the next day.

The car windows were rolled down and the doors were open, but conditions remained miserable. A pair of folding chairs and a card table served as their new reception area. Luckily, a large oak tree supplied much-appreciated shade. Unluckily, it appeared that the card table had been bombed by birds.

"You two want to explain why you're sitting out here supervising Gus, who's supervising the construction?" Theo dabbed at the back of her neck with a sodden tissue. "It doesn't make any sense and it's ghastly hot."

Busy spraying the bird residue with some cleaning product that relied on bleach as the main ingredient, Martha snorted. "That's what I think, too. But no, my partner in this enterprise," she said, pausing and glaring at her sister. "She seems to think if we are not out here to guard the donations, no one else will contribute."

"I just feel so responsible for what happened to the murder quilt. Those bloodstains are never going to come out." Jane opened a faded patio-type umbrella and tried to jam the base into the ground.

"I doubt a few more bloodstains are going to matter." Martha laughed without true amusement. "Plus, you don't want to take a chance of removing the original stains. What kind of display would a spotless 'murder quilt' make? People will pay to see blood."

Jane made a moaning sound in the back of her throat. "I don't care. The second Tony gives us the thumbs-up, I want to dash in there and get it soaking in cool water."

Theo didn't remind Jane there was most certainly a bigger mess inside than a few stains on an antique quilt. In fact, Theo had already talked to three different companies that claimed they could clean up biological messes and crime scenes. It wasn't going to be inexpensive and it wasn't going to be fast. Jane and Martha would probably be better off buying a new trailer and moving the artifacts.

Furthermore, Theo suspected the quilt in question wasn't even in the trailer. She guessed it was locked away in an evidence locker in the bowels of the law enforcement center. It might even have been sent away to a laboratory. She would ask Tony before saying anything.

For the moment, Jane seemed to have forgotten how Patti had bled out on their floor. And the murder weapon was one of their donated artifacts. And the construction of the new building and reconstruction of the antique barn were costing more every day.

Theo saw no sense in reminding her mother-in-law of the reality of their problems.

Tony's arrival distracted her.

When Tony pulled into the museum parking area, he groaned. He wasn't exactly surprised to see his wife, aunt and mother together at the museum site. Why would he ever expect it any other way? Life was never easy.

He was not delighted to see them.

They all looked quite pleased to see him, however. Happy smiles greeted him and he felt like an old grump as he approached. "What are the three of you doing out here?"

What he meant of course was "Why don't you go away?"

Some of his feelings must have shown on his face because Theo stared at him for a moment, her eyes widening behind the dark lenses clipped to her glasses. With a smile, she tipped her head to one side, inquiry etched on her sweet face. "Shouldn't we be here?"

Tony didn't answer. There wasn't a good answer so he watched as Gus headed toward them, moving at a leisurely pace. Behind him, Tony saw Quentin handing Mac and Kenny some tool he didn't recognize. Nothing he saw made him think construction during a heat wave was a rational business to get in to. Quentin's T-shirt was soaked with sweat, making it stick to his skinny frame. He probably hadn't worked this hard the rest of his life put together. Mac and Kenny wore abbreviated T-shirts, cut-off jeans, work boots, ball caps and bandanas tied around their necks. They were covered with dirt, making it hard to distinguish where the tan ended and the dirt began.

"Hey there, baby brother," said Gus. A wide smile creased his face. "What brings you out to our mess? Going to take down your yellow tape any time soon?" He gestured toward the trailer still festooned with miles of yellow plastic.

Tony sensed no real impatience on his brother's part. Murder had been committed and Gus would wait with great good humor until Tony released the crime scene. "It shouldn't be much longer. Archie will want to go over the evidence before we release it. I expect him to swing by later today."

"Archie? So you're ready to bring in our fearless prosecutor?" Gus lightly punched Tony's arm and feigned a broken hand. "Does this mean you've solved the case?"

"I have. Actually, Wade did." Tony couldn't keep the smile from his face. "I hate disorder in my county the same way you hate it when someone borrows a hammer and leaves it on the ground."

Gus shuddered at the comparison. "That's no laughing matter."

Wade arrived in his patrol car, parking crossways, blocking the driveway. Instead of climbing out, he lowered his window and remained inside, talking on his cell phone.

"Do me a favor, Gus." Tony leaned closer so only his brother could hear his words.

Gus nodded, his expression wary.

Although Tony kept the genial expression pasted on his face, his focus was not on his brother. "Your truck's not blocked. Take the ladies for a drive will you?"

"Where? For how long?"

Tony pretended to talk about trivia, not changing his expression. He lowered his voice so the words didn't travel farther than Gus's ears. "I need them out of the way. It'll only take a few minutes. I can't be worrying about them, or you."

The pupils of Gus's eyes contracted and Tony knew he understood.

Gus shook his head, his expression comically morose. Speaking in a fairly natural tone, he was careful to keep his eyes away from Tony's sidearm. "I guess I lost our bet, huh?"

"Of course." Tony grinned and slapped Gus on the shoulder. In a voice loud enough for the women to hear, he announced Gus's punishment for a lost bet was springing for pie and coffee at Ruby's. "I feel like chess pie today. Get me a slice in a go box, will you?"

Gus nodded as he moved the women toward his pickup with gentle determination. "Theo, if you'll move your van."

Theo shot a quick glance at the silver-blue minivan partially blocking Gus's truck and slipped her keys into her hand. "I'll lead the way to Ruby's and go on back to my shop after pie."

Tony thought there were definite advantages to having a smart wife. Her reward was a grateful grin.

"Aren't you coming with us, Tony?" Jane almost reached Gus's four-door pickup when she turned back. Without breaking his stride, Gus turned to collect her.

Tony sighed. Leave it to his mom to complicate any situation. He told the only lie that would work. "I'm going into your trailer. I really don't think you want to be here or see that."

Jane's eyes flickered to the trailer and she stopped. Somewhat paler, she let Gus help her into the big pickup.

Tony rested his fists on his hips and watched until Gus managed to get her settled on the passenger seat. He could only hope his brother would lock the door before she could change her mind and bolt again.

The moment the pickup moved out of sight, Tony headed for

the trailer. Wade joined him. They stood outside the broken door and stared hard at it, almost willing it to tell them what had happened. Whoever broke the latch didn't need much strength, just a crowbar and a bit of determination.

Tony spoke softly, his words meant only for his deputy's ears. "Where do you suppose the car is?"

Wade adjusted his sunglasses and glanced around. "If I didn't want to drive it away, it has to be around here."

"My guess is he drove it the other direction instead of heading for the road." They strolled around the outside of the trailer, checking the windows. "We were so certain the body was Doreen's, we didn't really search this area very well."

Tony noticed three pairs of curious eyes following their every move. Kenny, Mac and Quentin hadn't moved from their earlier positions.

Tony surreptitiously loosened his sidearm. This wasn't the OK Corral. On the other hand, their prey wasn't exactly helpless. He didn't know the range of a nail gun or even if it was possible to shoot nails like they did in the movies, and he wasn't interested in finding out. "Make your way around to the other side." Tony watched Wade move off before he ambled toward the three workers. He smiled. He hoped it looked more natural than it felt.

"Sheriff?" Quentin spoke loud enough to startle a pair of nearby birds. They flew into another tree and scolded the men.

"Quentin." Tony thought Quentin looked like a rabbit about to bolt. The teeth hanging over his lower lip did nothing to contradict this assessment. Some of the damage caused by his meth addiction would not improve, like his teeth. At least his skin seemed to be clearing up. Scarlet from heat and exertion, Quentin's face dripped. His hands trembled as he untied his bandana and used it to wipe off some of the moisture. With hands as shaky as those, Tony thought, he'd be hard pressed to keep water in a cup. Even though he smelled bad, for a change it was the aroma of sweat and not chemicals. "Hot enough for you?"

Quentin said, "It ain't been this miserable in a long time."

Tony nodded. He looked at the other men. "While Gus is away, I've got a couple more questions."

"Sure thing," said Kenny. His Adam's apple moved under his skin like he was having a spasm and his eyes moved constantly, never quite meeting Tony's gaze. He couldn't have looked more guilty if he'd tied a sign around his neck that read, "I've been very bad."

Staring into Kenny's face, Tony wondered what bothered his conscience.

"Time to hit the water bucket again," said Mac. He turned away and moved toward the big yellow water container sitting on a thick board straddling a pair of sawhorses. He didn't stop there but headed for his truck. Not quite running, he was traveling fast.

"Mac, stop." Wade's voice carried across the construction site. The chattering birds fell silent.

Mac ignored the command. Increasing his speed, he vaulted over a pile of debris.

Tony's fleeting glance at Quentin and Kenny revealed their absolute confusion. They seemed frozen in place. With his left hand, Tony pulled his handcuffs from his belt and with his right he slipped his gun free. "Get down."

Quentin and Kenny didn't have to be told twice. The pair dropped to the ground like stones, their arms wrapped around their heads.

Wade fired.

The bullet slammed into the dirt, inches from Mac's flying feet. That was all it took. Mac stopped and raised his hands above his head. He didn't move a muscle until Tony's handcuffs locked his wrists together behind his back. At the click of the second bracelet, Mac's shoulders drooped and his head fell forward.

Tony read him his rights as they walked to Wade's vehicle. Within seconds, Mac was locked inside and on his way to the jail.

When Tony turned around he saw Quentin still stretched out on the ground, his skinny arms wrapped around his head. He shivered. Next to him, Kenny wasn't looking much better. Although the gravel under his bare skin had to be cutting into him, he seemed not to notice it. Tony touched Kenny's side with the toe of his boot. "You two can get up now, but don't go anywhere."

Kenny pulled his knees up under his chest and squatted, his weight balanced on the balls of his feet.

Tony used his cell phone and called Rex. The dispatcher sounded a little miffed he hadn't been able to hear anything on the radio. "Send Sheila and Mike over here."

"Nobody tells me a thing, Sheriff, I'm supposed to be on top of this stuff and you like to keep me in the dark." Rex whined. "What's going on?"

"No, Rex, I'm not hiding from you. I just hate it when people with scanners pick up everything that's going on. We're not running a damned home entertainment service."

"I can't get you help if I don't know what's happening."

"You're right." Tony realized that he had done a stupid thing, cutting Rex out of the loop. Luckily he and Wade had been able to handle the situation. "I'm sorry. It won't happen again."

"Okay, okay, I get it." Rex still sounded aggravated. "Sheila and Mike are on their way. Sheila sounded like she is practically on your doorstep now."

Sure enough, by the time Tony disconnected the call, Sheila had parked her car where Wade's had just been. "What's up?"

"We've arrested Mac for the death of Patti Yager."

"Wow!" Sheila glanced around the construction area and looked carefully at Quentin and Kenny. "I trust you'll fill me in later."

Tony nodded. "How were you at Easter Egg hunts?"

"My basket was always full." She smiled at him and poked a loose strand of blond hair back into its braid. "I suspect we're not looking for old eggs."

"By now, we'd be able to smell an old egg. This is bigger."

Sheila peered at him over the top of her sunglasses. "Let me guess, Mrs. Yager's car?"

"Yep." He glanced over her head and saw Mike arriving. When the two deputies were standing together, out of earshot of the remaining construction crew, he told them about the earlier arrest. "If I hadn't been distracted by the Doreen misidentification, we would have done this earlier. Let's see what we can find."

They each headed in a different direction. Dense undergrowth and encroaching kudzu made it impossible to see clearly for more than several feet. Carefully checking for tire tracks and broken vegetation, they worked their way deeper into the brush. The construction vehicles had churned up a lot of the area. Their search churned up an array of biting insects.

"I've got it." The vegetation muffled Sheila's voice and then finding her became the challenge. "I almost missed it."

Tony moved to stand directly behind her and still didn't see it, even with her lifting a thick kudzu vine and pointing out the direction. At last his eyes adjusted to the low light and he focused on the dark green car trunk. Weeds and tall grasses shielded the tires and bumper. "Good work, Sheila. No wonder you filled your basket."

"Thanks, boss." Slapping an insect on her neck, Sheila pushed the vine she held in her other hand over to Mike. "I'm going back for the camera. If I'm not back in two minutes, we might have to play a little Marco Polo."

CHAPTER TWENTY-EIGHT

Tony couldn't believe hiking in the jungles of South America would be worse. It felt like a claustrophobic's nightmare underneath the canopy of vegetation. There seemed to be no available oxygen. Hot and humid, the organic cave sucked the air from their lungs and the moisture from their pores. Within minutes, sweat ran in rivulets down his back and dripped off his face. A glance at his deputies showed they were just as miserable. Sweat darkened their chocolate-brown uniform shirts making them appear black. Looking more like paint than cloth, the shirts clung to the bodies wearing them, outlining their protective vests.

"Miserable" didn't quite cover the situation.

"Where's Wade?" Sheila pressed her face against her sleeve, wiping the sweat from her eyes before she returned to taking photographs. "I'd hate for him to miss all this fun because he's somewhere busy flirting with Mike's fiancée."

"Ruby's not interested in a pretty boy like that." Mike shifted his grip on the kudzu vine he held out of Sheila's way. "Can't we just cut this damned thing? It'll grow back before morning."

"Just a few more photographs, okay?" said Sheila.

Tony wasn't sure if that was a question to him or a statement addressed to Mike. He spoke into his radio. "Rex, if Wade's done with his delivery mission, tell him I need him out here pronto to do his fingerprint thing. You can also tell him he'll enjoy this one. No blood."

Rex's reply began with a shout of laughter loud enough for all to hear, then he moved on to his report. "The suspect is locked up where I can keep an eye on him."

"Hey, Rex?" Tony said. "Have Wade bring us some bottles of cold water. Big bottles."

"You got it."

Watching from their comparatively pleasant occupation of holding the vegetation away from the car, Tony and Mike and Sheila offered countless words of encouragement to their comrade. Wade bent over the car, twirling fingerprint powder on the car door. If anything, it was getting hotter with the afternoon sun pouring through gaps in the canopy. Wade's suggestion they tow the car out first and then he'd lift prints fell on sympathetic ears.

"No can do." Tony shook his head. "Frank and Joe Thomas can't hook up a tow cable without running their greasy hands over every last inch of a car and you know it. It's nothing conscious; they just like to touch cars."

What Wade said in response was muffled, which was probably just as well. Tony doubted it was something he'd want to hear. He grinned at his other deputies. "At least we didn't have to glove up. It makes my hands sweat just thinking about it."

Wiping her dripping face against her already sweat-soaked shirt sleeve, Sheila started to giggle. "By the time he finishes, he's going to have prune fingers." She lifted a bottle of cold water to her lips.

Tony heard the sound of the garage's truck arrive with a heavy-duty winch and a flatbed trailer. He went out to explain what he needed. Stepping into the sunlight was a shock. Even as hot as it was, it felt at least twenty degrees cooler than it did in the shade.

★　★　★　★　★

Theo left the ladies and Gus lingering over their pie at Ruby's Café. Her mind churned, moving from questions about Tony's actions at the museum site to her own need to get the boys from day camp and the ever-present question of what to have for dinner. She drove to her quilt shop and parked in the front, knowing she wouldn't be there for more than a few minutes.

Theo inhaled deeply, needing to relax just a bit, and noticed a sour smell coming from the back of the minivan. Wondering which boy left something to mold or die under the seat, she frowned and added an item to her mental shopping list. Time to get a new air freshener. Extra strength.

She climbed from the van and paused on the sidewalk, glancing at her watch. The boys would be done at day camp in half an hour. Luckily, she didn't plan to stay long at the shop, just check to make sure no one needed her.

Between the boys' baseball practices and games, Tony's work schedule and hers, it felt like weeks since the whole family had sat down to eat at the same time. Although she knew it hadn't been very long, Theo liked having dinner with her family. She loved the commotion. The boys would wiggle and spill and Daisy would lurk under the table waiting for fallen snacks. Tony would tell them silly stories and corny jokes.

When Theo was a little girl, she had dreamed of such chaos. Her grandmother placed the food on the table. Her grandfather would read a long Bible passage, say grace and then the three of them ate in silence. If it hadn't been for the books she smuggled into the house from the library, she would never have dreamed life was different in other families. Although she had often been invited to Nina's home for dinner, she was never allowed to go.

"Miz Theo?"

A man's voice boomed into her head. Theo gasped and spun around. Claude Marmot grinned and sidled closer until his face stopped only inches from hers. It suddenly struck her that under the swagger and layers of dirt was an attractive man. His terrible teeth gave him the rodent appearance. Claude could stand to lose a few pounds but he wasn't grossly overweight. A larger shirt would cover the hairy belly and if he shaved off the constant stubble, his face would be better than average. His hair was thick and dark with golden highlights. A little shampoo and elbow grease should make it gleam. She considered it patently unfair he was blessed with long, thick eyelashes that every woman of her acquaintance would kill for. Those lashes shaded clear, dark eyes that glimmered with intelligence and a hint of mischief.

"Can I help you, Claude?"

"Yes, ma'am, I do hope so." He shifted from side to side and his eyes flickered to the ground and up.

Theo stared at him, waiting for his next comment. In all her years, Theo had never seen Marmot-the-Varmint without his customary self-confidence. She prompted him. "What do you need?"

Hesitant, Claude idly scratched the portion of his bare stomach left exposed by the short, rattyatty orange T-shirt. "I was wondering, that is, if I paid you, that is, if it's not too much, that is, would you make a quilt for my fiancée? You know, as a kind of welcome present?"

"Fiancée?" So, a rumor she'd heard in the shop was true. Claude had sent for a mail-order bride. "When's the wedding? How much time would I have?"

"Maybe two weeks, maybe three months." A rumble like thunder shook the air as Claude laughed.

Another first, Theo thought. Claude wasn't prone to outbursts of merriment, usually spending more time complaining than working.

"She don't get here till Wednesday next."

For one insane moment, Theo ignored the work involved and actually considered the idea. "I'm sorry. I would like to, I'm afraid I just don't have that kind of time."

His crestfallen expression compelled her to suggest an alternate plan. "If you like, I'll ask my quilting group." She thought surely each of the "bowlers" would pitch in and make a few quilt blocks and the group quilting on the frame in the shop made quilts for charity. A monetary donation from Claude would get the thing finished in next to no time. "I think something can be arranged."

A burst of honking horns brought her into the present. At least ten cars were blocked by Claude's converted car/truck. He ignored the noise. "That would be great, Miz Theo."

"I, uh, you'd better unclog the road before there's a riot, and I need to go pick up my boys. We can talk about this later. You know, discuss colors and sizes." As she spoke a tourist, a middle-aged man in hideous plaid shorts, climbed down from his pickup and strode toward them. His face was purple and steam seemed to rise from his whole body.

"Somebody better move that piece of crap." The tourist pointed at the car/truck. "It's probably not legal to even have it on the street."

Claude nodded and ambled toward his vehicle. The tourist's attitude produced the effect Theo expected. Claude made a production of inspecting each tire and every inch of the car/truck before he yawned widely and climbed behind the wheel. He took his time starting the vehicle.

Theo was surprised the mollified tourist managed to drive away—without having a stroke.

Theo abandoned her plan to go into the shop. Her mind filled with the news of Marmot-the-Varmint's upcoming nuptials, she stepped off the sidewalk, headed for the minivan. She always liked to give herself a few extra moments of leeway when it was time to pick up the boys. Surprised at the speed of passing time, she realized day camp would be over in fifteen minutes. It should only take two minutes to drive there, unfortunately, just because the minivan ran minutes ago, there was no guarantee it would start now. If it didn't, she would use the extra time to walk over and meet the boys.

She stared at the silver-blue menace. It was unlocked, as usual, because the lock on the driver's door broke over a year ago. To lock it required pushing the button on the door and climbing over the console and out the passenger door. Getting in again required the process in reverse. There was never anything of value inside the van. Not even a moron would steal it, but she could dream. In her rosiest thoughts, it would simply disappear, removed from her life by providence. If it was stolen or wrecked, their insurance company wouldn't pay. It wasn't worth carrying anything more than liability coverage.

Theo felt as if she'd reached the breaking point. If it failed to start one more time, she might just borrow one of Tony's guns and put it out of her misery. She could be a news item, "Sheriff's wife kills car."

With a honk and jaunty wave, Claude and his car/truck vanished around the corner.

She returned the wave, then squeezed past a shiny red motorcycle as big as a car, and climbed into her minivan. It was hot inside, as only a closed car in a heat wave could be, so Theo left her door open for air. Gasping for breath, she turned the key, and the engine shuddered and started. The moment she was sure it wouldn't die, Theo hit the button to lower the window. It stopped halfway down. That, too, had become normal.

Knowing the Abernathys' budget limitation, the Thomas brothers had checked out several used vans for them. So far they fell into three groups, "too expensive," "needs work" and

Theo's favorite: "Why buy someone else's problem?"

The air conditioner rumbled into action, spewing tepid air. It was definitely cooler than the outside air, now it smelled like rotting garbage. Not only was her nemesis unreliable, it was starting to stink more and more by the second. Instead of its usual dog and boy smells with an overtone of dead skunk, it smelled like rotting food mixed with heavy perfume.

Maybe some critter had climbed into the undercarriage and died and the sweltering heat had rotted it. The swirling air coming from the vents circulated the vile results.

She backed out of her parking spot and put the van into "drive."

"Let's go to your house, shall we?" A whispery voice came from behind her, sending a wave of warmer fetid air over her.

Something poked into Theo's neck. It was cold and metal and smelled of gunpowder. About its use, there was not a shadow of a doubt in her mind. It could only be the barrel of a gun. It didn't matter that she couldn't see anything from the corner of her eye. Theo didn't move.

Chapter Twenty-Nine

"Now." The voice from behind her vibrated with anger.

"Home?" Theo's brain couldn't seem to process the word. "Where's home?"

"Stupid woman." The muffled voice grew louder. "Your home."

Adrenaline surged through Theo. Although her pulse raced, she turned her head a fraction of an inch toward her shoulder. It was enough. Now, she could identify the object poking her. She knew enough about handguns to recognize the barrel of a revolver pressed to the tender flesh under her chin. It was big, at least a .38 caliber, maybe even larger. Inside the cylinder, dark gray lead caught the light, proving to her the revolver was loaded. Tiny spots danced before her eyes.

"If you want your family to live, drive." The person in the back seat pressed the barrel deeper. "Carefully. Don't try to attract any attention."

Theo drove steadily toward her house, her mind racing as fast as her heartbeat, to no avail. Not a single halfway decent idea came to her. She turned left onto their short street. On the right side were three houses before a dead end at the creek. Theirs was the last house. The neighbors probably weren't home.

To the left was the park. This side of the park was deserted; picnic tables and the playground were at the other end. Theo slowed, waiting for instructions.

"Park in the street, next to the curb."

Theo complied. What else could she do? At least the boys were safe. No one would be home.

"We're going inside. Bring your keys and purse."

More fetid air. Whoever was behind her needed breath mints. Bile rose in her throat. Theo swallowed it and opened her door. The person with the gun climbed between the front seats and followed her closely, never moving the gun barrel away from her. Theo turned her head a fraction. Her mouth fell open.

Icky Vicky Parker held the revolver.

"Vicky? Why are you doing this?" Theo could barely form the words. Nothing made any sense.

"Inside." Vicky walked close to her, prodding her with the gun. If anyone spotted them, their demeanor would not seem abnormal.

Together the women went into the silent house. Daisy met them at the front door. The golden retriever's plumed tail wagged softly. After a quick doggy kiss on Theo's hand, she stared at Vicky and backed away. Her eyes never left Vicky as she emitted a low rumble, not quite a growl. Theo was surprised. The golden retriever loved everyone.

"Get away from me." Vicky kicked at Daisy.

The big dog snarled, displaying a formidable set of teeth. Theo feared Vicky would shoot the family pet, so she made soothing sounds and pushed her away. "Daisy, sit."

"Get a piece of paper." Vicky spoke in her normal voice.

"What kind?" Theo tried to envision a way out. For a moment she considered just turning and punching Vicky. She ignored her impulse. That was suicidal. Daisy would either help or make things worse. She couldn't take the chance.

"Don't be stupid. You're going to write a note. I don't give a shit what you write it on." Vicky glanced around the entryway before pushing Theo down the hall and into the kitchen.

Theo couldn't think of a way to stall or hide the notepad on the counter next to the phone. It was a wide roll of adding machine tape in an oddly shaped holder. Chris made it in Cub Scouts. Tears flooded Theo's eyes as she reached for the attached pen. Vicky dictated her message, watching to make sure Theo didn't write anything else on the paper.

Vicky smiled. "Put it on the table along with your cell phone."

Theo followed her instructions.

"Give me your cash and put the purse in the trash." Her little rhyme amused Vicky and she repeated it several times, laughing after each time.

If Theo had thought Vicky was crazy before, she knew for certain now. She hurried, following Vicky's instructions. The wallet held less than ten dollars. When Vicky reached for the cash, Theo lifted her eyes, looking at the clock on the microwave. Day camp was over. The boys would be looking for her. Maybe they had already called Tony. What if they were walking toward the house? Theo felt an icy chill and shuddered as she dropped her purse in the trash.

"Let's go." Vicky jabbed the barrel of her gun into Theo's back. "Walk out the back door like nothing is unusual."

Theo led the way. The moment she reached for the knob, Daisy began pacing in circles, barking again. It was the dog's usual behavior when she wanted to go out, Vicky wouldn't know what she wanted. "Not now, Daisy." Theo tried to sound natural. It wasn't working. Her voice was barely more than a squeaky whisper.

"Make it shut up." Vicky waved the gun. "Now."

Theo grabbed Daisy by the collar and wrestled the big dog away from the door. Once she and Vicky were outside and the door almost closed, Theo released her. Daisy began barking in earnest. At least she was safe. Unless Daisy jumped through a window, she would be there to greet the boys.

Theo felt the gun rub against her spine as they walked into the yard. A series of sharp pokes, rather than words, directed Theo across the grass and toward the creek. Like two old friends off for a walk, they moved without haste along the path. When they reached the next block with houses, Theo could see Vicky's parked car. The homes in this part of town were all old and set on large lots with mature trees, making efficient spying on the neighbors impossible. Even if someone should see them from an upstairs window, there was nothing suspicious in their behavior.

What was Vicky planning? Terror made Theo's stomach clench and she paused, bending over to throw up, accidentally scraping her face against an overgrown japonica bush. The vicious thorns ripped a red metallic thread from her patchwork vest.

Vicky laughed and prodded Theo unnecessarily, and none too gently, with the gun barrel. She reached into her pocket and dragged out the car keys. "You drive."

Theo knew she should resist. She should scream. She should fight. Climbing into the car with a crazy person was stupid. She did it anyway.

"Too bad we can't stay to watch the show." Vicky glanced over her shoulder in the direction of Theo's house. She leaned close and whispered, "I think it's going to be lots of fun, don't you?" She lit a cigarette and blew smoke into Theo's face.

Theo gagged, exaggerating the sound and pressed the button, lowering the window.

"Don't you dare puke in my car." Vicky's spittle landed on Theo's arm.

"I need air." Theo had a plan now. Whether or not it would work, she wouldn't give up.

Vicky jabbed a fingernail into Theo's rib. "Turn right here."

Theo shivered and drove carefully, following Vicky's instructions. As they left the town limits, headed toward the mountains, theirs seemed to be the only car on the road.

CHAPTER THIRTY

Tony waited at the table in the "greenhouse," the interview room named for the bright lights and beige-tiled walls and floor. A drain set in the center of the floor completed the comparison.

Ruth Ann once claimed it would be perfect for growing things like African violets. Today, nothing as lovely as a flower passed through his thoughts.

Tony wrapped his laced fingers around the back of his neck and leaned his head against them. Marshaling his thoughts, he waited for Patti's killer and his attorney to arrive. The photograph Wade obtained that morning was still in the paper bag, resting on the top of the file.

Mac and Carl Lee Cashdollar, his attorney, entered the tiny room. The two men sat, elbow to elbow, across from Tony. No one smiled. Mac stared at the paper bag, showing no sign of curiosity.

Wade checked the recorders. Satisfied that everything worked as intended, he remained standing next to the closed door.

"Is this you?" Ever so slowly, Tony lifted the bag and let the framed photograph slide onto the table. Mac's eyes focused on the action. Tony could see in them a flash of pain and then nothing but despair, the moment Mac recognized himself standing with his arms wrapped around the deceased woman.

"Yes."

"Did you kill her?"

"Yes."

Carl Lee whispered something into his client's ear but Mac shrugged it away. The game was clearly over. It was confession time. The attorney frowned. The decision was not his and he surrendered. His mournful blue eyes met Tony's. "Might as well get my esteemed colleague, our prosecutor, down here."

Tony made the call, relieved to learn Archie was available. Only minutes passed before the redheaded man charged into the room, briefcase in hand.

"Start from the beginning, Mac." Tony made himself as comfortable as possible in the small room filled with his deputy, the suspect, two lawyers and himself. The place was taking on claustrophobic dimensions. Archie was the smallest of the five and he wasn't exactly tiny. "You met Patti in Chattanooga?"

"Yeah. She was nice, you know, and I thought we had a good thing going. Food, fun, sex—you know, no strings, no commitment."

"Did you know her husband had recently died?"

"Yeah. She was pretty broken up by his death and all, but still wanted to have some fun." Mac curled his fingers into fists and rested them on the table. "Maybe I'm not the hero type, I'm not a bad guy, either. I don't mess with kids or married women." His shoulders rose and fell as he shifted on the uncomfortable chair. "I was married once and didn't much care for it. My wife was okay. Too bad she brought along her folks, her sisters and her friends. Every damned one of them wanted a piece of me. I felt like I was hacked to death with a paring knife. When our divorce was final, I swore I would never marry again."

"Did Patti know your feelings?"

"Oh, yeah. When we met, she was fun, sexy, not looking for a relationship. She said she couldn't get pregnant. I was a fool and believed her." Mac scraped a chip of mud from one of his knuckles onto his shorts. "Looking back, I think she was just looking for a stud to father a baby. When she told me she was pregnant, she said it was a miracle. A miracle? Hardly!" His eyes searched Tony's as if looking for understanding. An angry flush stained his neck. "I doubt she even liked me very much. I didn't have a prestigious job or anything. Suddenly she wanted to get married and swore we'd live happily ever after."

Tony felt a grudging sympathy for the man. His story was not rare. In this case the result was disastrous for everyone involved. "You ran?"

"Like the weasel she accused me of being." Shaking his head, Mac slid down on the base of his spine. "I didn't want any part of her family plans."

"Do you know how she found you?" Wade asked.

"No." Mac's confusion was obvious. "I did wonder."

Wade showed him a newspaper clipping found on the front seat of Patti's car. "She saw your photograph in the *Silersville Gazette*."

"Is that how? I thought maybe she'd hired a private detective to track me down and make me do the decent thing." He scrubbed his temples with the heels of his hands.

Tony felt a surge of impatience. He wanted the whole business cleaned up and closed. "Tell us what happened at the trailer. Was it your idea to meet her out there?"

"Hell, no." Mac leaned forward in his chair and rested his elbows on the cold steel table. "I went to the Okay with the guys for a beer after work. Then I left for my girlfriend Allison's place. The shortcut between the two takes me right past the work site."

"What time was this?" Tony watched as Wade wrote the information in his notes.

"Almost seven." Mac's eyes moved to his wrist as if he was checking an invisible watch.

"So, how long after you left the Okay did you drive past the museum?"

"Maybe five minutes."

That sounded about right to Tony. "Why did you stop?"

Mac gave a half shrug. "I was almost past it when I saw Patti's car parked out there. I recognized it, all right. She's needed to have it painted for as long as I've known her." Shaking his head in either disgust or despair, he paused. "If I'd kept on driving, nothing would have happened."

"So what did happen?"

"I pulled in and parked next to her car. I glanced around and didn't see her anywhere. Then I looked at the trailer door, it was ajar. The whole hasp had been pried off and dropped on the ground, discarded like a piece of junk." Mac looked directly into Tony's eyes. "That pissed me off. If it weren't for that, I might have just walked inside and told her to leave, or gotten back in my car and gone to Allison's. Your mom and aunt have been real good to me, always smiling and bringing cookies and iced tea out there and Gus ain't a bad guy to work for neither. He's fair and pays regular, you know."

Tony nodded.

"I jerked the door open and got one foot inside when Patti went ballistic. It was a nightmare. She came at me like a wild animal. I didn't know what she was doing there, and she couldn't have been expecting to find me inside a locked trailer. I never heard anyone talk like that, much less a lady. The way she was carrying on about my causing her to lose our baby and something about the quilts belonging to her and not Doreen, and man, oh man, I don't know what all she said. She was chattering a mile a minute and none of it made any sense to me. Then she made this screeching sound that made my hair stand on end. I never heard anything like that before." He squeezed the edge of the table with his fingertips until they were bloodless, gripping it like a lifeline. "All of a sudden she jumped at me, her fingers like this." Mac released the table long enough to form claws with his hands. "I was afraid she'd rip my eyes out."

"What happened next?" Tony could guess. He needed to hear it from Mac.

"I reached behind me and picked up the first thing I could wrap my hand around and swung it, hoping to scare her so she'd let me go." His face paled and his eyes roamed sightlessly around the room. "Next thing I knew, I looked down and she was lying there like some broken doll. Her eyes. Oh, God, her eyes were wide open, staring right at me over that evil-looking thing I hit her with, I didn't mean to do it, you know."

Tony heard an ominous gagging sound and pushed the empty paper bag across the table.

Mac grabbed it and opened it but took a deep breath instead of throwing up.

Tony glanced down and focused on a color photograph that had been under the bag. It was the initial photograph taken at the scene. Patti's body with its hideous neck wound and staring eyes drew everyone's attention. It was almost as awful as seeing it in person must have been. He heard Wade shifting positions behind him, and wondered if Wade might need a barf bag as well.

Mac composed himself, continuing to hold the unused bag. "What was that thing? At first I thought it was a scrub brush. Then I saw how it stuck in her neck and I ran outside to throw up."

"So you killed her by accident," said Carl Lee, not looking at his client. He stared at the sheriff and prosecutor.

"I believe that's possible," said Tony. "That was serious enough." His eyes locked with Mac's. "Then you covered it up. If it really was an accident, why'd you try to cover it up instead of calling it in?" Tony stared at Mac, torn between anger and understanding.

"I did try to hide it." Mac scrubbed his face again with the heels of his hands. "What would you do? I knew no one would believe it was an accident, so I drove her car as deep into the brush as I could and then sort of fluffed the vines up behind me as I left." Mac lifted his shoulders and let them fall. "It was stupid. My brain was scrambled. I remember thinking I didn't need to hide her body. Then I thought if I did, I'd have time to sort everything out. I needed time."

Wade placed a pen and a stack of paper on the table. "Just write it down the way you remember it."

Mac nodded. He sat for a long time staring at the blank paper. As if operating without his input, his fingers flipped the ballpoint pen end over end. Finally, he released a deep sigh and began to write.

Tony's cell phone rang, playing the calypso tune that signaled Theo's phone. He stepped out of the greenhouse to take the call. "What's up?"

"D-daddy?" Reedy and high-pitched, the voice belonged to Jamie. The fear in the little boy's voice chilled him to the bone. Tony had often heard the expression. Now he knew such a sensation was possible. Jamie snuffled into the phone and Tony knew he was crying.

A flare of panic shot through him. "What's wrong, son?" He forced himself to concentrate on calming the boy and not on any of the million possibilities ranging from funny to tragic. All of Jamie's emergencies weighed as equals to the six-year-old.

"Where's Mommy?" A juicy sob followed his question. "We can't find her."

Mommy? Tony's hand tightened on his phone. He signaled for Wade to come to the greenhouse door and pointed a finger at Mac. "Lock him up. I've got to go."

He didn't wait for a response from his deputy before he began running toward his parking bay. Jamie hadn't called Theo "Mommy" since he started school, saying it was for babies. Tony also knew Theo. His wife always kept her phone close. Knowing that Jamie had the phone, and that he wasn't with Theo, sent a shock of something close to panic through his veins. His gut twisted.

He struggled to make his voice calm. "Where are you, Jamie?"

Tony jumped into the Blazer before the answer arrived. He felt his heart rate increase as he waited, hearing only whispers of sound. Finally the boy answered.

"We're at home."

"We? Is Chris with you?" Tony felt a loosening of the vise clamped around his chest. The boys were smart. If not exactly streetwise, they weren't goofy, either. Six-year-old Jamie was a take-charge kind of kid and frequently pushed his older brother aside.

"Yes."

"Can I talk to him for a minute?"

Rustling and static preceded Chris's voice. "Mom never came to get us from day camp." More static almost covered his words. "We walked home."

Like his younger brother, Chris sounded scared.

"I'm on my way." Tony's brain ran through a list of possibilities. None were good. Even on what Theo called her "brainfree" days, she was a dedicated, protective mother. Tourist season with its influx of strangers passing through the town only increased her vigilance. He forced himself to sound calmer than he felt. "Where did you find your mom's phone?"

"On the kitchen table with a note to call you. She didn't put the face on it." Chris began to hiccup. "Daddy, where's Mommy?"

"I'm not sure." Tony pressed harder on the accelerator and flipped on the light bar but not the siren. His wife always signed personal notes with a drawing of a face surrounded by curly hair. If someone else wrote the note, they'd probably sign her name. If she wrote the note herself, leaving off the drawing was a clear distress signal. "I'm almost home. Get your brother and Daisy and go outside and wait for me in the front."

"Okay." Chris hiccupped again, gulping air, and disconnected.

Tony dropped his phone into his shirt pocket. Imagining the little boys' terror, he drove faster, praying as he made the turn onto their street.

At first, he didn't see the boys. Theo's unreliable silver-blue minivan sat in front of the house. Seeing it there meant nothing. Several times in the past few weeks she had abandoned it in various places and walked to meet the boys or called him to do it.

The Blazer skidded to a stop. Tony released his pent-up breath the moment he spotted the boys and dog clumped together behind a bush. His car door wasn't fully open when the boys and Daisy ran toward him. Daisy barked continuously, as if she too had a story to tell him. Chris and Jamie were incoherent, their words tangled, and tears washed strips of dust from their pale cheeks.

The instant Tony stepped clear of the Blazer, Jamie climbed him like a lineman going up a telephone pole and wrapped both arms tightly around his neck. At the same time, Chris flung his arms around his thigh, pressing his tear-damp face against him, and clung there like a barnacle. Tony could feel the boys tremble and tightened his arms around their shoulders.

Tony didn't feel any better than his sons. His eyes stung with unshed tears.

Facing the house, the three of them formed a breathing statue. Shivers coursed through each of them, showing Tony no one believed Theo had simply left her phone on the table with a note. No way. And she hadn't forgotten them. Theo might forget to put detergent in the washing machine. She would never forget her family.

He tried speaking but his throat felt like someone had jammed a dry sponge down it. It took several attempts before he could force air out. "I need to see the note, guys."

The boys nodded. He could feel their heads move. Neither boy released him. So, like a single giant crab, the three of them moved to the front steps where they managed to disconnect.

"Will you guys stay out here with Daisy while I go inside for a minute?" Tony hugged them again.

"No. Don't leave us out here." Chris clung to his father's hand. Salty streaks coated the lenses of his glasses. "We'll wait by the door."

Jamie nodded his agreement. Tony wasn't sure what he was agreeing to but suspected it was Chris's plan.

Tony didn't attempt to dissuade them again. He led the way up the steps. Daisy followed. The door gave its customary squeak when it opened. He walked into the eerily empty house and halted just past the doorway. He left the door open and pushed the boys behind him, wedging them between his body and the wall. "Wait here. Both of you hang onto Daisy's collar."

He could feel their heads nod.

He couldn't, he wouldn't, take the boys any farther into the house until he was certain no danger lurked inside. If something had happened to Theo in there, his sons did not need to see it. He pulled the phone out of his pocket and hit speed dial number three. Two was Theo.

Dispatcher Rex Satterfield didn't ask useless questions. He listened. Seconds later, his preternaturally calm voice assured Tony help was on the way. Nothing would be broadcast that any scanner could intercept. No sirens.

There was no sign of a struggle in the entry. Tony walked to the kitchen. The only thing out of the ordinary was the note, written by Theo, on the table. "Call your dad, Mom." No drawing—she'd been told what to write.

The only sound was the hum from the refrigerator and the thudding of his own heartbeat. There were no odors except the usual ones. Nothing like blood or burnt gunpowder.

The kitchen phone rang. The sudden shrill tone sent his pulse into overdrive. He jerked the receiver out of the cradle and slammed it against his ear. "Theo?"

CHAPTER THIRTY-ONE

"Sheriff? It's Claude Marmot. Kin I talk to your wife for a minute?"

Marmot-the-Varmint and Theo. Tony frowned. "Sorry, Claude, she's not available right now."

"That's okay. You kin give her a message for me." He cleared his throat about four times. "Tell her my fiancée's favorite color is pink but, you know, I'm really not all that keen on sleeping under a pink quilt if you get my drift. And if she could find a way to make it pink and yet not seem pink, I'd be much obliged."

Tony felt his eyebrows rise. "Sure, Claude, I'll give her the message. I guess she knows what it means."

"Well, her and me was talking about it only a little bit ago, so I imagine she does."

"Where was that?"

"Right in front of her shop." Claude coughed. "You're not thinking that something improper is going on between us?"

"No." In spite of his concerns, Tony had to smile. He couldn't even begin to believe that scenario. He hoped Claude might have information he needed. "Just curious about the time."

"Well, she was standing next to that piece-of-garbage van of hers and had her keys in her hand. She said something about needing to go get your boys."

Tony tried to imagine what happened to change that and failed. At least they had a better idea of what time she went missing. "Did she seem worried or nervous?"

"Nope. She was just her regular sweet self and said her quilting group would help out with my bride's quilt."

"Anything else going on around there at the time?" Tony suspected he didn't sound very nonchalant.

"Say, Sheriff, is there something wrong?"

"Please, Claude, just answer my question."

"Had a tourist get all hot under the collar when I stopped to chat. I did kinda leave the truck in the road."

"Did he seem violent?"

"Naw, he was a heart attack looking for a place to happen." Claude paused. "If he was going to get violent, he was coming after me."

"Thanks, Claude. I'll give Theo your message." The knot of fear wedged in his chest seemed to grow. Why had Theo come here and abandoned her van instead of picking up the boys?

Tony put the receiver on the cradle and flipped open his cell phone. He backed out of the kitchen, already dialing Gus as he climbed the stairs. Holding his breath, he peeked into the bedrooms. Nothing seemed disturbed. He didn't touch anything, just turned and made his way back down to the boys.

Gus answered. "What's up?"

"You still in town, big brother?" Tony was surprised he could speak through the tightness in his throat. He knew his voice didn't sound normal.

Gus didn't waste time on small talk. "How can I help?"

"Come to the house." Tony couldn't think what to say that wouldn't panic his sons. He relied on Gus to understand.

Gus didn't hesitate. "I'm on my way."

Relieved, Tony sighed and led the boys back outside and down the steps, just as Wade and Sheila drove up. Even Daisy seemed subdued. The big dog anxiously pressed against him instead of greeting his deputies with her normal exuberance. An odd whine rattled her chest. Tony would bet the dog wanted to tell him something.

"Hey, boss. Chris. Jamie. Anything new?" Wade climbed from his car, giving the boys a reassuring grin. Behind his sunglasses, the bleak expression in his eyes told Tony that he already knew the answer.

Sheila glanced around and smiled warmly. Her smile did not reach her eyes, either. "Say, Sheriff, why don't you and the dog and boys go over to the park while we look around inside?"

Tony knew it was a good idea. It was the right thing to do. He certainly hadn't checked all the rooms. Still, he might have protested if the boys hadn't tightened their grips. In spite of their attempts to appear calm, the arrival of the deputies had only increased their anxiety. He nodded. Still moving as one unit, Tony, the boys and the dog crossed the street and stood in the shade, silently watching the deputies enter the house.

Gus arrived, leaving his pickup at the end of the short block. His smile faded as he studied their faces. He glanced at the gathered patrol cars and back to them. Uncertainty clouded his eyes.

Tony swallowed hard and tipped his head toward one boy and then the other. He pleaded with his eyes and could only hope Gus would understand what he needed.

"Hey, guys!" Gus tried smiling again.

Tony thought it looked almost natural.

When the boys finally smiled at their favorite uncle, Tony felt some of their tension release. Their whole world had not turned sideways, only the heart of it. "We seem to have misplaced Theo."

The color left his brother's face. Gus gulped, regrouping, then said, "Let's take Daisy for a little walk across the park, maybe get some ice cream, and let your dad do his sheriff thing."

Two blond heads shook from side to side. At least the dog quit moaning.

With Tony encouraging and Gus almost promising the moon, the boys finally let go of their father and reattached themselves like barnacles to their uncle.

Tony glanced at his front porch. As he watched, Sheila appeared on the front step. With a short shake of her head, she indicated what he'd guessed. His cursory check was right.

Theo was nowhere in the house.

The moment the boys moved away from him, Tony headed for the house. As long as they hadn't found Theo dead, there was hope. What had happened? Who would take Theo? Ransom seemed unlikely. Certainly no one who had any idea of their family's net worth would have bothered. The house Theo inherited had been mortgaged to the hilt to finance the construction of her shop.

If not money, what? Revenge? His career in Silersville couldn't have sparked that much animosity, and several years had passed since his days in Chicago. Even there, he had just been another cop, nothing special.

The reason for Theo's disappearance had to be something darker.

Tony mentally searched for anyone who hated him. It was patently ridiculous to think Theo had such a powerful enemy. His wife might not be gracious all of the time, and yet, she was well liked by most of her acquaintances.

Sheila watched him with what he suspected were tears shimmering in her eyes. "I saw the note by the phone. I can call the FBI or the TBI for you, Sheriff."

His knees felt unexpectedly weak and he sat, dropping onto the porch steps as if his tendons had snapped. He watched his sons walking away, holding hands with Gus, still too frightened to worry about being seen by their friends. Was he supposed to wait for instructions? Would there be instructions?

"What do you want us to do?"

Tony blinked, suddenly realizing most of his deputies had gathered at his feet. Rex had called up the night patrol. The tiny force was ready to battle demons and slay dragons.

Who was the dragon?

Where had the demon taken Theo?

Theo glanced away from the road and into Vicky's eyes. In the shadowed light of the car's interior, they looked black instead of blue. Flat black, as if not even sunlight could penetrate into those shadows. It didn't surprise her they were full of anger. She thought everything Vicky said and did now simply screamed her rage. Vicky couldn't contain the madness any longer.

"Where are we?" Theo felt as if she had driven a hundred miles instead of less than ten. The road ran in long stretches then turned back on itself, zigzagging up the mountain. It was easy to see the town below. Finally, following Vicky's instructions, they turned off the paved road. This wasn't even a road, simply a pair of ruts worn in the vegetation. Grasses grew over the ruts. She doubted anyone had driven through here recently. A thicket of rhododendron straddled the road, scraping the sides of the car as they passed.

"Keep driving." Still holding the revolver, Vicky ripped apart a pack of cigarettes with her teeth, sending the contents flying all over her lap. Grabbing a cigarette, she lit it and inhaled deeply, then exhaled, blowing smoke in Theo's face.

Nausea bubbled in her throat and Theo turned her face toward the window. Theo hadn't exactly been keeping track. She guessed her abductor had already worked her way through most of one pack of cigarettes and now had started another. The smoke cloud was unpleasant and pervasive, even with the window open.

The open window did allow Theo to breathe some fresher air but more importantly she could touch her left fingers to her lips and casually flick saliva away from the car. Maybe it would help Dammit find their trail.

Theo clung to the steering wheel, fighting the uneven terrain. Vicky's silver sedan hadn't been designed for off-road travel. Ominous scraping sounds rose from the undercarriage with every bump. Each time there was a scrape, Vicky used the leather strap on her purse to slap Theo's wrist.

It didn't take an expert to see how much enjoyment Vicky got out of hitting her. Terrified, Theo considered this glee a bad omen. Being on the far side of nowhere didn't exactly calm her fears. Her thoughts swung from looking for a way to escape to missing her family.

At least Vicky had not taken the children.

Eventually, even the ruts ended. Forced by nature to stop the car, Theo clung to the steering wheel and prayed for inspiration and courage.

Staring straight ahead, too frightened to look at Vicky, she saw a tiny log cabin about the same size as a child's playhouse. It sat, abandoned and forlorn, in what had once been a clearing. The number of small bushes and the height of the grasses made it appear that years might have passed since the last visitor arrived.

So much for the idea of screaming for help. Theo couldn't be more alone with her abductor if they had flown to the moon.

Behind the cabin was an even smaller building with a crooked chimney. Theo guessed it was an old smokehouse. Closer to the road and slightly downhill sat the remains of a privy. It had no door. Wild vegetation spilled through the open doorway. Kudzu tendrils wrapped around the three buildings. A jungle of honeysuckle and wild roses formed an impenetrable hedge. A wild turkey, fierce and beady-eyed, dared them to come closer.

Vicky pulled the key from the ignition. "Get out." She wasted no time or energy on conversation as she pulled an almost full roll of duct tape out of the glove compartment.

Theo had no choice. She shoved with her shoulder, forcing the door open. Bees buzzed loudly as they swooped and soared. Taking a deep breath, Theo reveled in the sultry air. Compared to the acrid aroma of Vicky's cigarettes, the scent of honeysuckle seemed dark and almost too sweet.

"Put your wrists together." Vicky walked up to her. She carried the gun in her right hand and the duct tape in the left.

Theo shook her head. Enough was enough. "No."

Vicky hit her right ear with the roll of tape. The force of the blow knocked Theo off balance; she still tried to scramble away. The second blow knocked her to her knees. Vicky didn't give her a chance to get up but jumped on top of her, pressing her knee into Theo's throat. The bigger woman had the advantage.

Instinctively, Theo's hands rose to push Vicky away. She couldn't. Then the lack of oxygen made her woozy and weak. There wasn't enough air in her lungs to cough.

Vicky jerked the end of the tape free and savagely wrapped Theo's wrists together. Using Theo's sore ear for a handle, she pulled her to her feet and dragged her toward the cabin and forced her to sit on a rickety ladder-back chair.

It seemed to take only a few seconds for Vicky to immobilize Theo, taping her to the chair from ankles to neck. Little tape remained on the cardboard center of the roll. The last strip went around Theo's head, sealing her mouth and capturing her hair in the sticky coating. Vicky pressed the tape on itself, forming a bond connecting Theo's head to the top of the chair. Her neck was bent into an odd angle and the tape pinched, pulling on her tender skin.

She barely noticed. Her thoughts were centered on determining where she was and not inciting more violence from her captor.

Her prison chair was parked on what had been a small porch.

Nothing remained of it now except a few warped boards. Those were riddled with termites. The overhang had fallen away, so there was no shelter from the blazing late afternoon sunlight. Each time she opened her eyes, the harsh light seemed to cut into her brain. Her glasses were askew, distorting her vision.

Theo's eyes filled with tears, the sunlight creating pain worse than she'd expected. She blinked, forcing them away. She refused to give Vicky the satisfaction of seeing her cry. Worse than her pride was the worry that if she started to cry, her nose would get clogged and she'd suffocate. No. She simply could not begin to cry.

Instead, she focused all of her attention on Vicky, narrowing her eyes against the light of the lowering sun.

Vicky paced back and forth near the outhouse, her movements jerky and erratic. Her left hand pressed the tiny cell phone against her ear. With her right hand, she waved the pistol in the air as she talked, gesturing. She made stabbing motions with the revolver.

Theo could see Vicky's anger growing fiercer with every moment, not unlike the building of a summer storm. Whoever she was talking to must not be saying what she wanted to hear.

Theo hoped it wasn't Tony.

She had no idea if Vicky was demanding a ransom and, if so, how much it was. Tony could probably borrow a bit but would it be enough? Everything was mortgaged to the hilt already. The house would be free and clear if they hadn't borrowed against it to build the quilt shop. Her inventory wasn't exactly cheap, either. Hoping to take her mind off her problems, she amused herself with offering Vicky the minivan. After all, the relic was practically an antique.

The idea entertained her for a while. Then she began to mentally design a new quilt. That didn't work. A yellow jacket hovered near the tender flesh of her inner elbow. If the wasp managed to sting her between strips of duct tape, it might just be the straw to break her spirit.

Her favorite scenario was living to see Tony's fury unleashed on Vicky. Her husband might look like an overgrown, if bald, teddy bear. He wasn't one. Theo knew him well. His easygoing nature only ran so deep. Beneath his benign exterior lurked an avenging soul. Above all, he was a man who abhorred cruelty.

Theo's biggest fear was not her own death, it was what might happen if she died. If Tony killed Vicky, he could end up in prison, or worse. Gus would take in the boys, their family would be destroyed. Maybe Vicky's goal all along was just that.

Efforts to distract herself from the aches beginning to scream in her shoulders and knees and the way the sun seemed to be broiling her failed.

She narrowed her eyes against the too-bright sunlight, leaving them open just wide enough to see what was happening. Vicky turned again and Theo watched as Vicky's finger tightened on the trigger.

The revolver was pointed at her face. Only six inches separated her nose from the business end of the pistol. The opening in the barrel looked huge. This was not a game.

Theo watched Vicky's thumb pull back the hammer, cocking the gun.

CHAPTER THIRTY-TWO

Tony paced while he waited for Mike to return with his pet bloodhound. The minutes it took seemed like endless hours, Dammit was their best hope.

Through the open doorway, he watched Wade systematically searching for fingerprints. Since neither he nor Theo was great at housekeeping, there were bound to be many to sift through.

"Did you do the phone and note first?"

"Yes, sir, and then I did the table." Wade showed no signs of impatience as he answered Tony's question for the twentieth time. "What will you do with your boys?"

Tony's chest felt tight. He wanted to be with the boys. Above all else he had to find their mother, and his sons couldn't be a part of the search.

"Gus will take them home to stay with him and Catherine in Townsend. I've asked Gus to wait here until their escort arrives."

"Escort?" Wade seemed slow to process the word.

Tony realized Wade had been working on the fingerprints while Tony had made a hundred phone calls. "I've called in favors from every agency but the CIA. The boys will be well guarded."

Wade stopped working and focused on Tony, his expression unusually grave. "Why would anyone do this to your family, sir?"

"I don't know." Standing just outside the front door, Tony

gripped a large jar of antacids as he paced in place, eating them like movie popcorn. At this rate, he would run out quickly. "I just don't know. We don't have any money, and revenge doesn't seem very likely. Revenge for what?"

Wade's response was cut short by a squeal of brakes.

Tony spun around and watched as Mike parked diagonally in front of the house. Leaving the dog in the car, Mike pulled on latex gloves as he trotted up the stairs.

"I need a scent sample." Mike didn't wait for Tony to speak. "How about one of Theo's shoes?"

Tony led Mike upstairs to the closet and pointed to Theo's slippers. "She wore those this morning."

"That's good, sir." Mike placed one in a plastic bag and sealed the zip strip.

"What are his chances?" Tony asked.

"It's hellaciously hot today but the shower this morning might help hold the scent." His eyes flickered to Tony's. "He'll do the best he can."

"I know."

Mike wasted no time after collecting his sample. Opening the car door, he talked softly to the bloodhound. Moments after the dog sniffed the slipper, he led Mike into the house. The dog wasn't fully trained. He was the best they had. His interest increased in the kitchen and soon led Mike out the back door. He checked everything. Pressing his homely face against the leaves, he examined each bush. His huge ears slapped against his wrinkled skin dislodging a fly. Dammit headed away from the house, across the backyard.

Trailing him, Mike released the leash and kept the dog on voice commands.

Tony sent Deputy Darren Holt with Mike. His job was to handle the radio and keep in constant contact. Only seconds after they left the Abernathy yard, Darren reported a strand of metallic thread on a shrub in the next street over. Dammit had found it very interesting.

"I'm on it." With bag and tweezers, Sheila hurried to collect it.

The first wave of outside support arrived. A pair of vehicles from the Blount County Sheriff's Department parked in the street, almost in the park. Three men and a woman climbed out. They were armed to the teeth.

Leading the reinforcements, Tony trudged across the park to talk to Gus and the boys. "You go home with Gus." He tilted his head to indicate the officers at his back. "They'll serve as your escort." At least the sight of armed officers was a familiar one to them. There was never a time in their lives when the boys hadn't been around men in body armor, guns and badges.

Jamie had his arms clamped around Gus's neck. After a moment, he nodded. Chris leaned against his uncle and finally nodded, too. He glanced up and his eyes met Tony's. The lenses of his glasses magnified his tear-filled hazel eyes. Theo's eyes.

Tony felt like crying, too. Through the helpless rage he felt a knot of incredible grief growing deep inside him. He shivered in the sweltering early evening heat. What would become of them without Theo?

"Bang, bang." Vicky laughed. Her laughter no longer sounded remotely human. "Maybe I'll kill your babies first and come back for you. Put you out of your misery."

Theo felt a terror deeper than she could have imagined. The blood rushed away from her head, leaving her woozy and weak. She could feel her heart pounding in her chest, constricted by the duct tape. Even knowing it was hopeless didn't stop her futile attempt to escape. Dark spots danced in front of her eyes.

Theo strained against her bonds. Nothing budged. If anything, they felt tighter than before. The sun beat down on her and although the temperature was hellish, Theo still felt cold. Having her mouth taped didn't stop her questions. "Why are you doing this? You said you liked me." To her ears it sounded like she was humming but Vicky grinned in response. Maybe she had understood.

Vicky ran the sharp-edged sight of the gun barrel back and forth across a patch of bare skin on Theo's neck. "I do like you. I just happen to like me better." She giggled. "You'd just be in the way when Tony and I leave on our honeymoon."

"Honeymoon?" Theo couldn't suppress the word. Not even the duct tape silenced that word. Theo stared at the woman, seeing the ever-increasing madness in her eyes. Vicky thought Tony would marry her? Having her mouth taped kept her from mentioning Tony's current marital status.

"Oh, yes, we've wanted to be married for as long as I can remember." Vicky's smile was indeed as radiant as a bride's. "Today's the day."

Theo didn't move a muscle.

"As for you, you'll be dead before long. He wouldn't want to commit bigamy. He's just not that kind of man, is he?" Vicky spun in a circle, laughing and singing. "Here comes the bride." The smile vanished like a light turning off and she pointed the revolver at Theo. "Don't go anywhere without me."

Theo watched Vicky saunter across the weeds to the car. She revved the engine and threw it into reverse. The vehicle jerked backward, barely missing the outhouse. Vicky threw Theo a kiss as she straightened the car and drove away. "Wish me good luck, won't you?"

On the heels of Vicky's departure, Theo's terror changed focus.

To be teased with a deadly weapon was bad enough. To hear Vicky talk about hunting her children was diabolically cruel. The idea of Tony marrying Vicky might have made her laugh under other circumstances. Imagining Vicky standing at some altar, holding her gun on the vastly larger Tony and convincing him to promise to love and honor her gave her happy thoughts and removed some of her paralyzing fear. Tony would strangle her with his bare hands before he'd say those words.

She would find a way to free herself. With Vicky gone, she could do this.

Theo tried twisting her hands back and forth, hoping to loosen the tape. If anything, it seemed to grow tighter. There was simply no way she could break the tape using only her own muscle.

If she could get free, she might be able to make her way downhill and phone Tony or his office and warn them in time. What was Vicky really planning to do?

There had to be a way to cut the tape. How? Maybe she could use a nail protruding from the old building, if there was one. Or maybe she could rub the tape against a sharp edge, wearing through it. Either of these plans would help free her. She couldn't see behind her. The way the tape held her head firmly against the chair, she had to use her peripheral vision. The only part of the log building she could see was so termite infested it barely stood. The weathered wood looked soft as a dirty gray sponge. Termites ignored her presence and continued their picnic.

Above her, curious birds circled. In her fevered imagination they were vultures waiting for her to die. Their shadows moved across the wild roses just beyond the clearing, drawing her eyes. Something silvery glinted in the changing light. She didn't know what it was, it might be a piece of metal or glass. Maybe it was the lid to a can. Would it be sharp enough to cut the tape? Could she even get there?

She had nothing to lose. She tried scooting forward by throwing her weight back and forth. The force of her movement and the unusual weight took its toll. The termite-riddled board beneath the front legs split and the chair pitched forward until it found footing in the packed earth.

Theo was well and truly stuck. Tears leaked from under her swollen eyelids. She promised herself she wouldn't cry. Well, maybe she deserved a few tears. She took a deep breath instead. What to do? What to do?

She rocked sideways, back and forth on the old chair until it fell over on its side. Her left arm took the brunt of the fall. It burned and sent a crawling pain through her entire body. Maybe it was broken.

She tried to cheer herself up by joking that since it was already in the duct-tape version of a cast, it couldn't get any worse. After a few deep breaths, the pain eased and she wiggled, hoping the chair would move. It budged a quarter of an inch, raising her spirits.

Like a crippled turtle dragging its shell, she inched away from the cabin. At the rate she was traveling, it shouldn't take more than a few hours to reach her destination. She would put her top speed at ten feet per hour.

Little by little, the shiny bit lured her over rocks and ant beds. Although the sun lowered, the temperature did not seem to drop.

A cloud moved in front of the sun, throwing everything into partial shade. The shiny bit disappeared in the shadows. It was lost to her.

With daylight fading, Tony couldn't be still. Knowing the boys were safe with Gus and every shred of evidence was being collected, he decided to join Mike and Darren. At last report, Dammit was still eager on the trail. Mike had to force him to rest.

Darren relayed their location and requested additional water for the dog and men. The water Mike carried in his pack Dammit finished on the last break. Darren also suggested light snacks would help them all.

Tony and Sheila headed uphill in the Blazer. They found the exhausted trio waiting at a fork in the road. The bloodhound's quivering tongue looked like a giant pink dishtowel. Rivulets of sweat ran down the men's faces and arms.

The paved road continued a zigzag path up the mountain and a pair of ruts veered away. It was impossible in this light to tell if either had recently been used.

Tony filled Dammit's water bowl before he handed bottles of cold water to the men. The dog was not a dainty drinker. His giant tongue splashed water from the bowl, flinging it onto the men and up onto his wrinkled forehead.

"Which way?" Tony glanced around. Nothing appeared out of place.

"The ruts." Mike gestured with his water bottle. "Dammit was ready to haul me that way until I forced him to take this break." He shook his head sadly, breathing deeply. "He doesn't know how to pace himself."

"Is he having trouble finding a scent?"

"Not much." Mike smiled. "I'm guessing Theo is touching the bushes or spitting on them because the trail seems so clear."

Sheila handed the men energy bars.

Mike offered the dog a pair of biscuits. Dammit sucked them up like a vacuum cleaner before he began to chew. He stretched out in the tall grass panting. When his heavy breathing eased, Mike smiled and stood.

"Let's all go together." Tony stared down at the ruts as if they would supply much-needed answers. To him, the marks on the grass looked fresh. They were in deepening shadow. He felt a stir of hope mixed with dread. He didn't know how far the ruts ran or if they dead-ended or connected with another road like the one they were on. Was Theo just around the bend ahead or on the way to North Carolina?

Darren drained the last of his water. "Let's do it."

Mike nodded and dumped the remainder of Dammit's water. He put the bowl in the Blazer. "Thanks."

Instead of climbing in behind the wheel, Tony handed Sheila his keys. "If I don't walk for a while, I'm likely to explode."

Clearly accepting his explanation for the truth, she climbed onto the seat and let them get a head start.

Refreshed from the short break, Dammit sniffed the scent sample again and surged forward, his enthusiasm undiminished. The three men on foot hurried to keep pace with him.

CHAPTER THIRTY-THREE

Theo was caught in a thicket of wild rose brambles. Her attempt to find a way out of the chair had ended with her sliding down the slope, past the can lid she might have used to cut her bindings. Now she couldn't move in any direction.

Her cheek rested on the rocky edge of a precipice. Maybe being stuck in a cage of vegetation wasn't that bad. It saved her from falling to the rocks below or beyond them to the town of Silersville.

As darkness approached, lights were coming on in the valley, twinkling like Christmas decorations. The town itself resembled a toy village, pretty as a greeting card, with tiny buildings and stores. She could see the park in its center and across from it her house. All the lights were on.

She imagined she saw Daisy in the yard and Tony and the boys playing in the park.

Where was Vicky now? What would she do next?

Straining to catch sight of her nemesis, she stopped, startled, when another yard caught her attention. It took her addled brain several minutes to decipher what she saw. Then she began to giggle. Tony might not know where the missing lawn ornaments had ended up. She did. Playing with possible reasons why they were in that particular spot, she entertained herself for a while. When everything near her vanished in the dark of night, she felt her hope of being rescued diminish as well.

Ants marched across her body as if she was a fallen log. Some of them nibbled on her but she guessed they were discouraged by the sheer quantity of silver tape. Knowing she wasn't worth the ants' effort was the last straw. Her forehead rested on some dandelions and her tears dripped onto the packed dirt.

A pair of raccoons wandered past. Not even their masked faces or their surprisingly human hands amused her. They stared for a while before continuing their rolling waddle to a fallen tree. Something inside the tree, insects or grubs, caught their attention.

Being dismissed by the raccoons brought a new discovery: she couldn't cry anymore.

Above her, the evening star twinkled in the darkening sky.

As she stared up at it, she lost consciousness. When she became aware again, there were many bright stars overhead. Somewhere, she could hear the sounds of crickets and a mockingbird. Also a deeper tone, a dog baying. And men's voices. She couldn't tell where they might be. In the mountains, sounds echoed oddly and could come from anywhere, even long distances.

Tony felt as if they'd reached a dead end when the big dog dragged the men into a clearing and Sheila was forced to abandon the Blazer and join them on foot. In the headlights, the grass showed signs of recent vehicle and foot travel. Heedless of any possible evidence he might destroy, Dammit dashed across the vegetation to the cabin.

The bloodhound bayed and paused only briefly at the porch before sniffing the ground and charging downhill. The humans in his wake waved flashlights.

Tony spotted his wife.

Light danced from Theo's glasses, showing them where she was. She lay on her side, half buried in a bush. A ladder-back chair taped to her back was all that prevented her from plunging farther down the mountainside. Dammit reached her first and licked her face, his huge brown body wagging with excitement. Mike congratulated the dog and pulled his training toy from the bag. They moved away, letting the others see to Theo.

"Theo!"

She didn't move.

Tony charged past deputies and dog, flinging himself onto his knees, he leaned forward over his wife's still body.

Was she dead? Tony couldn't be sure. He held his breath and touched her neck. Her skin was warm but the only pulse he could feel was his own. Adrenalin fueled, his heart pounded in his chest. What if they were too late?

Theo's eyelids flickered but didn't open.

Relieved, Tony gulped air into his starving lungs and reached for the silver tape on her face.

"Wait!"

Tony turned, and Wade jumped forward waving his camera. He snapped three photographs, the flash blinding in the darkness, and stepped back.

Tony tried to juggle his flashlight and pull the tape from Theo's face.

"Let me do that, sir." Handing him her flashlight, Sheila knelt next to Tony. Her hands were covered with disposable gloves as she reached past him and eased the first strip of duct tape away from Theo's mouth.

Theo whimpered.

Trying unsuccessfully to block out the sound, Tony checked his wife for obvious injury. Sunburn made her fair skin scarlet on the right side. He was relieved to find only hundreds of superficial injuries. Multiple insect bites swelled, between wide straps of tape, leaving welts on every inch of her face, arms and legs. At least he found no knife cuts or bullet wounds.

Her glasses were still on her face, the frames were twisted

and the lenses smudged. Sticks, leaves and dirt clung to her blond curls. She was a mess.

Tony had never seen such a beautiful sight. "Who did this?"

Although weak and raspy, the single word was clear. "Vicky."

"Vicky who?" Sheila looked confused.

"Vicky Parker. Her uncle is Nelson. She's visited here only off and on."

"Why ever in this world would she do this?" Sheila asked.

"Vicky is a vicious killer," muttered Tony. The idea that his wife had been at the mercy of Icky Vicky Parker made him feel sick.

His deputies worked around him, letting him talk to Theo. Sheila used her radio to contact dispatch, identifying Vicky Parker as the culprit.

"Do you need an ambulance, sweetheart?" Tony didn't want to move her if she was injured.

"No." She panted softly. "Boys?"

"They're with Gus. I'll call them in a second."

"Good." Her lips could barely form the word. Tony thought she smiled. "Water?"

"I'll ask Doc Nash." Sheila reached for her phone.

Wade seemed intent on photographing everything from Theo's condition to the trail of crushed vegetation leading to the porch. Camera busy, he stood behind Tony, clicking the shutter, the flash continuing like a strobe light.

"What do we do with the tape on her arms and legs?" Tony asked. "I don't want to destroy any evidence. I can't take a chance that bitch will get off on some technicality or screw up on our part."

Wade thought for a moment. "If you try unwinding it, you'll end up with a tangled mess and no prints."

Mike, having rewarded Dammit for a job well done, joined them while they debated the best approach. "If you cut through all the layers and pull it off in chunks, would that work?"

"Sounds good to me. I'm sure as hell not leaving it on her any longer." Tony reached for his knife. Before he made his first cut, he leaned forward. Theo's lids opened slightly in her puffy face. He thought he saw her try to smile. Residue of gray tape clung to her skin, contrasting with the scarlet of her sunburn on one side and greenish pallor on the other. "We'll have you free in no time."

Tony sliced through the layers of tape holding his wife to the chair.

When the blood rushed into her hands and wrists, Theo jerked and screamed. Surprised, Tony rocked back on his heels as he realized how close he'd been to nicking her with his knife. With shaking hands, he massaged her hands and arms, soothing her pain. "I still have to do your legs."

Sheila disconnected her call and handed Theo a bottle of water. "He says to sip a bit, not too much."

Theo nodded and lifted it to her lips and managed to swallow a little water. She was unsteady but able to hold the bottle for herself.

Bracing himself for her next reaction, Tony jerked his knife through the next wad of tape, the one holding her legs to the chair. She didn't scream this time. She spat a mouthful of water into his face and grinned as if proud of her accomplishment.

Everyone laughed. All was well. Theo acting sassy meant she would be fine.

Sheila tried again. "Why did she do this, Theo?"

"Icky Vicky Parker thinks she's going to marry Tony." Theo's eyes drifted shut again. "Over my dead body."

Her words echoed in his thoughts, making Tony recoil. The idea was not only ludicrous but repellent. He'd sooner marry Nellie Pearl. He reached for his phone and dialed Gus. "She's safe. Will you put the boys on?"

Tony held the phone to Theo's ear. As she murmured comforting words to their sons, he looked up at Sheila. The last few minutes were a blur. "Did I hear you radio Rex?"

Sheila nodded. "He's already putting out a description of Vicky and her uncle Nelson, in case he's involved or knows something." Sheila spoke softly into Tony's ear. "Rex knows what Nelson drives. He needs a description of Vicky's car."

Nodding his understanding, Tony let each boy talk briefly to Theo before he took charge again, promising to call again later. "Can you tell us anything about Vicky's car?"

"It's a silver Ford, not real old or new, with four doors. It does have North Carolina plates on it and one of those air freshener trees hanging from the mirror. A red one." Theo frowned. "The car was full of smoke."

"That's enough." Tony listened as Sheila talked to Rex. "Let's get you to the doctor." He lifted Theo in his arms and headed for the Blazer. He looked at Sheila. "You drive."

They left Mike and Wade setting up lights and stringing crime scene tape with Dammit supervising. They'd have all the help they could use in a few minutes.

Sheila opened the back door for them and Tony climbed in, holding Theo high against his chest. It was awkward. He managed it without banging her head on anything. He couldn't say the same for his own. He whacked his forehead on the back door frame but he didn't drop Theo. Still very concerned about her, he thought she felt boneless in his arms, reminding him of a bird that once flew into a window. He'd picked it up and it rested in his hand, panting, bill open, eyes wide. He put in on the grass and guarded it until it was recovered enough to fly away.

Theo stretched across the seat, her head in his lap, clutching his forearm to her chest. She held on with both hands and drifted away, whether into sleep or unconsciousness, Tony couldn't tell.

Sheila drove down the narrow mountain road as if she were being chased by one of Orvan's banshees. Watching over her shoulder, Tony saw the headlights flash off trees growing by the side of the road. The world was a gray-and-black blur.

The radio crackled incessantly. Rex sounded almost bored as he monitored the calls. Tony knew better; the more tense the situation, the calmer Rex's voice. Everyone was looking for Vicky Parker and her uncle Nelson. No one had seen either one of them.

Light bar flashing, Sheila steered the Blazer toward the clinic, making it there in record time. Tony thought she might have taken them off-road for a bit. He didn't care, as long as they arrived safely.

The ambulance area was eerily empty. Only the reflective paint that delineated the helicopter landing area greeted their arrival.

Doc Nash and the indomitable Nurse Foxx stood just inside the double doors, waiting with a gurney. The moment the Blazer parked, Doc trotted forward and opened the vehicle's door, leaving Foxxy to bring the wheels. His alert brown eyes swept over Theo, assessing her obvious injuries. Ignoring Tony, he asked questions and waved his flashlight over her. His smile was reassuring, if tinged with anger.

Tony understood. The doctor had no tolerance for cruelty.

"You and your family are my very best customers," Doc teased Theo as he gently lifted her onto the gurney. "Not everyone gets curb service."

Theo nodded and lay back onto the spotless sheets and closed her eyes. Tony thought she might have passed out.

After the darkness, the light inside the clinic seemed intolerably bright. The gurney was barely through the clinic doors before it turned right into the fully stocked emergency room. Nurse Foxx and Doc Nash went to work without fanfare.

Foxxy made soothing clicking sounds with her tongue as she gently peeled off Theo's clothing and dropped each item into a separate paper bag. The doctor began his examination.

Tony wasn't offended when he got pushed aside. He perched on an incredibly uncomfortable plastic chair and watched the process. The doctor and nurse worked together with the speed and efficiency honed by long practice.

Within seconds that felt like hours to Tony, they took a sample of Theo's blood, inserted an IV into her arm and began hydrating her as they asked her a series of questions. He couldn't hear all the answers.

Nurse Foxx left the room several times, either carrying a vial or returning with something Tony couldn't identify. She changed the IV once. Drawers were opened and closed, revealing bandages, bottles and jars, basins and mysterious sealed bags.

Doc Nash continued to ask Theo questions, often making them simple so all she had to do was nod or shake her head. Wielding long tweezers, he pulled numerous thorns, stingers and splinters from her skin, dropping them into an orange plastic basin. With no apparent haste, he checked every inch of her skin.

Nurse Foxx handed the doctor a paper and spoke with him, her voice no more than a whisper.

Finally Doc waved Tony over to Theo's side. He thought the doctor's expression held a curious combination of anger, satisfaction and amusement. Amusement?

As Tony reached for Theo's hand, he noticed that her eyes looked brighter and she breathed more easily. When she smiled and twined her fingers with his, he felt a wave of relief surge through him. He looked into the doctor's face. "She's okay?"

"Yes." Doc's eyes twinkled. "We'll keep her here for a bit longer and get some more fluids into her. She was pretty dehydrated."

"That's all she needs?" Tony's knees wobbled, threatening his balance.

"Yes. And a bit of rest and time." The doctor's amusement seemed to grow. "I think that I can promise even the fainting will stop in about six months."

"Six months?" Tony and Theo spoke in unison. "Why so long?"

"You're pregnant." The doctor patted Theo's shoulder.

"No way." Theo stared. "It's not possible."

She looked as stunned as Tony felt. He looked into the doctor's face, searching for any sign that the man was joking. "There must be some mistake."

Shaking his head, Doc snickered. "I thought you two were still on friendly terms."

Theo's eyes filled with tears. The sight of them erased the doctor's grin.

In a voice as soft as a whisper, Theo said, "You know we wanted another baby. We finally gave up."

The grin returned, wider than before. "I guess you kept practicing anyway."

Theo blushed. The pale side of her face matched the burnt one. Crimson.

"Is that why she's been fainting?" Tony was elated and scared. Jamie had been a difficult pregnancy and Theo had miscarried baby Anna in the fifth month. "I thought it was the heat."

"That certainly didn't help." Doc nodded. "I'll leave you two alone."

Tony leaned over the gurney and kissed her. She smiled and whispered. "A baby?"

Too stunned to speak, he nodded as he smoothed the springy blond curls away from her face and gazed into her bright eyes. They seemed more gold than green in this light. "Doc Nash is pretty good at his job. If you think he's wrong, we can get a second opinion."

"I never guessed." Theo laughed then. "I thought it was just the heat that was making me sick. Heat and all those carnations."

Without releasing her hand again, Tony hooked a foot around the leg of the uncomfortable chair and pulled it close enough for him to sit. He more or less collapsed onto it. "It's been quite an evening."

Theo grinned. "I think we're getting too old for this much excitement. I want to go home."

"When Doc releases you, I'll call Gus and get him to bring the wild bunch home. He and Catherine are older than we are. They're probably sound asleep sitting in their chairs."

"And I suppose you have some questions to ask?" Theo ran her free hand over the side of his face and smiled when he turned his head and kissed her palm.

He nodded. "Wade will be up on the mountain for hours, so I'll get Sheila in here and you can tell us both how you ended up sliding downhill with a chair taped to your back."

CHAPTER THIRTY-FOUR

Theo's narration was brief and chilling. Sheila handed Tony a small recorder and she sat, taking notes while Theo talked.

Tony knew his wife could have easily died up there on the mountain. His cell phone rang, cutting into his angry, morbid thoughts. A glance at the screen forced a groan from his throat. "It's Martha."

"You'd better talk to your aunt or she'll call your mom to get information." Theo pushed against his shoulder with her index finger.

Normally he preferred she not do that; tonight the annoying gesture reassured him. He nodded and cleared his throat before he pushed the green button, connecting the call. "Hello, Martha."

"Tony." She hesitated. "Is everything okay with Theo?"

At her simple question, Tony felt the muscles of his stomach tighten. What if she'd made this call when he couldn't see Theo or smell the residue of a killer's cigarettes on her hair? "Why?"

"I just received a very disturbing phone call from one of my old students." Martha's normally musical voice sounded harsh and strained. "It was all about Theo and sounded really bad."

"I'm with Theo now." Tony considered his options. "Who's the student?"

"Vicky Parker. She was a student, only briefly, hmm, maybe twenty years ago." The pitch of her voice rose. "Frankly, Tony, I was afraid of her and was happy when she moved away. She said Theo died in an accident and also said we'd soon be relatives. What's going on?"

He saw no choice but surrender. "I will tell you only in strictest confidence, and only if you swear you can put a muzzle on mom until we locate Vicky."

Martha groaned. "I can only promise to do my best."

Theo watched Tony and Sheila, gratified by the anger and outrage on their faces. She'd told them everything she remembered and now that she was safe, her brain began operating again. Every other thought she had touched the idea of being pregnant again. Terrifying and wonderful.

Still talking to his aunt, Tony held the phone to his ear with one hand and kept the other arm wrapped around her waist. Theo pressed it closer with both hands. The idea that Vicky was still loose was simply too frightening to ignore. "She thinks I'm dead by now and called your aunt to gloat."

"Yes." Tony's head came up and he met her gaze.

"So, let's give her what she wants." Theo lifted a hand and pressed it to the swollen side of her face. She wouldn't mind if Vicky ran into a brick wall. "We can make her believe I'm dead. We can even make her believe I was unconscious when you found me and I never recovered. It's close enough to the truth."

Tony told Martha to stay off the phone and that he'd call back and explain the whole thing. He disconnected before she could ask a question.

Sheila grinned at Theo. "You're right. If she thinks she's succeeded in killing you, she's probably crazy enough to think the rest of her plan will work."

"You'd have to disappear." Tony looked reluctant. Theo noticed a glint of amusement in his eyes and guessed he had already considered the idea. "I could call in a favor from Calvin. The man owes me big-time."

Theo giggled, remembering Tony's description of Calvin packing up Doreen's stuff and unpacking it again when she returned from the dead, so to speak.

Tony quickly called and explained the situation to Martha. "With any luck, it will all be over before Mom has a chance to get involved somehow." Still looking apprehensive, he flipped the phone closed.

"Can we play it low key?" Theo didn't mind going into hiding, although she didn't relish the idea of everyone believing she was dead. "I'll hide at the shop, upstairs in my office. There's the daybed, and I'd have a kitchen and bathroom. It would be like a mini quilt retreat. You can put a message on the phone and a note on the door stating a 'family emergency' forced the shop to close temporarily."

Sheila frowned. "Wouldn't you have to sit in the dark?"

Theo shook her head. "When we moved back here and built the shop, I had two little boys and was expecting another baby. I wanted the office to be a combination of workspace and nursery/playroom so we put up heavy curtains to block most of the light."

"And if Tony turns on the lights while he's inside, she would think nothing of it," said Sheila.

"And if I accidentally leave them on, Vicky wouldn't be able to see you moving around. I like that." Tony reached for his phone. "As long as they can talk to you on the phone, we can tell the boys to stay with Gus because we're playing a spy game. They love spy games."

"No, you're the one who loves spy games." Theo giggled. "You always did want to be James Bond, didn't you?"

"No, I wanted to be Marshal Dillon."

"We've got extra help from agencies all around this end of the state. We'll have to notify them what we're doing." Sheila wrote a series of names in her notebook. "Other than that, we'll have to tell Calvin, Doc Nash, Nurse Foxx, Gus and the kids. Who else?"

"Don't forget Mom and Martha." Tony sighed. "If there's a leak, it will be from one of those two. If they don't know what's going on, they'll blow us out of the water for sure. We'll have to trust that Martha can handle Mom so we've done all we can to plug that one." He stared at Theo. "I'm not leaving you alone up there."

Theo laughed. "Maybe you can find some handsome deputy who doesn't mind hanging around a fabric shop all night. That daybed is a trundle bed and big enough for two."

"Sheila will stay with you." Only after the words were out did he seem to realize how he sounded.

"Call Calvin." Theo grinned, pleased by Tony's flash of jealousy. It served its purpose and defused some of the tension. "It's time to drag me off to the mortuary."

Tony and Doc stood under the lights, watching Calvin. Whatever sixth sense Tony possessed told him Vicky Parker was watching as well. Calvin carefully maneuvered the "body," stacks of towels and some wadded up newspapers zipped into a long, white bag, placing it in the hearse.

At the same time, Tony knew Sheila was escorting Theo around the back of the clinic and into the alley. The women, dressed in dark sweatpants and hooded sweatshirts delivered by the grateful mortician, vanished into the shadows. Even though he knew where they should be, the strong lights on the back of the clinic threw everything nearby into absolute darkness.

He didn't find it difficult to appear grief-stricken as the hearse from the Cashdollar Mortuary pulled away from the clinic's emergency entrance. Chilled to the bone by his deep fear, followed by an almost unbearable sense of relief, he shivered. Even the sweltering night air couldn't melt the ice in his veins. It was a miracle Theo had survived.

Doc gave Tony a sympathetic pat on the back and headed into the clinic. Sarah Foxx walked slowly over to Tony and gave him a hug.

"She'll be fine." Her soft words barely reached his ears before she turned and followed the doctor.

Tony nodded and let his shoulders slump as he wandered over to his Blazer. After the long roller-coaster day, it wasn't difficult to appear exhausted and dazed. Knowing Vicky could be anywhere and was most likely keeping an eye on him, he'd have to maintain his façade of bereaved husband.

Dragging, he climbed into the driver's seat of the Blazer and sat with his forehead pressed against his hands as they clenched the steering wheel. He hoped Calvin hadn't overplayed his role. Surely a funeral director would exhibit less outward anguish about a client. Then again, most men either loved their wives or were irritated by them. Not much middle ground.

He wondered where Theo was now. She should be in the alley behind her shop, waiting for him to turn the lights on and unlock the back door. As he started the Blazer, Tony replayed Theo's words in his mind. "The best thing about living in a town this size is we can walk to the shop as fast as you can drive there."

So much had happened this day, from the drive to Chattanooga to Mac's arrest and now Theo's "death," it surprised him that the town was busy. A line of customers still waited to get into Bud's BBQ Café. Tourist vehicles occupied all the downtown parking spaces, so he left the Blazer by the fire hydrant on the corner and made his way to Theo's shop.

He opened the front door and took a deep breath, half expecting Vicky to leap out of the shadows. The moment he was inside, he relocked the door behind him and flipped on all of the overhead lights. The store was empty. The classroom was empty.

Pretending to check the back door, he unlocked it. A syncopated knock let him know Sheila and Theo waited for him. He had ten minutes before they would enter.

The answering machine was connected to the phone behind the counter. He fiddled with the buttons for a while and cleared his throat several times before he began to talk. "Due to a family emergency, Theo's Quilt Shop will be closed today. To leave a message, please wait for the beep."

He dragged himself up the stairs into Theo's office and flicked the light switch. He found acting as if he'd lost Theo beyond painful. It wasn't difficult for him to look disheartened. Without her, the normally cheerful workroom was just a large, messy room. The children's alcove with its trundle bed, television and toy box was too quiet. Dragging his weary body to the window, he stood there for a few moments watching the tourists.

People milled around, especially in front of Gormet's Coffee and Ice Cream Shoppe. Late diners and window shoppers ambled along. Some carried ice cream cones that dripped like crazy while they peered into the shop windows. No wonder Theo refused to keep the shop open after normal business hours, even in the busiest season. She'd tried it the first summer and found the sign asking people to leave food and drinks outside was largely ignored. She lost money because she couldn't sell dirty fabric.

Zoë the office cat, just past the baby kitten stage, stared at him from the doorway of her carpeted tower. Her amber eyes blinked a few times before she emerged. He picked her up and rubbed her ears as he returned to the window, waiting, wanting to be sure Vicky saw him.

After a full two minutes, he tugged on the cord, drawing the heavy curtains over the window. From the sidewalk below, a woman's voice rose to his ears. "Someone's in there. I just saw the curtain close. Maybe if we knock, they'll open for us."

Returning Zoë to her nest, careful not to switch the lights off, Tony wandered downstairs. Nothing looked out of place. There were no obvious signs Vicky had ever been there. He couldn't guess her next move. Would she arrive, ready to replace Theo, or would she put a bullet into him?

He turned the classroom light off and those in the back of the store, leaving only the ones over the counter on. Feeling like an actor in a grade-C movie, he dug around under the counter and found a paper bag. Clumsy, he picked up a pen and dropped it. He groped on the floor, stalling. It felt like weeks passed before he heard the back door open and close. He released the breath he held and lifted his eyes. The soft footsteps behind him belonged to Theo and Sheila. In spite of the heat, they kept their sweatshirt hoods pulled forward to shadow their faces. With their hands in the kangaroo pockets they moved silently, slipping from shadow to shadow until they reached the darkened classroom.

Standing up, he used the wide black marker he'd found under the counter and wrote a note on the paper bag. Carrying a roll of blue masking tape and his notice, he walked to the glass front door. Even as he used a couple of strips of tape to attach the sign to the glass in the door, a cluster of women standing on the sidewalk looked elated to see him and then downcast as they read the notice. "Closed. Family Emergency."

"Psst, Tony?"

As casually as he could, Tony made his way into the darkened end of the store. When he cracked his shin on a display, he swore softly and fluently. It released some of the tension of the day. "Theo?"

She didn't lower her hood but leaned against him for a moment. He wanted to grab her and kiss her but couldn't take the chance. Vicky could be staring at his back right now. His skin crawled at the idea.

"Do you have to close the shop tomorrow? Couldn't Gretchen open it as usual?" Theo's voice was a breath of sound. "I hate to see shoppers turned away."

A bubble of laughter almost choked him. "You feel sorry for the shoppers or just hate to miss the business?"

"Both." She managed a quiet giggle.

"Okay, I'll amend the sign and I'll call Gretchen and explain her role in our little melodrama." His thanks arrived in the form of a soft kiss planted in the center of his chest. Although he couldn't really feel it through his vest, he knew it was there, and that was enough.

"Good night, Sheriff," Sheila's voice came from the darkness. "I'll take good care of her."

"I know you will." As he turned back toward the light, he whispered, "Good night, ladies."

Pausing at the door, he amended the sign to read "Shortened store hours because of an emergency." Hoping everything would fall into place before he had to involve too many people in the secret, he turned off the last of the downstairs lights. Gretchen would definitely have to know. He locked the front door and stood for a moment, head lowered, his hand pressed against the glass. It didn't take any acting skills at all to look tired and lost.

As he waited, he heard the phone ringing inside Theo's shop. After the fourth ring, he heard the message he'd left begin to play.

The caller disconnected without leaving a message.

He trudged along the sidewalk to the Blazer and climbed inside. Tony couldn't help wonder if the caller's phone number would be on the caller ID list in the morning. A glance at the upper-story windows showed a hint of light but no sign anyone was inside.

Gretchen answered her phone on the second ring.

Tony explained only the role she was to play in their

melodrama. With her stage training, she'd be fine.

"Can I ask one question?"

"Sure."

"If she comes into the shop, do I have to let her leave or can I knock her down and tie her up?"

"Do whatever you think best." Tony felt the knot in his chest ease. "Be safe."

"You, too." Gretchen disconnected the call.

Uncertain of his next expected move, he drove to his house and parked in the front. Instead of going inside, he sat, staring at it. Without Theo or the boys, his home would be too empty to bear. He grasped the door handle, preparing to go in and at least rescue the dog. He thought poor Daisy was probably pacing in circles, and then he remembered that Gus and the boys had taken her with them. She was probably curled up between them on the floor, watching some super hero save the world.

He could use a super hero to help find Vicky.

He settled back into his seat, waiting for inspiration. It didn't come fast enough. He fell asleep almost immediately.

CHAPTER THIRTY-FIVE

What awakened him, he couldn't guess. His eyes had grown accustomed to the dark. After a moment he noticed a shadow, darker than the others, moving along the grass next to the creek running parallel to his house and the park. The shadow staggered as it neared his home and his focus sharpened. Was that Vicky?

The shadow moved closer to the house and into the circle of light cast by the nearest streetlight.

The extra light helped. Still, Tony could only make out the shape. It looked like a man, not a woman, a small man with broad shoulders and narrow hips. The shadow carried a large, and obviously heavy, duffel bag. Struggling with his burden, the man paused frequently, resting the bag on the ground before grasping the handles with both hands and swinging it forward as if momentum would help move it along.

Tony had his hand on the radio when a shaft of moonlight penetrated the overhanging trees and struck the shadow's face. Roscoe. Tony recognized him immediately. Harmless, loopy Roscoe.

Mesmerized, Tony stared, considering possibilities, and came up with none. He simply couldn't imagine what Roscoe was doing. And why here? And on foot? Roscoe wasn't generally disposed toward exercise for fun of it. His trailer park was on the far side of town and he usually spent his evenings watching television with a vending machine for company.

At that moment, Roscoe stepped into a slight depression and staggered. The bag stuck in the bottom. Wrestling with it failed to move the bag forward. He dropped it and jumped up and down, flapping his arms like wings. It looked to Tony as if Roscoe was talking to the bag while trying to fly.

The bag moved.

Roscoe wasn't touching it.

Fascinated, Tony leaned forward and eased the window down, listening. Roscoe didn't kick the bag, he gently nudged it with his foot. Tony heard Roscoe's nasal twang travel through the night air. "Be still."

The bag growled in response. Sort of. It wasn't a dog's growl. The unfamiliar snarl raised the hairs on Tony's arms. Before he could identify the sound, the bag began to move up and down like someone was inside it dribbling basketballs. Roscoe lunged for the handle and missed. At the same time the sound intensified, becoming a banshee yowl, and the bag bounced toward the creek.

Scrambling after the runaway duffel, Roscoe shrieked, a shrill, extended, "Noooooooo!"

"Sweet mother-of-pearl! What is in that bag?" Tony couldn't stand it any longer. Thoughts of Vicky receded as he grabbed his flashlight and jumped out of the Blazer.

Theo wouldn't exactly classify the night with Sheila as a slumber party or a quilting retreat.

They weren't suffering, either. The two women explored the contents of the tiny pantry as soon as they got upstairs. Now that she was safe and knew that her family was safe, Theo's stomach growled like crazy. She was starving! She didn't even want to consider how long it was since she'd last eaten.

The tiny pantry held packages of microwave popcorn and macaroni and cheese, a variety of canned soups and fruits, tuna, crackers and even hot cider mix and hot chocolate. There was plenty to feed them both. The air-conditioning worked perfectly. They snacked for a while and watched a movie with the sound turned low.

Sheila made frequent checks of the doors and windows. Nothing looked out of the ordinary. The telephone probably rang twenty times, and each time the sound startled them. No one ever left a message. Sheila happened to be standing next to it when it rang. The caller ID screen glowed neon green. "Caller unknown" read the display. She glanced at Theo. "Is this normal? Do you usually have messages in the morning?"

"No. I've spent a lot of evenings here, and I swear the phone didn't ring more than once." Exhausted, her eyelids felt as if lead fishing weights were attached to her lashes. She struggled to sit upright and lost the battle. Sinking onto the mattress, she whispered, "Do you think it's Vicky?"

Sheila considered the question. "Yes, it probably is. Why do you think she keeps calling? It's the middle of the night."

"Maybe she thinks Tony is here." Theo sighed and pulled a vibrantly colorful flannel quilt over herself. "Maybe she knows the whole thing is a setup. Right now, I'm too tired to care."

Tony ran toward Roscoe. The poor man grabbed for the handle of the duffel bag and missed again. The canvas bag yowled again and bounced faster. In Tony's estimation, only a couple of good bounces separated the bag from the water in the creek.

Roscoe yelled. "Stop, Baby!"

"Baby?" Tony lunged for the bag at the same time as Roscoe. Neither of them got a grip on the handle, they each grabbed a fistful of canvas. The bag bounced and yowled again, nearly pulling the men into the water.

"On two," said Tony.

Roscoe nodded, never taking his eyes from the bag.

"One, two." Tony tightened his grip and heaved. Roscoe did the same. The bag came to a gentle stop three feet up the bank. It was silent for a moment. Then it bounced and yowled again. This time it moved away from the creek.

"Baby!" Roscoe grabbed the handle and clung to it like the tail on a kite.

"Open it," said Tony.

"No, sir." Roscoe tightened his grip on the bag and sank his teeth into his lower lip.

"Now." Tony was not amused. Roscoe caring for a baby was clearly a disaster in the making. He reached for the zipper. The bag growled. "What the hell kind of baby is that?"

Roscoe's body sagged. His hand trembled as he reached for the tab and slid the zipper partway down.

Tony focused the flashlight beam on the opening. An empty baby bottle flew from the bag and landed at Tony's feet. He leaned over and peered inside. Staring up at him was Baby. A black bear cub with a white patch of fur on its chest lay on its back blinking at the sudden bright light.

The cub growled at him.

"What is that?" Moving the light to Roscoe's face, Tony glared at the man. He felt like Theo looked when she was interrogating the boys about some misdeed. For a moment it looked like Roscoe planned to feign ignorance.

"This is Baby." Roscoe reached into the bag and began scratching the white spot on the cub's chest. The little bear immediately made a humming sound and settled down.

Tony didn't know if bears could purr, although it sounded like one to him. "Tell me about Baby."

Roscoe's eyes crossed with the effort he made to comply with Tony's request. He looked surprised that he needed to explain. "Thought you could tell. Baby's a bear."

"No? Really?" Tony reached into his pocket for an antacid

but came up empty-handed. "I never would have guessed."

"Gee, Sheriff, I'd a thought anyone could recognize a bear." Roscoe appeared awestruck by Tony's lack of education.

"I was kidding. I know what it is." Tony sighed heavily. He didn't feel particularly interested in Roscoe's opinion. "Where'd you get the bear?"

Roscoe stared at Tony's badge but said nothing. At their feet the bear cub burped.

Suddenly weary beyond reason and tolerance, Tony leaned against a nearby tree and crossed his arms over his chest. After the day he'd had, he could probably fall asleep in that position. The nap in his car had probably lasted less than fifteen minutes.

Roscoe didn't show any signs of answering his question.

Tony waved him away, knowing he could always find the man again. He suspected Roscoe knew as well as he did that Tennessee law prohibited keeping a wild animal for a pet. It didn't matter if the critter was a frog, a raccoon or a bear. Roscoe wasn't well educated. Still, he was smart enough to keep his mouth shut. Tony sighed, saying nothing as Roscoe and Baby bounced their way past his home and climbed into Roscoe's truck on the next street over.

Tonight Tony just didn't care. If he thought of it, he'd report the violation in the morning. The game wardens would have a field day trying to get a straight answer out of Roscoe. That thought made him smile. Someone else could deal with Roscoe and his illegal Baby.

He couldn't bring himself to enter the house. Without even the dog for company, the silence would keep him awake. If he got any sleep, it would have to be in his office, at his desk.

As he pulled away from his home and drove along the quiet park dotted with lights on decorative poles and the streets surrounding it, he thought he could feel someone watching him.

Being paranoid didn't mean no one was out to get you.

275

CHAPTER THIRTY-SIX

Vicky's car, the silver sedan, turned up shortly after daybreak. Evidently, while the entire sheriff's department searched for Vicky and Tony dug through paperwork on his desk, someone had driven the car into the parking lot shared by the law enforcement center and the municipal offices and abandoned it.

Wade discovered it and ran a check on the license plates. To no one's surprise, the car had been stolen in Asheville. The owner, a high school kid working at a fast-food restaurant, had been knocked out and his keys taken from his hand. He never saw his assailant.

So, if not the silver Ford, what was Vicky driving now?

An envelope taped to the steering wheel was addressed to "Tony. Personal."

Treated as the most valuable piece of evidence ever collected in the history of law enforcement, the note inside was transferred into a protective cover. Then it was read by no fewer than twelve people. So much for personal. Tony thought the idea of personally strangling Vicky with his bare hands held real appeal.

Written in block letters and adorned with myriad hearts drawn in red marker, reading it sent chills down his spine.

Dearest,

Soon we will celebrate our blessed union. Our eternal adoration will no longer be interfered with by that interfering bitch, your late wife.

You will know such joy as never before. Until then, my love, remember our vows to each other.

Fury surged through Tony, obliterating all pretense of a civilized man. He would strangle Vicky with his bare hands if he caught up with her first.

No one found a morsel of humor in the situation.

At one minute after eight that morning, Calvin called Tony. "I just got a call from a woman asking if I collected your wife's body from the clinic. She said she wants to send funeral flowers."

Tony jumped to his feet and began pacing, the phone pressed to his ear and the blessed lack of a cord giving him freedom of movement. Maybe their plan was working. "And? What did you say?"

Calvin sounded miffed but he repeated it anyway. "I said that it was my understanding the family is not yet prepared to deal with condolence calls and asked the caller to respect your wishes and privacy."

"Excellent." Tony wandered to the lunchroom and poured himself a cup of coffee. "She'll probably keep calling. Just keep telling her the same thing."

"I'll take care of it."

"Thanks, Calvin." Tony knew this plan wouldn't work at all without the undertaker's cooperation.

"I'm glad I could help." Calvin's voice echoed through the phone. "There are worse places I could be this morning, you know. Like at home."

"Doreen's still upset, is she?" Tony felt a smile lift his lips. It would take a brave or desperate man to go home to that angry woman. A hungry bear cub in a duffel bag would be a snap to deal with in comparison.

"Yes, yes she is." Calvin gulped loudly into the phone. "I do believe she's somewhat calmer than she was. Oops, call coming in." He disconnected.

Lowering his receiver, Tony thought it sounded like Calvin had a pair of gym socks stuffed down his throat. He suspected "somewhat calmer" was an exaggeration.

Tony dropped by Theo's shop to check on his wife and deputy. A couple of tourists, the same women he'd seen on the sidewalk the night before, stood peering through the glass. With their hands cupped over their eyes to cut the glare, they looked like bird watchers holding binoculars.

He cleared his throat and the women jumped. One of them emitted a shriek that drew the attention of a couple of men standing nearby drinking coffee from tall paper cups. The men just grinned widely and continued downing their coffee. Tony would bet the unsympathetic men were the women's husbands.

While the women regained their composure, he considered what he would tell them.

Gretchen's arrival eliminated the need.

Transforming their two-minute conversation from the night before into a performance piece, the former opera student employed her acting skills and imagination to extend her sympathy as she ushered him and the women inside. Keeping up a constant stream of chatter, she began flicking on the lights.

Slipping away unnoticed, Tony made his way upstairs, opening Theo's office door without knocking. Sheila had her sidearm pointed at his heart when the door swung wide, making him think his surprise visit was ill advised. He raised his hands into the air and grinned at her until she holstered the gun. A glance around the room made his smile widen. Theo's office and work area were cluttered with bright pieces of fabric. Scraps littered the floor and new blocks were pinned to Theo's design wall. He didn't know if Theo was working or if Sheila was being converted into a quilter.

Tony heaved a sigh of relief. Either scenario meant Theo was fine.

His wife half-reclined on the daybed. The kitten slept on her lap as Theo used a seam ripper to pick out stitches in a small quilt square. She looked only slightly the worse for wear, her face bruised and sunburned. She grinned at him and he could see that some of the puffiness had receded. In a few days, she would look like nothing had happened to her.

He doubted he would ever be the same. If he had hair, it would have turned silver in the night. His cell phone rang, effectively stopping his morbid train of thought.

"Sheriff?" Wade sounded like he was still sleeping. "Are you coming back in today?"

"Yes. I'll stop by the Cashdollar Mortuary, first. It has to look like I'm planning a funeral." Tony felt a chill as he said it. "Dollars to doughnuts Vicky's watching the place."

"If only we knew where she was watching from."

"True. So true." Tony waved to the women, pasted on his sad face and made his way down the stairs and out onto the sidewalk. The heat hit him like a fist, and it was still early in the day.

It took only moments to drive the three blocks to the parking lot shared by Doreen's Gift and Flower Shoppe and the Cashdollar Mortuary. Because Doreen stocked a large number of gift items for brides and new babies, as well as flowers and sympathy cards, people often called it the "beginning to the end."

Tony released the breath he discovered he held and went through the outside mortuary door. The business office was on the right. He could see Calvin at his desk, typing something into a laptop computer. The hallway and door that separated the gift shop from the funeral home was to his left. Straight ahead was a set of double doors. They were closed.

He'd chat with Calvin for a respectable amount of time and return to his own office. Maybe Ruth Ann's computer skills would have discovered the owner of the abandoned farm, Theo's prison. Maybe she'd even have search warrants. He could dream.

Ruth Ann was talking on the telephone when he arrived. She scribbled a note and handed it to him as he approached her desk. As usual, her research skills were impeccable. Her familiarity with the law didn't hurt, either. Her concern regarding Theo's situation manifested itself in her setting aside her customary preoccupation with her fingernails.

The note simply said, *"Cabin and land belong to Nelson Parker. Archie's working on getting warrants. He didn't seem to think there'd be a problem."*

Tony hadn't even gotten his mail open when Park County's prosecutor, Archie Campbell, strolled through the open doorway. His wide smile told Tony what he needed to know.

Archie ran a hand through his red hair. Tony watched. Maybe the hair wasn't quite as dark as it had been when he was younger, but it was still thick and glossy.

Tony's envy was dispelled by the knowledge that Archie was on their side. Without a warrant, there was little they could legally search. "What's the word?"

"Two warrants. One for the abandoned cabin, all buildings and the property it sits on. I've included a map of it. A separate warrant for his current residence and all possessions." Archie handed him a fat document. "Everything on the Parker properties, inside the Parker buildings and vehicles." He grinned. "You can dig up the old man's corn and tobacco and sift through every speck of his dirt and anything else that appeals to you."

Momentarily speechless, Tony fanned his face with the warrant, bringing a whiff of Archie's expensive aftershave to his nose. Maybe his department could buy the man another bottle of the stuff as thanks. "What judge and why so generous?"

"Since Nelson's niece was Theo's abductor and she stayed up at his place, it wasn't hard to get a warrant." Archie shifted around until he was comfortable on the vinyl chair. "Judge Smith would make a good 'hanging' judge. I barely mentioned the victim's relationship to you before the cap came off his pen."

Tony studied Archie's face. The man looked like he might explode if he didn't get to finish his story. "There's more?"

Lots of shiny white teeth greeted his question. "He offered to sign an extra one, blank, you know just in case."

"I like that idea. A lot. I'll pass." Tony thought Archie's smile looked forced. The shadow in the prosecutor's eyes exposed the depth of his anger about Theo's abduction.

"You want to come with us?" Tony pressed the button connecting him to dispatch. Archie didn't immediately respond. Tony said, "Rex, call out the troops. We're going to search the Parker lands."

Archie straightened his tie. "I know y'all will have fun digging in the weeds and climbing through and under that rat trap of a house. Instead, I'll mosey on back to my office. It's got better air-conditioning than yours."

The search for Vicky began at the cabin where she abandoned Theo. In broad daylight, it looked even more remote. The back of the cabin's roof had a hole in it the size of a washtub and the floor beneath it had rotted away to the dirt below.

The smokehouse was intact but showed no signs of recent use. Judging by the size of the bush growing in the privy, no one could hide in there.

Leaving a couple of deputies combing the woods around the cabin, Tony and the rest headed for Nelson Parker's current home. He figured they could walk between the two properties faster than they could drive. Walking was a straight line to the south. Driving took them north and then west before circling to the far side of the mountain.

He glanced into his rearview mirror. Thank goodness for interagency cooperation. A line of law enforcement vehicles followed him. There weren't that many entries in the Fourth of July parade.

In the chaos and aftermath of Theo's abduction, Tony had lost sight of his one-time goal in getting onto the property. What would they find there? Might there really be a freezer containing the remains of Vicky's high school madness with Harrison Duff? It felt like thirty years since his drive to Cincinnati. In fact, it had been less than a week.

"Nelson Parker." Tony spoke into the Blazer's microphone. "Come on out. We have warrants to search your place." He waved a sheaf of papers, not the actual warrants, above his head, half expecting a bullet to rip through them. Nothing.

The sound of his own voice echoed from the surrounding hills. Nothing moved. Nothing. Not even Nelson's normal greeting of a shotgun barrel presented through the open window.

No ugly chickens pecked in the dirt. The old man's pickup sat in the driveway. There were no other vehicles. No shotgun-toting man in overalls met them at the gate this day. Three strands of scrap wire held the gate closed. The fence post wobbled when they began untwisting the wire. The little farm appeared abandoned as they lifted the gate and set it aside. They walked in, leaving their vehicles parked on the road. A line of heavily armed deputies fanned out behind Tony.

If anything, Tony thought the corn and tobacco looked more pitiful than ever.

Echoing his thoughts, Wade said, "Parker needs to water his garden." Bending over, he poked a finger into the dirt. "It's dying of thirst in this weather."

Tony nodded. Maybe he was punchy from a lack of sleep. The little patch of land gave him the creeps. What else had to die? What was buried beneath it?

A sudden rustling in a shrub snapped their heads around. Guns pointed, they watched a spotted hog emerge from the underbrush and amble past. It didn't even seem to see them. A whisper reached his ears. "We could have a pig roast later."

"With a skinny pig?" Tony pointed to the animal's ribs. "Who would eat a skinny pig?"

Tony and Wade led their group to the front of the house. Mike took another group around back. Radios tuned to the same band kept the groups in touch.

The boards of the porch sagged, just like the roof overhang above. The door was latched from the outside with another piece of wire, wrapped around a pair of long, rusting nails.

Wade began untwisting it. Tony stood, shotgun raised, pointing through a broken windowpane. "Nelson Parker."

A faint but human cry was the only answer.

Accompanied by the borrowed SWAT team, they surged into the main room. It was half kitchen, half living space. No one. Two closed doors were set into the opposite wall.

A flick of a wrist turned the knob of the first. The door swung inward. Sparsely furnished and surprisingly tidy, it appeared to be Nelson's bedroom. A threadbare quilt covered a sagging mattress. Instead of a closet, a row of hooks held the old man's extra overalls and shirts. There was no place to hide.

The cry came again.

They opened the next door. Either the floor was warped or the door was. It screeched as it dragged and opened halfway before sticking. The room was bare except for a cot and a bright green and yellow playpen.

Standing, hanging onto the edge of the playpen with one hand, a baby boy gurgled and waved a soggy cracker in his other hand. From the smell of it, his diaper needed changing.

Wade snapped a handful of photographs before Tony approached the playpen. With the ease of long practice, Tony reached over and lifted the little guy, careful not to smudge any possible fingerprints on the playpen or get dirtied by the infant.

An open package of diapers sat in the corner along with some baby wipes. Tony cleaned the baby and discarded the dirty diaper and soiled shirt, putting them into an empty grocery bag. He tied a knot in the open end of the plastic grocery bag, hoping to keep the stench down. The baby didn't seem hungry or upset. He was quickly intrigued by the shiny gold badge attached to Tony's shirt and reached for it with sticky fingers.

"He hasn't been alone long." Tony offered his opinion. "There's no sign of a rash. He's pretty laid-back about the whole thing."

"How'd she get away?"

"I can answer that." Mike's voice rattled through the radio. "We've got a small still up here, maybe fifty yards from the house." The radio crackled. "There's a tunnel, too, that shows signs of recent usage."

"Fabulous." Tony never expected this to be easy but couldn't they catch a break?

"Sheriff?" Mike's voice came again. "I'll go through the tunnel, I'm not sure you'll pick up my transmissions."

"No. I don't like it." Tony propped the baby into the crook of his arm. "Vicky or Nelson or both of them could be in there, waiting for you. You wouldn't stand a chance against a shotgun blast in a tunnel. Come up with a better plan."

"Okay, sir. We'll get back to you in a minute." He paused. "Did I understand correctly? Does Vicky have a baby?"

"I doubt it." Tony stared down into a face that looked like it belonged in a baby food ad. The baby grinned, exposing four little teeth, and tried to bite into Tony's badge. "I'll bet this is the baby missing from the shopping mall in Charlotte."

"At least someone will have good news today." Mike cleared his throat. "What are you going to do with him?"

"I'm going to get Ruth Ann to come up here with a car seat and a couple of deputies. I want Doc Nash to come, too. After he checks the baby, I want him to be on hand when we open that freezer, if it's here."

"It's here. I think I passed it on the way to the still. It's covered with a bunch of stuff, but you can't hide the shape."

"Leave someone, several someones at the still in case someone pops out. You come back, Mike," Tony said. "You can show us the freezer. I'll borrow a robot if we need it to search underground."

CHAPTER THIRTY-SEVEN

Tony and Wade waited until Doc Nash declared the infant as fit to travel in a car seat. Minutes later, Ruth Ann, the baby and two escort vehicles headed for town.

Doc Nash looked as if he'd like to follow them. No one seemed anxious to proceed. They stalled for about five minutes before making their way, single file, following Mike around the side of the house to the site of the old shed. He pointed to his discovery.

The freezer sat exactly where Harrison had sworn it would be.

With the building gone, hauled off to Claude Marmot's home, the freezer sat in the open. Even so, if they hadn't known where to look, they might have missed it during a casual search of the property. Someone had attempted to camouflage the thing. Not only was it draped with an olive-drab canvas tarp, but a few cut branches and some loose dirt had been scattered on the lid. The bottom of the once-white freezer sat on packed earth that blended with the rust, the color of autumn maple leaves, creeping upward from the ground.

Photographs were taken before they carefully removed the tarp, exposing an ancient full-size chest-type freezer.

A shiny new, stainless steel padlock held it closed. Fingerprints, if any, would most likely be found on the lock.

Wade waved his magic dusting brush. Nothing. Not even a creature had left a mark. It was anybody's guess when the lock was added. It had to be sometime after Harrison moved the body to McMahon Park. Three months to three minutes.

Armed with a pair of industrial-strength bolt cutters, they managed to cut the lock off and dropped it into an evidence bag. Maybe something would turn up under the microscope. Maybe the state lab people could find some special clue that would prove the case and land them on a television forensics show.

"No more stalling," said Tony. "We might as well do it."

Wade nodded and tried the lid. It didn't budge. Mike added his muscle. Without warning, the hinges, rotten with rust, broke and the lid slid down the back, crashing into the packed earth with an ominous thud.

Nelson Parker stared up at them. Even enclosed in a large sheet of heavy, clear plastic like a disposable drop cloth, he was recognizable, right down to his overalls. Whoever had wrapped him up had used a lot of silver duct tape, until the body resembled an Egyptian mummy.

The wrapping wasn't airtight. As quickly as the door fell, the putrid stench of hot, decaying flesh rose like steam in the sultry air. Shocked and sickened, Mike and Wade jumped back, out of range. Doc Nash stood like a statue staring at the body.

Wade jogged away before pausing for his ceremonial upchuck.

Tony walked away, sucking in deep breaths of fresh air through his mouth, trying to avoid joining his deputy puking in the brush. He stopped and studied the body from a distance. He was damned sick and tired of looking at corpses.

It didn't take a great mind or a pathologist to see that Nelson's body hadn't been here long. As hot as the weather was, Tony guessed maybe only a day or two. He glanced at the ground. Who could guess how much evidence they'd trampled?

"Well, that's not what I expected to see in there." The doctor sounded as weary as Tony felt. "What do you suppose is under him?"

"I can see fingerprints on the plastic." Wade pulled out his camera again and began taking a series of photographs. He took care not to inhale near the remains. "We should leave him there until we can process the scene."

Tony nodded. "If only we knew where the scene is." He gestured widely. "We've trampled every damn inch of this place, and I want to know what's underneath Mr. Parker. Now."

Four borrowed deputies arrived just in time to help. Looking like they'd prefer to leave, they watched as Wade and Mike put on double layers of gloves and lifted Nelson, still in his plastic shroud, and lowered him into a body bag. The moment the zipper closed, they all inhaled.

"He's as skinny as his pig," said Wade.

Mike nodded. "The old guy weighs nothing. My granny could lift him."

Tony leaned forward, looking into the freezer and saw an assortment of bone and some bits, maybe mummified remains. Harrison's claim of three more bodies in there was incorrect. Tony could see five skulls.

Tony began punching the buttons on his cell. He needed lots of help.

Tony called the Feds. He wanted them to come collect the older remains. If they were in fact the remains of the murders committed in the national park, those murders had taken place on federal soil and they should process the scene, or at least help, and then prosecute. He didn't care who took the bodies and the case—the FBI, the National Park Service, or the CIA.

He stared at the body bag. It felt like the weight of the world rested on his shoulders.

No matter how he looked at the problem, Nelson Parker's murder was his to deal with. It was easy enough to figure out who had stuffed him into the freezer. It was not so easy to guess why. In the long run the why wasn't the issue. Guesses wouldn't convict a stray dog much less a wily murderer.

They needed proof.

Tony stood in Theo's office, wondering how long they could maintain the charade of her death. The ringing phone snapped him into the present.

"We have Vicky Parker's whereabouts, sir." Rex's voice boomed from Tony's tiny phone.

"Where is she?" He felt Theo's hand on his arm and looked down. His wife's face was pale and concerned. He squeezed her hand. "Is she alone?"

"No."

Tony thought Rex sounded agitated. Not at all like Rex.

"She's in Doreen's Flower and Gift Shoppe. From what I gather, she went into Doreen's to get a bridal bouquet." Rex cleared his throat. "The Queen asked who the groom was and when Vicky said it was you, Doreen laughed in her face. I guess it's turning into a real cat fight."

"Not good." Tony was appalled and afraid of what might happen. Vicky was as volatile as gasoline and Doreen might be the flame to ignite it. "Calvin didn't explain the situation to his wife?"

"I guess not, or if he did, she forgot about it. There's more."

"What?" Tony headed for the stairs, thinking Rex sounded scared.

"There's a high school girl in the back room. She's the one who called. Her name's Chandra Wilson. I still have her on the line." He cleared his throat. "Sir, she's my sister's oldest girl."

Tony felt like if it weren't for bad luck, they'd have none at all. "Keep her on the phone and keep her calm, and for heaven's sake tell her not to make any noise."

Tony tried to visualize the interior of the shop. It wasn't a place he often entered and if he was inside, he was usually looking for the way out. There was stuff everywhere and he was just too big to feel like he wasn't about to knock everything over. Literally a bull in a china cabinet.

He did know the general layout. The front doors were set in the center of the narrow end of the rectangular building. Just inside those doors was the counter and cash register. Myriad floor-to-ceiling glass shelves held everything from fine crystal to key rings that looked like Hollywood versions of outhouses. In the back of the shop was a bank of tall coolers filled with fresh flowers and another counter. To the right of the cooler was the door that connected it with the mortuary. To the left was a short hallway that held restrooms, Doreen's office and the door into the stockroom. A door from there opened into the parking lot.

Entering from the front seemed out of the question. Mortuary or stockroom? Tony weighed the pros and cons as he ran from Theo's shop.

"I'm sending everyone I can find. Should be about twenty vehicles arriving soon. Do you want them to hold back?"

"Yes. I don't want Vicky looking out those windows and seeing anything different. Have them fan around the back and park on the mortuary end." He began to hear voices on the radio. "Keep Chandra on the phone line with you and tell her to stay in the back room unless she is absolutely positive she can get into the mortuary safely. I don't think she's near the connecting door."

After a moment's pause, Rex answered, "She says she's stuck in there and is crawling into a corner behind some boxes of pots and pans."

"Smart girl." Tony exhaled sharply. "She should be as safe there as anywhere. Make sure everyone knows her location."

Tony stopped next to the Blazer and stared up at the Cash-dollar businesses. With summer traffic and the desire for the element of surprise, he took off running. It would be faster. Sure enough, there was a veritable parade of law enforcement vehicles headed toward Doreen's. A borrowed SWAT van parked off to one side. Tony thought it would be a great time to rob a bank. Every town and county in the eastern half of the state had sent at least one car and one cop. Some had sent more.

When this was over, he'd owe more favors than he could pay in a lifetime.

A Sevier County car rolled to a stop next to him and Tony jumped in. "Drive around back."

"Yes, sir." The deputy steered the car in a wide loop and parked near the SWAT van.

Tony jumped out and gave the deputy two thumbs up even as he continued his conversation with Rex. "Is everyone on the same frequency now?"

Sounding much calmer than he had, Rex answered in the affirmative. "What's the plan?"

"I'm not sure I'd call it a plan, I seem to be the one Vicky wants to impress, so I think I'll let her." Tony didn't want to admit his lack of a plan. "Link me to Chandra."

"No, sir. I don't like it."

"Rex, you're not getting paid to like it." Tony strode toward the front door of the Gift Shoppe with his recent chauffeur hot on his heels. A glance to the side confirmed Wade and Mike approaching from the opposite angle. They looked like commandos.

"Sheriff?" A girl's voice whispered in his ear. "Where are you?"

"I'm just outside the front door."

"The Queen and that other woman are screaming at each other."

Sure enough, Tony heard sounds of a cat fight coming through the radio or the door or both. "Hey, Chandra?"

"Yes?"

"How do you know if a customer comes in and you're in the back room? Is there a bell?"

"No. There's a light that flashes in the stockroom."

"Good." She might have said more, Tony cut her off. He stared through the glass of the door. Doreen stood on the far side, almost facing him. Vicky stood with her back to him. The marble counter between them held a bridal bouquet of long-stemmed white flowers and lots of ribbons and bows. His stomach churned.

Easing the door open a crack, he released the aromas of perfumes and candles and the sound of two exceedingly angry female voices.

Without warning, Doreen grabbed the long-stemmed flowers and began whacking Vicky across the face with them and swearing at the top of her lungs. For her part, Vicky pulled the revolver's hammer back with her thumb and pointed it at Doreen's chest.

In the split second before Tony and the first three deputies lunged inside, Tony realized he'd never suspected the Queen to have such a command of profanity.

Swearing the entire time, Doreen went ballistic, leaped over the counter like an Olympic hurdler and planted her fist into Vicky's jaw.

Before she could hit the floor, Tony grabbed Vicky's gun hand, squeezing it hard and pointing the barrel of the revolver at the floor. With the hammer back, it wouldn't take much to make it discharge. Doreen continued slapping Vicky with the barren stems she clutched in her free hand. When he shifted positions, she turned on him, hitting his nose with the sap, or whatever gel-like goo comes out of broken flowers, shoving a thorn into his lower lip.

Two deputies each grabbed one of the Queen's arms and dragged her away.

While the extra deputy clung to Vicky's free arm, Tony managed to wrestle the revolver away from her without shooting anything. Vicky wasn't going down easy. She lashed out with a foot, caught the edge of a glass shelf filled with crystal gewgaws and sent it crashing into the one behind it. The chain reaction of shattering shelves and glassware moved across the store like dominos falling.

Above the sound of breaking glass and a string of curses, Tony heard a scream that made his skin crawl. Doreen sounded like a banshee.

The deputy clinging to Vicky let out a pain-induced, "Bitch."

Without releasing his grip on her, Tony glanced at his assistant. Vicky's teeth pierced the man's forearm. He was swearing a blue streak but wasn't giving up. Tony signaled a SWAT member to join them. He guessed the man weighed about two hundred pounds and carried close to another hundred in gear. "Sit on her."

"Sir?" After a quick glance at the situation, he happily complied, lowering himself onto Vicky's thighs, holding her firmly in place while Tony snapped one of the bracelets of his handcuffs on her. Seeing she still had her teeth set in the deputy's arm, Tony reached across and under her chin and squeezed her cheeks with his fingers, pressing against her teeth. When she opened her mouth, he picked up a fallen package of cornbread mix and wedged that into her mouth in place of anyone's body parts.

The instant the handcuff snapped on the second wrist, he

sent the bite victim out to see the doctor. "Tell Doc she might have rabies."

CHAPTER THIRTY-EIGHT

Theo paced around her office making herself and Sheila dizzy. The Queen wouldn't put up with interference of any kind, especially in her own business. Theo knew that for a fact.

Finally her phone chimed. "Tony?"

"Everything's fine."

She guessed, "Doreen shot Vicky with her own gun?"

"Not quite. She was holding her own, though, and swearing like a sailor."

"I guess you'd know all about that." Theo began to giggle. "No offense."

"None taken." Although he rarely used profanity, Tony'd had a fair command of it by the third grade and added to it each year after that. His Navy days served as graduate studies.

"Where's Vicky now?"

"She's locked up. I can see her from here. She's in the holding cell pacing, spitting and screaming."

Theo heard Rex's laugh echoing through the phone. "So everyone's okay?"

"Vicky bit one of the loaner deputies. We owe him big-time."

Theo thought he sounded tired. "He'll be alright?"

"Yeah. Doc cleaned it up and gave him some antibiotics." His voice lightened. "He's in the lunchroom, laughing his fool head off now and trying to write up his report. He says Vicky is bad news. He also claims he never, ever, met anyone who scares him more than Queen Doreen—and he did two tours in Iraq. The man knows scary."

In the middle of the night, Tony lay awake. The breeze moving through the bedroom, propelled by the ceiling fan, felt pleasantly cool. He was sweating like crazy. He opened his eyes, staring through the darkness at a wicker chair on the tiny balcony outside. It would feel so good to sit out there and let the fresh air clear his mind and dry his skin.

This felt even better. This was heaven.

The big bed was overcrowded. Theo lay pressed against him. Where her skin touched his, he baked and she sweated. The dog panted. To welcome Theo and the boys home, Daisy had been allowed to join them and now lay across the foot of the bed. Jamie and Chris slept soundly, their warm bodies draped over their parents like puppies sharing a box.

Excitement and relief kept them all awake until the early hours of the morning. Only when allowed to sleep next to their parents had the boys finally settled down, fitful even in their sleep.

Tony felt tears welling in his eyes. He'd nearly lost Theo to Vicky's madness and he'd barely had a chance to see her today. The relief of finding her safe brought another wave of adrenaline racing through him. The backwash was stunning. A new baby or another heartbreak? The last pregnancy had been so difficult for them all, but especially Theo, and then had ended in a miscarriage.

He was happy about the prospect of another baby, wasn't he? Awake, though, he worried about Theo and how they could afford another one.

Mostly he worried about what would happen to all of them if they ever lost Theo.

★ ★ ★ ★ ★

The boys wanted to stay with Theo. They begged to go to work with her and keep her in sight. Theo agreed, mostly because she needed the reassurance of seeing their precious faces. She expected they would tire of the quilt shop before noon. In truth, it was closer to eleven.

Theo laughed as Jamie grew restless, knowing he probably wanted to tell everyone he knew what had happened. The little boy loved being a storyteller. He would embellish a story beyond recognition. In his version, Theo was sure he would have rescued his mother from a cartoon villain, complete with top hat and mustache.

He'd have to make up his own details. They hadn't shared many of the facts, believing the boys didn't need to know how close she came to dying or being crippled in a fall down the mountain.

Chris was comfortable in the window seat of her office, reading a book with the sleeping cat draped across the back of his neck.

It made her sweat just looking at the pair.

Jamie poked Chris in the ribs. Chris shifted. Jamie attacked again. Chris looked over the top of his book. "Mom?"

Theo didn't bother to glance up from her sewing machine. She knew exactly what was going on. "Jamie, stop it."

Jamie persisted, never quite crossing the line that would result in lost privileges, or worse, total grounding.

On the edge between irritation and laughter, Theo reached for a paper on her desk. "I have to go deliver this clue to the mystery quilt to my friend Caro. Do you want to come with me, stay here, or finish the day at camp?"

"Camp." In a rare moment of total agreement, the boys dashed down the stairs.

Theo trotted behind them, pausing to tell Gretchen where

she was headed. "I'm going to drop the wild bunch at day camp and take this clue to the mystery quilt to Caro."

"She hasn't been in the shop for a while." Gretchen's look of concern was reflected in the face of the customer, one of the regulars.

"No." Theo agreed. "She didn't even make bowling the other night, and she only misses if her son can't come stay with Gregory."

"I'll hold down the fort."

Theo dropped the boys at day camp, sure that the high school kids who were the paid staff would earn their money. Maybe earplugs were supplied by the supervisors.

At a quick knock on his door frame, Tony looked up and saw Mike and Dammit ease into his office. Mike's expression told him he wasn't visiting. "What's happened?"

"Ruby just got a phone call from one of Hub's relatives. One of the ones we talked to a few weeks ago."

Tony felt his heart beat faster. "And does this mysterious relative claim to know something about Ruby's baby—not a baby now—Ruby's girl?"

"Yes." Mike's attempt to restrain his smile failed. "She claims she can give Ruby an address. The address of the girl and her new family."

"No kidding?" Tony laughed. Even if the lead turned into another failure, another one could turn up, a true one. "Ruby, with your help, has broken through the family wall of silence and with a clan like that, it's the biggest hurdle."

"I hope so." Mike's fingers massaged the bloodhound's floppy ears.

"And what does Ruby expect?" Serious now, Tony settled back into his chair. "Does she think the girl will be happy to see her, happy to learn she was sold like yard sale goods?"

"Ruby is a realist." Mike's eyes were clear, untroubled. "If the girl is happy, living with a good and loving family, she won't interfere. She might hope to become a family friend, you know, one invited to birthday parties." His face hardened. "If it's not a good situation, we'll both fight."

Tony nodded. "When do you leave?"

"As soon as you say go."

"Go."

With a salute, Mike turned and left, the dog trotting at his side.

"And good hunting."

CLUE #4

Draw a diagonal line on wrong side of 24 of the 2 1/8" squares of Light #3.

Place one right side down on the end of each 10 1/4" by 2 1/8" Medium #1 strip. Sew on the drawn line, press to light. This creates a light triangle on one end. Make sure all triangles are sewn in the same direction. It does not have to be the same direction as the blocks in Clue #3.

On 7 of these strips, create triangles on both ends. If the point is up on the left end of the strip, the one on the right end should be down, forming a wide parallelogram.

Lay out quilt top.

Alternate A and B blocks, 3 across and 4 down, leaving space between the blocks for the sashing. Place a 2 1/8" square of Light #3 in each intersection. Arrange plain end of sashing strips to the outside edges. The sashing strips with triangles on both ends should be placed in the middle of the quilt. The sashing strips and setting squares should form a small four-pointed star.

Sew top together.

Borders:

Using the 1 3/4" squares of Light #3 and the 32 squares of Medium/Dark #1 sew four star blocks. Make 16 star points by placing the right side of light to right side of medium. Stitch diagonal from corner to corner. Press to light. Arrange with Light #3 square as center and Medium/Dark #1 as block corners.

Measure corner blocks—trim all length-of-fabric strips to that width.

Measure quilt length and width. Trim 2 of the length-of-fabric strips to length of quilt and 2 to the width of the quilt.

Sew long borders onto quilt sides.

Sew one corner star on each end of strips cut the width of the quilt. Sew onto top and bottom.

Quilt as desired. Use remaining 2 1/2″ strips for binding.

CHAPTER THIRTY-NINE

At Caro's house, Theo rang the doorbell. She thought she heard Caro's voice but wasn't certain. There was definitely someone moving around inside. She leaned to one side and peeked into the window. Caro's husband stared back at her.

Concerned that Caro hadn't opened the door, Theo rang the bell again. The door was jerked open in her face. Gregory loomed. An angry expression contorted his face and he held a broom in his hand. There was no hint of recognition in his face.

"Hi, Gregory, is Caro at home?"

He shook his head and stared. He remained silent.

Theo studied his eyes. Alzheimer's had robbed him of so much. Now it had even robbed him of his wife. She heard Caro call out from the kitchen. "Theo, is that you?"

Theo smiled. "May I come in?"

"Why?" A hint of confusion alleviated some of Gregory's rage.

Remembering Caro often said lying was often the best option, and the bigger the lie, the more easily believed, Theo said, "I'm supposed to come clean your floors." She held out her hand. "Is that the broom you want me to use?"

Gregory handed her the broom and turned and shuffled away. Theo dashed into the kitchen where Caro lay on the floor, helpless.

"Oh, Caro, honey." Theo knelt by the old woman. "How badly are you hurt?"

"I can't get up." Caro's eyes filled with tears. "I think my hip's broken."

Theo glanced over her shoulder. Gregory sat on the edge of his recliner, staring with empty eyes at the flickering image on the television. Pulling out her cell phone, Theo called Doc Nash, explaining the situation. Then she sat on the floor and held Caro's hand. "What happened?"

"He didn't know who I was and it frightened him." Tears slipped down Caro's cheeks. "He would never hurt me on purpose."

"I know, Caro, but now he has." Theo pulled the dishtowel from the counter and wiped the tears away. "I'll call your son."

"He's in Kansas City on business. That's why he couldn't come stay with Gregory last Thursday."

"Then who else should I call?"

"I don't know."

Theo felt so hopeless and helpless. She hurried to let Doc Nash in and secure the high latch behind him so Gregory couldn't unlock it and wander off. Only because Caro was with him had the door been unlocked; otherwise they would have had to break it down.

Doc Nash greeted Gregory like the old friend he was. Moving quietly, he made his way into the kitchen. A cursory examination was all he needed before calling the ambulance. "It's the hospital in Knoxville for you, my dear."

"And Gregory, what about him?"

Doc Nash looked thoughtful. Glancing at Caro, the house, and Gregory. "He can't stay here. He loves you best and turned on you. A stranger would be too disturbing for him. I guess he'll ride along with us in the ambulance. I'll send him to the geriatric psych ward to get his medications adjusted. After that, we'll see. Maybe you can both recuperate at the same nursing home and come home together if that's what you want."

303

Theo hurried off to pack a couple of small bags, one for each of them. Out of habit, she glanced out the front windows into the yard. Caro's favorite flowerpot was gone. The thing was huge and heavy. Her nephew had taken a small barrel and covered it with broken ceramic tiles, making a mosaic design of cardinals.

Still depressed from the trauma at Caro's home, Theo tried to busy herself.

The moment Tony walked into her studio, Theo knew he came to hear her news about Caro. She looked up from her sewing machine and focused on him. He wasn't smiling.

"Are you okay?" Tony ruffled her curls.

She nodded. "Caro and Gregory will never be the same. In a way, this might work out better for them both. He'll be well cared for, entertained, get his medications on time; everything Caro couldn't do for him. Caro will visit him often, of course, but she'll be able to heal and sleep at night." Theo frowned. "Did you know she had to get up with him about eight times a night? He wandered around banging on the walls, searching for something that only he knew about."

Tony smiled but the sadness in his eyes bothered her. She'd never shared with him all the terrible or terrifying moments Caro lived with. People without personal experience with dementia rarely understood its impact on patient and caregiver. Time to change the subject, she thought. "It seems like months since we talked. What happened in Chattanooga and out at the museum? You sent us all away."

Looking surprised by the number of events in the short time, Tony sat on the window seat and the kitten jumped up next to him. "We arrested Mac."

"Mac? Why would he kill Doreen's look-alike?" She frowned, more at the exhausted expression on his face than at the news.

"Did he know who she was?"

Tony nodded and handed her a newspaper clipping encased in an evidence bag. "Actually I'm hoping for your opinion. This was in her purse." He paused. "We found it on the seat of her car which was pushed deep into the underbrush."

"Oh, my." Theo swallowed hard. The photograph showed Doreen and Bathsheba holding up the murder quilt. Doreen sported her latest hairstyle and most dazzling smile. In the background, Mac's face was captured, smiling widely, exposing a distinctive gap between two of his teeth. "This is the reason she drove up here."

Tony nodded. A frown still creased his face. "I doubt it will take long to find the hairdresser who transformed Patti into Doreen's look-alike."

Theo agreed. "If she had a regular hairdresser in Chattanooga, I'd guess she transformed Patti fairly often."

"What do you think? As a woman?" Tony looked up from the photograph. "Was it seeing the man or the woman or the quilt that compelled her to drive up here?"

Theo pushed her glasses up her nose. "Probably the combination. I'm certainly no expert. I'd guess she felt cheated all her life. Her father says he loved her but he didn't insist she could take her place in the family album. You've got her grandmother and half sister holding an heirloom for the family she felt had rejected her." Theo sensed an even deeper pain had driven Patti. "Her husband deserted her by dying. The only child she ever conceived she miscarried. I feel sorry for her." She felt tears welling in her eyes and blinked them back.

"But?" Tony massaged her shoulders, easing some of her tension.

"I don't think Mac ever intended for any of this to happen, do you?"

"No." Tony studied the picture. "If Mac had been standing in a different place or had turned his back when this picture was taken, Patti might still be alive and he wouldn't be in jail. When you think about the power of coincidence, it's amazing."

"True." She firmly believed in coincidence.

"If he had called me when it happened, it would probably have been ruled manslaughter, not murder. When he tried to cover it up, he made the situation much worse." With a frown, he lifted the kitten off his lap and stood. "I guess it's time for me to go back to the salt mines."

Theo laughed. He looked like Jamie when she told him to clean up his toys. "Putting off the paperwork won't make it get done faster."

"I know. I just thought you'd want to know what we learned."

Theo realized she hadn't told him about her discovery of the lawn ornament stash. "Speaking of learning, I know who has the lawn ornaments. I want Caro's flowerpot back in her yard before she gets home. And I want blooming flowers planted in it."

"You don't." Tony stared into her eyes. His widened. "Yes, you do."

Tony returned to his office, feeling better. In fact, he felt like jumping in the air and clicking his heels together.

Ruth Ann sat on the floor next to her desk, playing with the toddler they'd taken from Nelson's cabin. She pursed her lips and puffed air into his face. Each time she did it, he laughed so hard he'd fall over if she didn't support him with both hands.

"The Feds and his mom and dad are on their way."

"I thought they'd fly in last night." Tony knew the baby matched the photograph on the bulletin, right down to the tiny scar on his eyebrow. "Footprints check out?"

"Yes." Ruth Ann puffed in the baby's face again. "There was a huge storm system that kept them grounded in Charlotte.

They'll be here any second."

Tony felt his last knot of tension dissolve. "He's okay?"

"Absolutely." She nodded toward the front doors and spoke to the baby. "Here's your mommy and daddy."

Tony turned to see Wade holding the door for a dazed, but ecstatic, young couple and a pair of smiling FBI agents. Life was good. He loved his job.

The baby teetered, roaring with laughter. His tiny hands opened like starfish as he reached for his parents.

"It should have worked." Kenny Baines stared into Tony's left shoulder. "She ruined it when she called you."

"Who ruined what?" Tony stared at Kenny. Even if he was strong as steel, it didn't seem possible that the small man could filch such oversized yard art.

"Blossom." The little man shrugged, the sadness in his eyes gave him away.

Tony saw nothing but heartbreak reflected in them. "You took Blossom's donkey cart in hopes of gaining her attention and affection." Kenny's cheeks darkened under Tony's stunned gaze.

"It never crossed my mind she'd call you." His eyes moved away. "I figured I'd be able to find the thing and she would be all happy and grateful and maybe she'd go to the movies or somethin' with me."

Tony's eyes widened as Kenny's plan became clear. He agreed. It should have been simple and straightforward. Kenny would "find" the donkey and cart and return it to her. Blossom would be so overcome by gratitude that she would fling her arms around him and clutch him to her ample bosom. He'd be a hero. Instead, Blossom was upset and so were many other people.

"You didn't stop with her ornament."

Slumped into his chair, Kenny stared at his hands. "It became a game, I guess. Sitting home alone without the girls was making me crazy, and I knew it was wrong and yet, it *was* kinda fun."

Tony watched his misery with some sympathy. Kenny Baines had moved to Silersville about five years earlier with his wife, Yvonne, and twin daughters. The girls, Stephanie and Kimberly, were the stars in Kenny's heaven. When Yvonne fell for a backup singer in some hopeful new country group and moved to Nashville, Kenny had been granted custody. Kenny and the girls made a nice family.

The only catch, and Kenny's downfall, was sending the girls to Nashville for a week each month to stay with their mother. Tony guessed that, lonely and bored, Kenny developed a crush on Blossom.

"The girls aren't in Nashville." Tony leaned forward. "Kimberly has been at all the games and practices."

Kenny nodded. "They're staying with Yvonne at her parents' house for a change. Y'know, so they don't miss anything."

Tony relaxed in his chair. Kenny looked miserable. It was difficult to believe the small man was strong enough to heft the yard art into his pickup. If Tony hadn't seen Kenny's abilities on the job site, he'd never believe it. He didn't look like a body builder, and he sure didn't look like tensile steel.

"How'd you get those things moved? You picked the biggest ones."

Kenny's embarrassment seemed to ease. "Haven't you seen my pickup? I'm a part-time bricklayer."

Tony suddenly recalled seeing a hydraulic lift on the tailgate of Kenny's pickup truck and laughed. Damn, he missed that one.

"My turn," said Kenny. "If it wasn't the pickup, how'd you figure it was me?"

"Theo saw your backyard from the mountain." Tony smiled, recalling Theo's giggle. "She said there was a lot of bright paint to catch the eye."

Kenny nodded. "Do you think Blossom will ever forgive me?"

What Blossom thought about Kenny, only Blossom knew. It sure wouldn't hurt Tony's feelings if she focused her affections on Kenny. Maybe, he thought, his office could work out a deal with the citizens whose ornaments had been moved. After all, the yard art had been safely stored and could be returned, undamaged, to the rightful owners.

If he played his cards right, Tony thought he could get Blossom off his neck, get the ornament owners off his neck, and maybe get a little community service work done. All in all, this might turn out to be a blessing. Kenny had done him and the county a favor.

After sending Kenny home, Tony propped his feet on his desk and patted his stomach. He'd miss the extra pies, of course. Even as his eyes drifted shut, he visualized the piles of brush and garbage Kenny would get to haul away.

Who knew? Maybe Blossom would bake Kenny a pie.

ABOUT THE AUTHOR

Barbara Graham began making up stories in the third grade and immediately quit learning to multiply and divide. Her motto is "every story needs a dead body and every bed needs a quilt." Most of her early stories involved her saving the world. Fortunately for all involved, she and her heroic skills have never been put to the test.

A prize-winning quilter and partner in a pattern company, her quilts have been in calendars and magazines, as well as displayed in shows.

Married to a man who can do math in his head and the mother of two perfect sons, she lives in Wyoming.

Visit her at www.bgmysteries.com.